TWELVE DAYS

PAUL WILLIAMS

BLOODHOUND
— BOOKS —

Print ISBN 978-1-913419-12-7

ONE

A PARTRIDGE IN A PEAR TREE

C astello di Rocca stood on the edge of a chasm. I stared at the dark windows, the heavy stone, the turrets. Castles like this had been built in the Middle Ages to look menacing to enemies, to inspire fear.

I looked back. Just cloud and fog now, as if the world behind me had been swallowed up.

'*Benvenuti nella casa propria del diavolo.*'

'Who lives here?' I asked the driver.

'A mad old man. He lets out the castle to the odd *mazzo di turisti.*' The driver punctuated his sentences with hand movements, nerve-racking because he kept taking his hands off the wheel, even on tight bends, to make his point. 'Usually they come to see the torture instruments. But the *museo* is closed in winter. Number one tourist attraction in Reggio Emilia in summer. Signor Rossi collects instruments of torture.'

It wasn't the thought of a castle full of contraptions of torment that worried me. The more intriguing question was why the Reverend James Miller had picked this remote castle for a reunion of the chosen.

If it were not for Suzanne, I wouldn't be here. Nothing else could have dragged me to meet these people again: the preacher who destroyed my childhood, and his surrounding group of gloating, smug hypocrites. But Suzanne was coming. For years I tried to obliterate her from my mind, outrun her, but that was impossible. The media had slathered her image over billboards and magazines; she waltzed across movie and television sets and her latest hairstyle, her daring dress at the Oscars, her new facelift were the subjects of whole articles written in women's magazines.

Seeing her again, I hoped, might lay ghosts to rest.

The Fiat Uno squeezed through a narrow passage between sheer rocks. Boulders looked poised to fall from the top. The sky pressed down.

'A storm is coming. Look!' The driver took both hands off the wheel to indicate the heavy low clouds.

I pulled at the neck of my sweater. 'Is this the only way in? The only road to the castle?'

'*Si, signore.*'

He pointed up the road, and I noticed the mark on his left hand. The driver saw me staring and explained. '*La volgia.* Birthmark.'

'I thought it was a tattoo.' The rough brown patch of skin was shaped like the hourglass silhouette of a woman's mid-section; dark hair grew out of it.

He laughed. 'The woman of my life. You have a woman in your life?'

'No.' I had no woman in my life. I had *women* in my life. A series of deflections, look-a-likes, bad copies. Trying to eradicate a prototype that had been written into my neural networks.

Her.

The Fiat Uno rounded one last bend and the castle rose before me, stretching into the cloud. I considered that perhaps this was not the optimum place to be trapped for twelve days with the remnants of what I now considered to be a cult.

Lichen clung to walls, turrets and crenulations. At this elevation, I could see why the castle had been built here; an impressive giant stone citadel dominating the medieval landscape and the Enza River valley below that isolated itself from the outside world. 'How do they get supplies? Food? Drink? *Mangia. Bere.*'

'That's my job, don't you worry. I'm the concierge. I will take good care of you. Plenty food, how you call it… *pernice.* I brought everything.'

'And wine, I hope.'

'Instruction from your *padrone* – no alcohol.'

So much for celebrating Christmas and the new year. This was the Reverend James Miller's doing. He had never tolerated alcohol, smoking or dancing in the congregation at Joyful Resurrection. Every Sunday as teens, we listened to his black and white morality. I wondered if he had softened his extremist views. Probably not. I leaned back against the seat, attempted to relax whilst considering that each bend in the road might be the last thing I saw.

The Twelve, we once called ourselves.

The driver parked on gravel in front of a wide entrance hall. He got out and opened the car door for me.

'*Grazie. Quanta costa?*' I almost didn't want to know the answer, because it was Christmas Day and I assumed the price of my ride would be inflated accordingly.

'No, no. All paid for by the *signore*'

We shook hands and I felt the texture of the birthmark. 'Drive carefully… looks like a snowstorm is brewing.'

'*Buon Natale!*'

Dark snow clouds sagged over the valley, with every moment increasing the chance of a white Christmas. I wrapped myself in my coat, took a deep breath of freezing air and stepped into the past.

The sense of unease in the pit of my stomach could not be ignored. But now that I was here, there was nothing to do but crunch through a thin layer of ice and snow to the entrance. Below-zero air froze my sinuses as I knocked and then pushed on the heavy door, which swung open on creaking hinges.

'Rafe. Merry Christmas! You're looking good. Still as young as ever.'

'Merry Christmas to you too, Reverend James.'

I called him Reverend because that is what he had trained us to do as teen converts in his church, the Church of the Joyful Resurrection, out of respect for his office, he had told us. But now the name stuck in my throat. 'Reverend' was a descriptor, not a title, and by insisting on it as a title showed that this pastor lacked appropriate boundaries, lacked respect for the power balance within the church, and had arrogantly invented his own title. But the habit stuck.

The Reverend James Miller had aged well. He was cleanly shaven, and his bald head shone. 'Been a long time. A long time. How are you?' He didn't wait for a response.

He ushered me in. A Christmas tree stood in the centre of a tall-ceilinged room, and two men with their backs to me pulled decorations out of a box and strung them up on the branches. Christmas lights flashed on and off. Two women hunched over a nativity scene, arranging the figures under the tree. I was surprised. Reverend James had never allowed Christmas trees in our church, considering them pagan symbols. Maybe he had softened his views. A 'Merry Christmas' banner hung between two large chandeliers. A fire roared in a large grate, and a mirror the size of the entire wall on the opposite side reflected the glitter and lights. I felt thankful for the warmth. My apprehension eased, for a moment.

The giant mirror reflected everything back, doubling the movements of the small group gathered there. I watched myself walk by. My clothes were too casual for the occasion: black Levi jeans, black Levi shirt, university sweater, a heavy black overcoat. The others were dressed for a dinner party. But then I remembered that they always dressed up like this for church and holy days – men in suits and ties, women in long, high-necked dresses.

One man decorating the tree turned. 'It's Rafe! Hey, Rafe!'

'Hi, Glen. How are you?'

'Rafe, you old devil, you! You still have all your hair.'

He put the long string of lights down and reached out his hand. To tell the truth, I hardly recognised the thin man with the crew cut, starched shirt, grey pants and shiny shoes whom I had once thought of as my friend. I say 'friend', but even then we had been competitive in our studies, in sports, popularity, and, of course, women. 'Merry Christmas, Rafe. You look well.'

I wanted to say the same, but Glen's face, arms and hands bore scars. Skin lesions and what looked like skin grafts crossed his nose, his cheeks. But I smoothed over my surprise at his appearance. 'You too.'

'After a career in the military, I think I'm pretty fit. Not as fit as you. You haven't aged at all,' he said. And then, looking cautiously around him, Glen lowered his voice. 'Hey, I know you've just arrived – and I don't know if I'll get another chance to say this – but would you come up to my room after supper? I need to talk to you.' He gave an anxious glance around the room.

'Sure.' I said. 'So where have they put us?'

'He's cooped you all up in little cells where the monks used to live. Men and women separated, as usual. But there are ten of us, so someone has to sleep in the old tower room. I didn't want to, but no one else wants to be alone up there.' He pointed to a dark stairwell in the corner of the room.

'I'll take the tower room if you want. I don't care.'

'It's okay. I'm a loner by nature.' Glen turned. 'Hey, Mike! You remember Mike?'

'How would I not remember one of The Twelve?'

Mike the machine; fit, tanned and bristling with energy. I shook his hand and he gripped mine firmly – too firmly, as if he still had something to prove. 'Hey, Mike.'

'I'm good, man, really good.'

'You still doing that fitness instructor and tour guide stuff?' I asked.

'Yep. And add mountaineer to that. Climbed them all. Everest. Kilimanjaro. Annapurna. Mont Blanc.' Mike wore his arrogance comfortably. Even back then, he had presented himself as way better than anyone else, and you had to believe it too. But now he looked worn, as if he had driven his body too hard over the years.

'Glen,' Mike said. 'You still a military man?'

'Retired. Good thing about the military, you can retire early. Lot of burnout.'

Mike nodded. 'What about you, Rafe? Still writing those controversial books?'

I pulled out the dog-eared paperback author's copy from my large overcoat pocket. I had been looking over it on the plane to add any changes for yet another print run in the UK. Gaudy red cover, dripping with blood. *God is Dead*. 'It's selling well. International bestseller, as you must know. Already into its fifth edition. So lots of travel and no rest for the wicked, I'm afraid.'

Glen shook his head, then looked about him again. 'Not a good time, Rafey. For a title like that. It's Christmas Day.'

I returned it to my pocket, perversely enjoying the discomfort I could see on their faces.

Mike turned to welcome another of The Twelve; a large man I for the life of me didn't recognise. He looked like a character in a Roald Dahl novel who had eaten too much chocolate and was about to burst.

'Hey, Rafe, it's Stephen, Stephen Smith.'

Stephen. Of course. We had clashed badly in the past over my questioning of the cult's truth. He still looked sour, but smiled broadly at me. All forgiven, apparently. We shook hands cold-fish style. Stephen was pasty-skinned, pampered, complacent. A look that said he had never suffered in his life. Never had to transform himself, pull himself out of the sludge of real life or wrestle with self-worth. He had been born into money. If it was easier for a camel to go through the eye of a needle than a rich man to enter heaven, Stephen would be on the outside of the pearly gates for eternity.

Glen clapped Stephen on the back. 'Stephen here's done the best of all of us.'

'Really?' After all, I was an international bestselling author. Suzanne was a Hollywood star.

Stephen waved a pudgy hand in the air. 'Finance. Stocks. Investment banking.'

'The nerd of the class,' said Glen, 'always has the last laugh.'

Status, money, career. The way we introduced ourselves. *Hi, I'm Rafe, backslider, atheist, writer of heretical books, university professor.*

To tell the truth, I thought I might probably have enjoyed eating live cockroaches more than endure these reintroductions. I had run from these people for a reason. But, I reconciled, I – like the other men, I guessed – had come back for a reason. A single one.

And I wondered how Reverend James had financed this

whole retreat. We had all been sent first-class air tickets. Stephen must have had a hand in it. I was sure of it, the way he was basking in self-adulation.

'Would you like a drink, Rafe?' Stephen poured sparkling apple juice into a champagne glass and passed it to me. 'It was quite a miracle how this all happened. A few of us old stalwarts got chatting, met Reverend James, and we realised that this is what God wanted.'

The Twelve always gave credit to God for everything good. And for things that went wrong? Well, Satan's fault. Their world views were watertight. So comforting. The world divided into the saved and the damned. If only life were that simple.

'Glen, you said there'd only be ten of us. Who's not coming?' I asked.

Glen shook his head. 'You didn't know? About Sean Philips and Jack Davies?'

Sean and Jack were the two dissenters who had left Joyful Resurrection shortly after I did.

'Sad, very sad,' Mike said. 'They were each killed in a car crash. Horrible. But sort of obvious that once outside the protection of God, anything can happen.'

I bit my lip. This was one of those statements I would never allow my undergraduates to get away with, based as it was on false premises. But I shut up. For now. I had to remember I was back in the old cult. They still believed in that shit. All of it.

'Which is why it's important that the remainder of us meet up,' Glen added.

'Exactly,' Stephen said. 'We're glad you could be here.'

I smiled. Enjoyed my own lie for a moment. 'I wouldn't have missed it for anything.'

'Praise the Lord,' said Stephen. 'I'm sure Reverend James is pleased to have you here.'

A clatter and a smash made us all turn to the Christmas

tree. A woman was untangling a green line of lights and had dropped some red and green baubles, which splintered into a thousand pieces. 'Sorry, guys.'

'Hey,' I said, and lowered my head to speak in Stephen's ear. 'Is that Alison Jones?'

Her glasses were still huge, with lenses that made her eyes look surprised the whole time. High neckline, thick, shapeless skirt to her ankles. Thin-lipped, she held out a limp hand but would not hug me. Girls and boys didn't touch or hug, back then. The distance between the sexes needed to be maintained as strictly as the demilitarised zone between the two Koreas.

Clinging to Alison's arm was none other than Reverend James' wife, Linda, as small, frail and beautiful – and ice cold – as ever. She wore a formal long skirt and a long-sleeved blouse that buttoned to her neck. The Ice Queen, we used to call her. I made the mistake of embracing her: she pulled back from me with haste. 'Good to see you,' she said.

'And Danny! Haven't seen you forever. Merry Christmas!'

Dark-haired and tanned, Danny Wilson hadn't changed either since he was a school kid. Still looked like a troll with those heavy eyebrows. Still stuttered. But he had done well for himself too, as a car mechanic. Fingernails black. Greasy hair. Family of five. 'M-merry Christmas, brother,' he said. 'I have p-p-prayed for this moment. Are you well in the Lord?'

'I'm well, Danny, but not in the Lord.'

He looked puzzled. And like Glen had done, he looked about him as if someone was listening.

Someone was. Reverend James stood behind me, placed his hand on my shoulder. 'Emily Barnes is held up at the station in Reggio,' he said. 'I've ordered a taxi to fetch her. She'll be here shortly. Then we're all present and accounted for.'

'So Suzanne is here?' I said.

'Oh yes,' said Reverend James. 'She's in her room, I believe.'

So here we were again: Glen, Mike, Stephen, Alison, Danny, Rafe. Emily to come and Suzanne to make an appearance. Reverend James and Linda. Ten of the original Twelve. Reverend James had intended an elite group in the Church, twelve apostles to lead the flock, to go out into the world and spread the faith. We had all made a pact, a vow to keep the faith.

I had broken that. My bestselling book was a radical damnation of James Miller and his Church of the Joyful Resurrection. I had likely infuriated them all. Some, I'm sure, hated me.

'Ladies and gentlemen!' Reverend James clapped his hands. 'Gather round! Huddle up! We are now on retreat.' He held up a straw basket. 'Remember to please deposit all your electronic devices here.'

'No way,' said Mike.

'There's no reception anyway,' said Danny, placing his laptop and cell phone in the basket. 'I've been t-trying.'

When he called it a retreat, a cutting off from the outside world, he was not kidding.

'Not much has changed, I see,' I said to Glen.

In the old days, granted, there were no cell phones or internet, but on retreats back then we had to surrender our Walkmans and cassette players, and any distractions from temptation that would hinder communication with God. Even books were discouraged, except of course the Bible. And we were segregated so that distractions of the opposite sex did not impede our meditations.

Glen took the basket. 'This will be locked up for safekeeping.'

Shortly thereafter, as Glen had said, Reverend James directed us to separate areas on the first floor – men to the old monks' quarters to the east side, women to the slightly newer quarters in a separate wing on the west side. Even Linda would be with the women while Reverend James went to be with the men.

Stephen distributed sturdy black rubber twelve-volt flashlights, one for every person, and spare batteries. 'Compliments of the castle owner. He apologises for the poor lighting. The power is not good.'

He also gave each of us a key on a key ring, numbered one through ten. 'These are your room keys. Please don't lose them as I don't have any spares.'

Each key, I was surprised to see, was slim, modern, flat. 'I'm a little disappointed, Stephen,' I said. 'I was expecting a large dungeon key made of brass.'

Stephen laughed. 'The castle for the most part has been entirely modernised, the owner assures me. State-of-the-art kitchen and bathrooms, but for some reason the lighting is faulty.'

'And the heating leaves something to be desired,' said Mike, hugging himself tightly. 'You'd think they'd have installed central heating. The corridors are like a deep freeze.'

'I was told heating would be adequate,' said Stephen. 'But you're right; it's a bit chilly in places. Don't worry. Each room has a heater, and with that marvellous fireplace in the living room, I'm sure we'll be able to cope.'

Away from the heated entrance foyer, the dark passage leading upstairs was freezing, and so dimly lit that it was almost impossible to see without the flashlights. Everywhere outside the living area smelt of rotting damp. And through each window we passed, I glanced out at the dark storm pressing closer, like an impending apocalypse.

Linda led the women to their quarters in a wing at the near end of the corridor to the left, and Reverend James led the men to our individual cells in a wing on the right. At the end of the corridor, once the women were all in their rooms, Reverend James stopped and turned. 'So Rafe, you married?'

It was a surprising question, unrelated to the task at hand. I frowned at him. 'No.'

'Now that surprises me.'

I shrugged. 'Too many to choose from.'

'And you, Glen?'

'With all those military tours of duty, I never had time for relationships.'

'I always thought you and Suzanne would have got together,' said Reverend James to me.

In response, Glen held out his right hand in his flashlight beam and turned the ring on his pinkie, taking it off. A white-gold ring with small amethysts encircling a diamond. We crowded around it.

'I remember that ring,' said Mike. 'I actually got to wear it for a day.'

Danny held the ring up to his flashlight. 'Not me. I never wore it. Never in her favour.'

'What about you, Rafe?'

'Yeah, probably. Can't remember.' I was not about to discuss my lifelong obsession with Suzanne with these men. I'd worn this ring all through GCSEs for good luck. I'd fantasised about her, almost failed an exam because I had been daydreaming about her. Seeing the ring again made me feel like I'd lost my balance, as if I'd just stepped in quicksand.

'I remember you wearing it,' said Glen. 'Of course it meant nothing to her. She played us like cards.'

Mike took the ring from Danny and placed it on his pinkie for size. He held it up to the dim light. 'So, Glen, you ended up with it. I wondered where it had got to.'

Glen laughed. 'After school, I just asked her for it. She said, "You idiots." I brought it to see if she still remembers.'

'She probably won't,' I said.

'Do not let your heart turn aside to her ways; do not stray

into her paths,' said Danny. 'Reverend James, that was the Bible verse you used to quote to me.'

Reverend James flashed his light at the doors at the end of the corridor. 'Proverbs 7, verse 25. I hope those foolish days of pining after Suzanne are long gone.'

'Long gone,' said Glen. He walked up a small flight of steps at the end of the dark, cold corridor to the left. 'The tower,' he said, 'is up here.'

Danny and Mike found their rooms, and Reverend James pointed to the end of the corridor on the right. 'Your room, Rafe, is over there. Bathroom to your right. Supper's at six. See you then.'

Though it had to be no later than five o'clock, night already surrounded the castle. Wind blew something, shutters perhaps, and a distant bang echoed through the corridor.

I fitted the key into what looked to be a brand-new lock and entered a room with narrow, tall windows. I turned on the light. The icy air stopped my breath. Particles of dust caught in the light and spiralled down. The spores caught in my throat. The history of this room spoke of centuries of misery and suffering and cold and isolation. The walls were thick enough so that a person could scream and no one would hear in the next room. Everything was freezing to the touch. I cranked up the heater to full and it ticked and radiated feeble warmth into the thousand-year-old air. Darkness reigned outside, although the lights in the castle did cast a faint glow. In that glow, I could see that sleet and snow had already covered all traces of the road up to the front entrance.

I wondered now if I could order a cab and hightail it out of here. Always have a back-door exit plan was my motto. But I could see by the way the weather was deteriorating that soon there would be little possibility of any kind of vehicle getting through this mountain pass.

I needed to shower, but the designated men's bathroom was occupied, so I stumbled down the corridor to the women's wing and found another bathroom at the end. I locked myself in and turned on the shower taps full blast. The castle may have been old, but the bathroom was all marble and glass. And the water was scalding hot.

I heard a rap on the door as I was towelling myself dry.

'Just a minute! Be out soon.'

I dressed and opened the door.

'Hello, stranger.' She stood in the dimly lit corridor, a towel wrapped around her, clothes in her hand.

'Suzanne. Wow, what are you doing here?' I was completely caught off guard.

She wrapped the towel tighter around her chest. 'This is the girls' bathroom, you know.' That ironic smile on her face. Her warm voice. The same Suzanne. Her lips were full, her cheekbones high and the skin under her eyes tight. Her blonde hair had been swept back into a ponytail, so the nape of her neck was exposed.

Her eyes fixed on me, and a dizzy past blew over me. 'You look well, Rafe.'

'You too.' Twenty years and she still treated me like a gawky teenager. 'I'm an author. And a professor. In that order.'

'Of course, your book. I've heard of it.'

'Have you read it?' I couldn't help feeling small, as if I was seeking her approval. Just like the old days.

She laughed. 'I don't have time to read!'

'No, of course not.' I was fighting a battle here, not so much within myself – I could watch this scene from a wry distance – but to not give her what she demanded. It was clear to me now exactly how it worked. Suzanne expected something, required it, from all men. She had been Miss Beauty

Queen at school, had gone on to be a model, and later, in a series of strokes of good fortune, made it to Hollywood – the big time.

She pushed past me and into the bathroom, where she stared into the mirror and inspected her face. She shook her hair loose. I followed her back into the bathroom and watched her in the mirror. 'I'm between movies at the moment,' she said. 'And you? I heard you have a PhD.'

'I teach philosophy at the University of California.'

'You were always the brains of the bunch. I knew you'd go far.'

'Far is a metaphor. A matter of opinion.'

She didn't respond.

'How's Jerry?'

The tabloids had followed her every step of the way, their courtship, marriage, honeymoon in the Seychelles, the growing bump in her stomach, her first baby. The paparazzi needed someone to follow, and she had led them a merry dance for years, until some new young thing had taken her place and she had contented herself in playing the role of a sexy middle-aged woman.

'Jerry's fine. We're sort of separated now, as you probably know.'

'I don't believe everything I read in the tabloids.'

'Well, they got that one right.'

'How's Hollywood treating you?'

She walked to the shower and turned it on. Tested the water temperature. 'Hideous place, as you know. We live up in Santa Rosa. Our two kids are almost grown up now.'

'Time flies when you're having fun.'

Suzanne looked uneasy. I vaguely remembered some scandal in Hollywood that she had become embroiled in, with some movie director, a media frenzy in the tabloids. But this was par for the course for her. She had constant media attention. I was surprised the paparazzi hadn't followed her here. But then, we were cut off from the world. Probably a relief for her.

I pointed to the door. 'I'd better…'

'Later then.'

I closed the bathroom door behind me. My heart pounded. But of course, she did that to everyone. That was why she was a movie star. They paid her millions of dollars to broadcast a carefully constructed yet entirely bewitching sulky smile into every man's yearning heart.

At 6pm, we gathered back in the living room; all except Suzanne. The men threw hungry looks in the direction of the stairs leading up to the women's cells, but she was, I assumed, playing her usual game of Being Noticeably Absent. She had perfected this art decades ago. Reverend James had an announcement to make. He clapped his hands for attention and we stood around him as though we were still teenagers. 'Some of you have expressed a desire to see the torture museum. It is officially closed for the winter, but the concierge has given me permission to take you all for a peek.' He held up a large bronze key. 'Just don't touch anything. Follow me.'

He led us up the stairs again, to a southern wing away from the bedrooms. Pushing through the large wooden door, we found ourselves in a cold, dark, high-ceilinged room with small windows. A shadowy object sat in the middle of the room. Stephen flipped a switch and the room was flooded with dim Gothic light from four cobwebby chandeliers. I stared up at a polished-steel blade at the top of a high wooden frame. At the base of the frame stood a platform, positioned below the guillotine blade.

'Whoa,' said Glen. 'See where the head is placed, just at the right angle for decapitation.'

Alison winced.

'Signor Rossi is well known for his rare collection of torture instruments. He keeps them in tiptop shape, for viewings,' said Reverend James.

Above the guillotine, Glen pointed out eight storefront dummies suspended by ropes from a bar in the roof, nooses around their necks.

Alison shuddered and after a quick glance, would not look up again.

'Ghoulish,' said Danny.

Linda was browsing items in a display cabinet. 'Gross!'

I read the inscription above the items she was staring at. 'Scottish thumbscrews, circa seventeenth century. Tongue-extractor, possibly Spanish, 1501–1800.'

'Eugh.'

Reverend James passed on to other items on display on the long trestle table. 'Hair shirt. Cat-o'-nine-tails for self-flagellation. And look at this mask!'

Mike shone his flashlight on an iron mask. The face of a demon had been etched on the outside – pointy ears, forked tongue, wild eyes. On the inside, two long spikes faced inwards for the eyes, two smaller ones for the nostrils, and a long, curved, two-pronged fork represented the mouth.

It looked to me as if Reverend James relished pointing out each torture instrument, dwelling on its capacity for cruel pain. I stared at him, and an old loathing welled up in me. It was absurd by anyone's standards to spend Christmas in an isolated castle full of macabre medieval torture instruments.

'It makes my eyes ache and my throat close up just to think of it,' said Alison.

'Hideous,' said Linda.

'A slow death by asphyxiation,' said Mike. 'It would gouge

out your eyes, stop you breathing, tear out your tongue and block your windpipe.'

'The Middle Ages were b-barbaric,' said Danny.

'Tell us more about this Mister Rossi,' said Mike. 'He sounds creepy.'

'Stephen and I met him when we were arranging our stay here,' said Glen. 'He's a businessman. Very handsome, polite, and totally obsessed with the past.'

'And the crowds keep coming, apparently,' said Stephen. 'People are fascinated by torture.'

'Look over here.' Mike shone his flashlight on an open, upright coffin in the corner of the room. The insides were fitted with sharp steel spikes top to bottom, bottom to top, like grinning teeth. 'You put a man in here and... spike him through.'

'Or a woman,' I said.

'The iron maiden', it said on the plaque. On the outside, a figure had been carved on the sarcophagus of a naked woman with full breasts, pudenda, and face in a mask of frozen terror and anguish.

Alison was holding her stomach tightly. She looked as if she was about to throw up.

Linda ran her fingers along a rectangular wooden frame, raised from the ground, with a roller at both ends.

'That's the rack,' said Stephen. 'You tie the victim onto here and stretch him until his joints are dislocated.'

'And this looks like a giant spinning wheel,' said Linda. She touched the crossbar, which was fixed on to a large wooden wheel, and turned it. It creaked loudly.

Stephen peered at the diagram above it and the explanation of how it worked. 'You tie the victim to the crossbar and spin him around – to break his bones.'

'A Catherine wheel,' said Mike, reading, 'named for St

Catherine of Alexandria, who was tied to its seven spokes and beaten. Let's go for a spin.'

'Sure,' I said. 'You first.'

'Whoever this Signor Rossi is, he's a sadistic creep,' said Mike, reading each inscription.

'It's history,' said Stephen.

'It's fascinating,' said Glen.

'I hate it.' Linda turned away.

Alison stood by a metal bull in the other corner of the room. 'And this?'

'The brazen bull,' Mike read from the plaque attached to its rump. 'This must be the worst way to die. They place the victim inside the bull here' – he opened a trapdoor in the bull's hindquarters – 'and stoke this fire underneath its belly until the victim literally is roasted alive and melts into fat. Ugh.'

I read out loud. 'The bull has an acoustic apparatus that converts screams into the sound of a bull for the pleasure of those watching.'

'They made a real fire here,' said Mike, pointing to the kindling and briquettes underneath the bull and the blackened underbelly. 'Do you think they demonstrate these torture instruments for visitors?'

Alison shook her head. 'Don't be silly.'

'Hey, this bull has udders.' I crouched down to examine the hind end of the bull, where hollow tubes with holes at the end had been welded onto the belly, and a bowl placed underneath. 'It says this is where the liquid remains and fat of the victim is collected.'

Glen tapped the brazen bull with his hand and it gave out a hollow ring. 'Those torturers were not good at anatomy, obviously.'

'Ugh,' said Linda. 'Why collect the fat of the poor victim?'

'It makes a nourishing soup,' I said.

'Stop it, Rafe.'

I read the plinth: 'The bronze bull was invented by Perillos of Athens, who presented his ingenious method of executing criminals to Phalaris of Sicily in 550 BCE. The Sicilian tyrant was so taken with the idea that he tested it out on no other than Perillos himself. Made to the exact proportions of a handsome bull, even to details such as its magnificent horns and prominent genitals, the bronze bull was bizarrely "improved" by the Romans with the later addition of udders, making it a transvestite bovine creature. The udders were added so that the juices of the victim would drain out of the bottom of the bull and delight spectators with "milk". It was rumoured that this "milk" was collected and imbibed. According to historical records, when the bull was opened afterwards, the bones of the victim "shone like jewels and were made into bracelets".'

'I'm suitably sickened,' said Mike.

Alison hugged her stomach. 'Can we go?'

'Just a moment,' said Reverend James. He held up his hands. 'There is a reason why I brought you to this torture museum today.'

Aha. There was method to his madness. He had organised this macabre tour as a prelude to an impromptu sermon. I knew this man too well.

'Tomorrow is the Feast of St Stephen, the first martyr,' said Reverend James. 'Each day I will read you a chapter of *Foxe's Book of Martyrs*, how the early Christians were tortured to death for their faith. They suffered horrific deaths for their faith.'

Moral lesson number one.

I had underestimated my staying power. I had come all this way to lay the ghosts of my infatuation to rest, but I hadn't bargained on what it would really be like to spend twelve days with a bunch of religious fanatics led by a lunatic. Especially if the object of my infatuation was not going to even play the game.

Supper was at six o'clock. I traced my way through labyrinthine corridors, down the stairs and into the dining room, guided by the smell of roast meat.

The fire crackled in the fireplace at the far end of the room, and on the mantel above stood a large advent calendar. The Christmas tree flashed its gaudy lights in sequenced patterns and the tinsel glittered. But I saw no presents under the tree. I stared at Reverend James in the wall mirror, which reflected every nuance of the gathering.

And who the hell is this Signor Rossi, I thought. Creepy rooms, torture instruments, mirrors everywhere. More like a scene for a Gothic crime novel. Or some seedy porn setting. 'The storm is getting worse,' I said.

Mike looked up at the window in surprise as if he had not noticed the howling wind, the sleet battering the window panes, the deepening darkness.

'We're here for the long haul, Rafe,' said Reverend James. 'Twelve days.'

'Don't you love a white Christmas?' said Glen. Every place had been set with our name written on a small white envelope. He found his nametag and sat.

The Reverend took his seat at the head of the table. 'I only hope Emily makes it. Assuming her taxi can get through, she should be arriving any minute.'

'I can't see any car getting through this storm,' said Mike.

I found my nametag on Alison's left and sat down.

'Who's the great cook?' asked Mike. 'Smells delicious.'

'Signor Antonio Alfieri, the concierge,' said Stephen. 'Not only is he a wonderful host and driver, he is also a marvellous chef. He prepared all our food for these twelve days.'

Reverend James leaned forward. 'Ladies and gentlemen, these are dark times. Thanks for heeding my call – no, God's call – to come to this retreat. Some have come far – USA, Canada, England.'

'Dark times indeed,' I said, gesturing at the windows. A bare tree branch scraped at the glass, like the claw of a ghoulish spirit trying to get in from the cold.

'Please take the envelope addressed to you on your place-mats and look inside, but don't let anyone else see. This is between you and God.'

'Shouldn't we wait for Suzanne?' said Glen, fingering his envelope but not opening it.

Reverend James frowned at his wife, who pointed up at the stairwell. She meant, of course, by the rolling of her eyes, that Suzanne was playing princess.

I took a quick look inside my envelope to see the number eight, and a picture of eight maids a-milking. I got it. We had each been assigned one of the twelve days of Christmas. So we were going to play some silly game.

Linda poured what looked like red sparkling wine into each person's wine glass, and Reverend James raised a toast. 'To the twelve nights of Christmas. May the good Lord bless us all.'

I tasted grape juice. I hadn't expected Gutturnio or Lambrusco, but it did seem a crime to be in one of the finest wine regions of Italy and not get a taste of its wine.

'Cheers!' I clinked glasses with Glen, Stephen and Danny. 'Good to see you all again.'

The front door banged open, and a gust of icy wind and snow flurries blew through the hall. In walked a bundle of scarves and coats. She unwrapped herself at the fire, fluffing out a mane of long, straight, red hair. Emily Barnes. My first feeling was joy – I hadn't seen her for years, and we had been close friends. My second feeling was guilt. I had not kept in contact with her for years either. I had simply disappeared.

'Emily!' said Reverend James. 'You made it. Merry Christmas!'

She shivered. 'Nearly didn't make it. God! It's frikkin' freezing out there. I don't know how we got through that mother of all snowstorms. We're right in the middle of it.'

Stephen stood up to help her out of her coat. She brushed her hand through her hair. 'Hi, guys,' she said. 'It's good to see you all again. How long has it been, hey?'

Stephen thrust the basket under her nose. 'Any electronic devices? Right here.'

She gave him a pained look, fumbled for her phone in her pocket and found it. Looking at it sadly, she dropped it into the basket and took her place next to me. She smiled and kissed my cheek. 'Rafe! I can't believe you came to the reunion. Good onya.' She leaned her head on my shoulder, fluttered her eyelids in mock affection. I gave her a sideways bear hug. The feelings of warmth and childish affection rushed back.

'I told you we shouldn't have let them sit together,' said Glen.

Reverend James pointed. 'Emily, your seat is actually over there. Nametag. Envelope. All the seats are designated for a reason. It's all part of the plan.'

'There's a plan?' But Emily did not switch seats, so Stephen handed her the correct envelope and nametag.

The concierge, who had donned a white cook's hat and apron, pushed a silver trolley of food out of the kitchen doorway. '*La cena è pronta.*'

'We're still missing one.' Glen craned his neck towards the dark stairwell.

Didn't we all know? But this was Suzanne. Any party, any occasion, she would sweep in late when the party was in full swing for maximum effect.

Alison poured Emily a drink, and she swilled it in her mouth. 'Hmm. Vintage bouquet. I'd say a good 1950s Cabernet Sauvignon.'

I nudged her under the table. 'Behave.'

She picked up the envelope Stephen had placed there.

'You may look, Emily, but please do not show or tell anyone else,' said Reverend James.

She slit open the envelope with her nail. 'Oh, I see. Wonderful.'

'Seven swans a-swimming,' she whispered to me. 'What's yours?'

'Eight maids…'

'Sexy.'

The others were distracted by an apparition descending the staircase in a low-cut green dress, her hair sparkling blonde as if she had arrived at the Oscars. Even the concierge stopped serving to stare.

'Sorry I'm late,' said Suzanne.

Sure you're sorry.

The effect was measurable. The men became instantly awkward and self-conscious; the women screwed up their faces at her as if she hurt their eyes. She upset the balance instantly. So much for being wise and mature. Danny was grinning like a schoolboy, Mike looked like a puffer fish, Glen sat rigid. All still under her spell. No change at all. I refused to give her more than two seconds.

Even Reverend James looked nonplussed. 'Now we're all here, we can begin.' He motioned Suzanne to her seat opposite me. 'Let's say grace.' His prayer droned on for some time. How we were all blessed to be together again, and were here for renewal and to listen to Him and His plans for us. And to revitalise our faith and commitment to The Twelve.

'Amen!'

'Please eat. And while we do so, I want to tell you about "The Twelve Days of Christmas". This song was sung by persecuted Christians in order to help them keep their faith, to remember and pass on the tenets of their beliefs without the persecutors knowing it. Each symbol means something. We will begin with today, Christmas Day, the first day of Christmas, and the partridge in a pear tree.'

Here we go again. The interminable Reverend James sermon. At the Church of the Joyful Resurrection, he used to go on and on for hours, delaying everyone's Sunday lunch. And as I used to do during those sermons all those years ago, my eyes sought out Suzanne's. Back then, if she looked back at me, my emotions would soar. Tonight, I kept my sentiments under tight rein. Reverend James took a slice of meat on his fork and raised it in the air. 'What meat are we eating here for this Christmas feast?'

'Turkey,' said Mike.

'Pheasant,' said Alison.

'*Pernice*,' I said. 'Partridge.'

The Reverend looked up at me in surprise. 'Correct.'

'I get it, I get it,' said Danny, beaming. 'And I bet p-pear is for dessert.'

Reverend James nodded. 'What does the partridge represent?'

'Christ.' This was Alison, wiping her mouth with a napkin as she spoke.

Reverend James placed the forkful of meat in his mouth and chewed before answering. 'The partridge, Christ, hanging on a tree for us, the centre of Christmas.'

'And,' said Linda, 'we eat of his flesh, of his body and blood. It's all symbolic.'

'Delicious,' said Emily under her breath. 'Tastes like chicken.'

'You haven't changed,' I whispered back. 'Actually, it tastes like old string dipped in garlic.'

She giggled and Reverend James gave us a sharp look.

Danny shot his hand up. 'I don't quite understand. If Christ is the partridge, then who is the "my true love" in the song?'

'On the first day of Christmas, my true love said to me…'

said Reverend James, his mouth full of partridge meat and gravy.

Alison was quick off the mark. 'Again, that is obviously Christ.' She pushed her glasses onto her nose.

I remembered why it was difficult to like her. She, and the others, knew the Truth with a capital T. And Truth was static. Had to be pronounced with the pious pomposity of fifty flipping Pharisees.

Reverend James pressed his fingers together. 'We are the bride of Christ. The Bible often refers to Christ as the true lover, husband. In the Song of Solomon…'

Ever the philosopher, I could not keep my mouth shut here. I had to point out the illogic of this symbol. 'But if my true love Christ' – fingering the air to signify quotes – 'gave me a partridge in a pear tree, Christ' – again, air quotes – 'gives me himself. That's nonsense.'

Suzanne smiled at me in forbidden admiration, as if I were the only person in the world. As if sharing a secret with me. She was good at this. But I was practising immunity. I did not feel it, that old fluttering of the heart. It was gone. Surely.

Stephen gave me The Look. You never question the Reverend James Miller, let alone interrupt him when he is expounding on the Truth.

Alison gave me the smug eye. 'Christ sacrifices himself for us. He gives himself to us. It's obvious.'

'Obvious,' said Emily, digging me in the ribs. 'You don't get it, Rafe.'

Again, I wondered how I was going to survive twelve days of Supercilious Stephen, Pious Danny and Machine Mike, Sour Grapes Alison, Holier-than-Thou Linda and the Reverent Reverend. My only ally here was Emily, and the only saving grace an amused look Suzanne offered me.

'Now eat,' said Reverend James. 'Enjoy, for this is His body, broken for you.'

'Delicious food.'

The concierge, still in the room, made a gracious bow. 'You need anything more, please call me. I'll prepare dessert.' And he wheeled the trolley back into the kitchen.

Suzanne had said nothing throughout the meal, but kept an ironic smile on her face. From time to time, she arched a characteristic eyebrow, as if she was above it all, an expression often exploited in her movies. It annoyed the hell out of them, I could see. She held the attention of all the men – yes, even Reverend James, who kept throwing her furtive glances as if even he was fishing for her approval. As for Danny, Mike, Stephen and Glen, they were drooling. Not so the women: Alison could not mask her disdain for Suzanne; Linda stared at her plunging neckline in distress as if it was causing her physical pain; Emily ignored her completely.

I could measure the distance between my teen infatuation and the damage done then and now. I could see all her tricks, and her illusions, and the spells that used to enchant me. Finally, Mike summoned the courage to speak to her directly.

'Suzanne, how do you do it?'

'What?'

'Play all those roles. How do you pretend to be so many different people?'

Suzanne winked. 'Aren't you ever someone other than yourself?'

'No,' said Mike. I noticed a glance between Linda and Glen. Only a millisecond, but a glance nevertheless, which I could not decipher.

'What about doing things you don't do in real life?' said Stephen. 'Like smoking. What was that movie where you were a chain smoker? *Fireball*, was it?'

'And that movie where you had to put on all that weight?' said Emily.

Suzanne showed her perfect white teeth implants and

crowns. 'It's a job. And all those people I act are not me. There's a glass wall between me and my role.'

Maybe, I thought, *we have something in common after all.*

'Is it t-true,' Danny asked, 'that you can c-cry at will?' His stutter, I noticed, was much worse when he addressed her.

She stared at him, blinked a few times, adopted a heart-broken expression, and sure enough, there were the tears, rolling down her cheeks.

'Amazing,' said Stephen. 'So we can never trust you?'

'Why would you ever?' she said.

I had to say it. 'We wouldn't.'

'Good. You shouldn't,' she said.

Behind the joke was a history of heartache. I knew that each of these men, in turn, had cracked hearts because of her, and by their reactions to her now, they had never quite healed. All through this exchange, Glen frowned, averting his eyes from her whenever she looked at him. Signs of possible continued infatuation. After all these years.

The concierge rolled out dessert, which was, sure enough, tinned pears and ice cream. Then he announced his departure. 'Enjoy the retreat,' he said. 'I will be back in twelve days!'

'Thank you, Antonio!' said Alison.

Reverend James clapped his hands, as a magician does to make something disappear. 'Let the twelve days of Christmas begin! I have placed a Bible and notepad and pen in your room. I want this to be a cleansing time. Confess to God. Purge yourself. Each of you write down a secret confession to God. Something you want to be forgiven for. A vice. A sin. A transgression. Pray over it. Then tomorrow morning, bring the piece of paper and we will burn it here in the fire.'

Emily nudged me under the table. 'You look like you're about to murder someone,' she whispered.

'Sorry. Just wondering why the hell I'm here.'

'Me too.' She linked her pinkie finger to mine under the

table, a gesture we had invented at school when we needed support from each other.

I knew Reverend James could draw a confession out of a saint. I could see the thoughts racing around in each person's mind, each one deciding not if they had a vice, but which one to confess. I didn't believe in sin, or God or any neurotic anthropomorphism of humankind's deepest insecurities. But I had plenty of vice I could share. Plenty. If he wanted sin, I had a bountiful harvest to offer him.

'I suggest we have an early night,' said Reverend James.

Glen stood. 'Listen up, people. The castle is a pretty derelict place, as you have discovered. There are several no-go areas where it is unsafe.'

'The tower, for one,' I interrupted, 'where you're staying.'

'The entire north side of the tower is a no-go area. My side, the south, is fine. But don't go prowling around at night. There's a collapsed staircase down to the basement. The whole cellar area has caved in. No one goes down there.'

'Goodnight, everyone,' said Reverend James. 'Tomorrow we start our programme, so be sure to get some rest. We start our Quiet Times bright and early. Prayers at 6am.'

Alison and Suzanne followed Linda up the stairs and along the left passage to the women's quarters; Mike, Stephen and Danny followed Reverend James down the right passage that led to the men's quarters. Glen lingered in the corridor and held Emily and myself back. He spoke quietly. 'I need to talk to you both.'

We followed him to the end of the men's corridor, along a narrow passage and up the winding stone steps to the tower. The tower room jutted out of the east side of the castle. I looked back at Emily and she shrugged her shoulders. We passed dark crevices in the stairwell covered in spider webs and Emily shivered. 'Ugh.'

'Dark times indeed,' I repeated.

'Smells like a sewer.'

'Welcome to the tower.' Glen closed the door behind us.

I took in the leaded windows on two sides and the narrow balcony leading out straight ahead. The large pentagonal room was fiery hot.

'It's not as bad as you made out, Glen,' I said. 'This is like a penthouse.'

'And cosy warm,' Emily said.

Glen pushed open the balcony doors and stepped out onto the tiny ledge overlooking the black void of the storm. A violent gust of wind blew a curtain of snow and ice into the room.

'You're crazy,' said Emily. 'It's evil out there.'

'Come on!'

We stepped out onto the balcony into the full force of a blizzard. Glen whirled around. 'Woohoo, this is something!'

'You sure this is safe?' I yelled. The balcony was a slab of rock jutting out from the wall, which looked as if it was about to crumble or break off if any weight was put on it. A wooden railing held us in. Above the balcony hung a large stone gargoyle the size of a human. A demon with its tongue out peered over the ledge. It looked battered and weather-worn too, as if any slight bump might dislodge it. I gripped the ice-cold railing. Snow and sleet stung my face, my eyes. The wind howled around my ears. 'Vertigo,' I said.

'Nice,' said Emily, her teeth chattering. 'Now let's get the hell inside.'

We stepped back in and Glen banged the balcony doors shut, sealing us inside the room, which had cooled dramatically. 'Sit, sit.'

I was shuddering with cold and my head spun. Emily grabbed my hand. 'My fingers are ice. Yours are warm.'

We sat on the couch while Glen paced. 'Rafe, and Emily, you must hear this too. I'm just guessing we're the only non-believers here. And maybe Suzanne. The renegades.'

'I thought you had kept your faith,' I said.

Glen smiled. 'On the contrary. We're the odd ones out.'

'Indeed.'

'And Suzanne.'

'And Suzanne,' he repeated wistfully. He held out the hand with the ring. Looked at it in the light.

'My God,' said Emily. 'You still have her ring.'

He nodded. Folded his arms. 'I'm worried about what the Reverend's intentions are here.'

Emily laughed. 'To see if he still holds us all in his magnetic power.'

'The man evidently has a vain but persistent hope that he can bring us lost sheep back into the fold,' I said.

'No. I think it's more sinister,' said Glen. 'He wants to bring things out into the open.'

'What things?' I said.

I saw fear in Emily's eyes. 'No,' she said to Glen. 'Not that. He wouldn't dare.' Her face went red.

'Something going on that I don't know about?'

Glen ignored me. 'Seriously, Emily—'

Emily stood. Something had upset her. 'I'm getting really tired all of a sudden. Rafe, please walk me to my room.'

'Sorry, Em,' said Glen. 'I shouldn't have… I didn't mean to bring that up.'

'No, just need to go now.'

'I'll let you out. Oh, please listen to me, guys, just one thing I need to tell you…'

And that one thing he said would niggle me for the whole twelve days to come.

'Please, guys, lock your doors. It's not safe.' Glen did not just look worried – he looked terrified. His eyes were wide, and he fiddled with the ring on his finger, moving it up and down, turning it, as if he couldn't get it off.

'What do you mean?' said Emily.

He ushered us to the doorway, held the door open for us to pass through. 'Just beware, things are not what they seem.'

'Glen!'

But Glen had already closed and locked his door.

Emily took my arm and we walked back along the corridor. We had accessed the tower room via the men's wing, but I saw that the tower room could be accessed from both wings, so we followed the right passage down to the women's side.

'He's acting a little paranoid,' I said. 'What's spooking him? Reverend James?'

But Emily said nothing all the way to her room. Outside her doorway, she turned. 'Rafe, sorry.'

'Please tell me what's going on.'

The darkness crept into the castle from the outside. The air grew colder, if that was possible. Sleet slid down the windows like ghostly fingers. Angry wind rattled the shutters.

'It all went so sour,' she said.

'What?'

'Some bad things went down after you left The Twelve.'

'Between you and Glen?'

'I don't want to say anything now. Maybe tomorrow. Okay?' She reached up and gave me a peck on the cheek, then after a second's hesitation, a hug. My face was buried in her hair.

'I missed you, Rafe.'

'You're freezing,' I said. She was trembling, but not just from the cold. She held me tight for a long few minutes and then pulled away. 'We were so much bigger then than now,' she said. 'We had such big ideals. Such hope. And now look at us. Adults. Shrunken hopes, fitting into a compromised world.'

'You don't look too bad.'

She stared into my eyes. She had clear green eyes that, even in the dark, seemed to sparkle. 'You're still in love with her. You should just bloody get over it. She's an empty vessel – let it go, dude, finally and forever, please!'

'It's not–'

'All of you. Really. It's sickening.'

'I don't… Not anymore.'

'C'mon, you can't argue with me on that one. Anyway, it's late. More later. Goodnight.' With elegance, she closed the door in my face then locked it.

I stared at the closed door. For the first time, I realised how it may have felt for her all those years ago, to play second fiddle, to be the girl next door, the sister, not the queen; to listen to our love-sick lamentations over Suzanne. How annoying that must have been!

I found my way back to my room, and though I didn't want to be paranoid, I turned the key in the lock. *It's not safe.* Whatever did he mean? I buried myself in my sleeping shroud, curled into a foetal position (the sheets were so cold they felt wet) and puzzled over Emily's reaction to Glen's comment. Something had soured after I left. I tried to figure out what she meant, but I was so tired, I quickly fell into a dreamless sleep.

TWO TURTLE DOVES

I woke around midnight. Sat up, stared at shadows, switched on the light. Nothing. I checked under the bed, behind the drapes. Perhaps it was just the rickety floorboards. The wind howled outside. An angry god pelted snow at the windows. Trees scratched at the glass to get in. Back in bed, I buried myself in the heavy duvet again and pinched my eyes shut. This was some storm.

Wait. I was sure I could hear something outside the door. Perplexed, I flung aside the duvet again, then wrapped myself in it as a dressing gown – damn, it was cold – unlocked my door and peered into the darkness. I could swear I saw shadows, heard voices. I crept along the hallway, then pulled back at the steps leading up to the tower. I could see two figures pressed against the wall outside Glen's room. One was tall – had to be Glen – the other a smaller figure, a woman.

I flattened myself against the wall and listened, but could hear nothing intelligible.

Glen's door creaked open and the two entered. I heard the click of the door being locked from the inside. Nothing more. I listened to my own heart pounding.

It couldn't be who I thought it was. And even if it was, I shouldn't care anyway.

An old inadequacy hit me in the gut. I was sixteen years old again. I thought of Suzanne's ring on Glen's pinkie, how he had insisted on showing it off to everyone, as if it was a trophy; that he had something of hers, something of her. Possession. Ownership. Jealousy. I thought I had left that behind years ago.

I waited. But my teeth chattered and my feet were ice. No sense prowling the corridor. I felt my way back to my room, locked the door with freezing fingers, and lay down again. My trembling came from more than the cold.

I must have fallen into a deep sleep soon after, for when I woke to a pounding on the door, I was disoriented and my head throbbed. Outside the window the night was still black. I untangled myself from the duvet and unbolted the door. The passage was unusually cold, wind tunnelling at me as I peered at two distraught faces outside. Stephen and Reverend James, in pyjamas and dressing gowns and slippers.

'What's going on?'

'We're looking for Glen.' Reverend James peered past me.

'Why?'

I saw the answer on their ashen faces.

'Rafe, Glen is missing.'

I threw my coat on over my pyjamas, pulled on my sneakers (without socks, which I regretted soon enough) and followed them to the end of the passage that led up to the tower room. The door was open (I swore I remembered him locking it from the inside). Danny and Mike were poking around in the entrance, picking up clothes. The first thing I noticed as I entered was that the doors to the balcony were wide open, pinned back by the wind. Flurries of snow blasted in from the outside. 'What the…?'

The balcony railing was missing. A duvet hung caught on the rotten wood that remained. I gripped the door frame and leaned out over the precipice. Snow and frozen rain stung my face.

'It's a blizzard out there,' said Stephen.

'Keep back, Rafe,' said Reverend James. 'The whole balcony isn't safe.'

'Where's Glen?' I grabbed the duvet and pulled it back inside. The room was a mess. The wind had played havoc here, and snowdrifts had already collected inside the door frame. It looked as if someone had violently tossed everything upside down. Glen's suitcase was on the floor, clothes scattered. A pillow lay sodden near the open window. An empty basket lay on its side near the window – I recognised it as the one in which we had all deposited our cell phones. And I detected a whiff of some sweet scent in the air.

'That's what we want to know,' said Danny.

'Stephen got here first,' said Reverend James. 'His room is closest to the tower.'

'I heard Glen's door banging open and closed,' said Stephen.

Danny nodded. 'I thought it was the st-storm. Thunder.'

'Here's the key!' Mike held up the slim new key he had found on the dresser.

Stephen took it from him, pocketed it. 'I found the door open, so I went in. Glen was nowhere in the room, and the balcony doors were flapping like this. The duvet and pillows…'

'Maybe he's in the toilet,' I said, 'or somewhere in the rest of the castle.' If he was with a lover, maybe they had sneaked back to her room. 'Maybe the women's rooms. The tower passage leads to their wing too.'

Reverend James shook his head. 'We don't want to disturb them yet…'

I hit my fist against the door frame. 'Damn.'

'Please, God,' said Mike. 'Let's pray he was nowhere near the balcony when the railing collapsed.'

'Lord Jesus, have mercy,' said Reverend James.

I peered over the edge again. The snow had covered every-thing, but I could make out a few patches of colour, an oblong shape that could be a suitcase. 'I can't understand why all his things are out there.'

Stephen shrugged. 'The wind maybe.'

And then I saw what I had been looking for. My blood froze. 'Look!'

About twenty metres below the sheer cliff edge, on a rock that jutted out, I saw the shape of two splayed legs, arms, and a head, haloed with red. The snow had covered, blown over and drifted, but I was sure of what I saw.

'He's there. Look!'

'Glen!' called Danny. It was a stupid thing to do – shout out into the wind, into the void, the dead snow. Reverend James grasped my arm.

'We have to get to him.'

'Do you think he could be… alive?' said Danny.

The snow stung my face. 'My God. His head looks bashed in.'

'We have to get help,' said Mike.

I pulled out of the Reverend's grip. 'Call the police. We need a phone.'

'Hey, guys, what's going on?'

I turned. Suzanne, Alison, Linda and Emily crowded into the room. Suzanne wore a pink dressing gown that looked like a marshmallow, Emily was in a baggy tracksuit, and Linda and Alison had wrapped themselves tightly in blankets that trailed on the floor.

'Who let the girls in here?' said Reverend James.

'Sorry, Jay,' said Linda, staring around the room, terror in her eyes. 'Emily insisted.'

Emily pushed past. 'What the hell is going on?' She peered through the balcony doors. Turned. 'Where's Glen?'

'Something t-t-terrible,' said Danny. 'Horrible.'

I reached out, took Emily's arm and guided her away. 'There's been an accident.'

'Looks like the balcony railing collapsed,' said Mike. 'Glen's body is down there on the rocks.'

'No!' Suzanne put her hand to her mouth. I looked back at her, thinking about the small shadow I had seen in the middle of the night. Something about her manner made me look again. Our eyes met. I saw fear in her eyes – maybe more than fear: guilt.

Emily held on to my arm. 'Rafe, we have to rescue him.'

I leaned over the edge again, as far as I dared, and stared down the rocky precipice. Glen's body was now half-buried in the snow, but suddenly a clump of snow tumbled away to reveal a head of dark hair – and a blue hand. I made a note of landmarks so that if the body was completely covered, the police would know where to search. I peered down the mountainside and saw at once that this was the most inaccessible part of the valley. A sheer rock face. 'Mike, could anyone climb down there? What's your view?'

Mike shook his head. 'We'd need ropes, climbing gear, and a winch.'

'People, I think we need to get out of here,' said Reverend James. 'The whole tower room feels unstable.' He herded the women away from the open balcony doors and back into the passageway. We followed. Stephen shut the door behind him, as if to block out the horror.

'Let's go to the living room,' Reverend James called out.

We clustered by the fire, which was still smouldering. Danny added some twigs and soon it was roaring bright. Reverend James took charge. 'Is everyone here and accounted for?'

I counted nine people. 'Everyone except Glen, yes.'

'Where's the concierge?' said Mike. 'Where does he sleep? We need to find him right now.'

Stephen shook his head. 'He left last night, after supper, remember?'

'He left in that b-blizzard?' said Danny.

I turned to Reverend James. 'Where the hell are the phones?'

He looked like death itself: pale, clammy skin, lips trembling. Using the word 'hell' bothered him more than the accusation itself. 'A retreat, Rafe. This was supposed to be a retreat. I didn't know this would happen.'

I had spied the landline, an old-fashioned black telephone with a large receiver, in the foyer. I walked over to it and picked up the handset. No dial tone. I clicked the button up and down. Stephen walked over and placed the phone down. His hand was trembling and his eyes were full of white terror. 'It's no use, anyway, Rafe, there's no connectivity,' he managed to say. 'We saw that yesterday.'

I pushed him aside to get back to the Reverend, who was huddling by the fire. 'But surely there must be an emergency channel. We need those phones.'

Reverend James glanced at Stephen and I saw what looked like collusion. As if they knew something I didn't and were trying to hide it from me. 'Glen took them all into the tower. He was in charge of them. I looked for them in the room. Gone!'

'You sure?'

Reverend James again flicked that conspiratorial glance at Stephen. 'We— we thought the tower would be the best place. Glen said he would lock them away.'

Stephen nodded. 'I gave him the basket.'

'That's what w-we were s-searching for.'

'The thing is, to remain calm,' said Reverend James, 'especially in front of the women. We don't want to frighten them.'

He looked so smugly self-enclosed that I wanted to hit him. 'I don't believe it! You're responsible for our safety here, and you don't even have a phone.'

Reverend James turned his back to me, crouched by the fire. He threw a heavy log onto the flames and worried the embers with a long fire poker. The fire burned angrily. I could feel that he wished it was me he was poking in that fire. In the mirror, a second blaze threw parallel flames on the side of the room. Nine mirror images of stunned old Twelve members huddled together in their nightclothes against the warmth.

'Poor Glen,' said Alison. 'He must have been out on the balcony, leaned on the rotten wood railing, and...'

I met Emily's eyes. Hell, we were out there with him last night.

'A freak accident,' said Stephen, more to himself than to anyone else. 'I was supposed to have that room. But Glen said he was fine with it.'

'You can't blame yourself,' said Reverend James.

'I can't bear to think of what happened,' Emily said. 'Poor Glen.'

Reverend James stood, the poker in his hand. 'Girls,' he said, 'let's have some coffee.'

I had forgotten how submissive the women in the Church had to be. Still it was a shock to see Linda meekly stand and obey. 'Sure.'

Alison joined her, and Suzanne and Emily followed, begrudgingly. Reverend James waited for them to disappear into the kitchen before speaking again, sotto voce. 'Let's all calm down. We mustn't scare the girls.'

Danny: 'C-could he be alive still?'

Mike shook his head. 'No one could survive that fall. Straight onto those rocks. I know. I've seen some tragic accidents like this on Mount Everest.'

Reverend James concurred. 'He was dead when he hit the ground. He didn't suffer.'

I stared at him. 'How can you say that?'

Reverend James returned the stare. 'I can say that. I know that.'

'We have to go and get him,' said Danny. 'What are we waiting for? Mike's a mountaineer.'

Mike shook his head. 'It would be suicide in this weather. And it's still too dark to see anything.'

'Emergency services should be able to get here,' I said. 'That's what they're trained to do.'

Reverend James brandished the poker at the fire. 'What we need to do is pray. Panic, fear and doubt are not the way of the Lord. The God who made the universe has counted the very hairs of our heads. We have to stay strong.'

I took the poker from him and stirred the fire, making sparks shoot up. I could not believe what I was hearing.

'We must stay put,' said Reverend James. 'It's a time for faith. We're being tested. We need to pray.' He held out his hands to Danny and Mike. Danny reached for my hand but I pulled back. Stephen gazed up at the ceiling, while Mike opened his palms and closed his eyes. Reverend James screwed his eyes tightly shut. I kept mine open.

'Lord, keep us safe. In your wisdom, you have kept us safe. Guide us, Lord, into what we should do here. 'We pray for Glen's soul, that he is in Thy peace. Amen.'

'Amen.'

The women arrived with coffee (caffeine somehow escaped the net of those things forbidden) and we sipped scalding over-sweetened drinks, grateful to stop the chattering teeth, the cold numbness inside. Wide eyes, steam, hands cupping mugs. I observed these people in the mirror. Something was not right here. Reverend James and Stephen kept exchanging sly glances. Linda chewed her nails and glanced nervously at her husband, but as soon as he looked back, she averted her eyes. This was not a normal reaction to a close friend's death. This looked like... guilt.

Suzanne smiled a Hollywood smile as she placed a mug of coffee in my hands. But her hands were shaking. She too looked guilty.

'Girls,' said Reverend James, 'we have put it all in the hands of God. Trust Him.'

I let the coffee burn down my throat. 'Nothing more we need to do? What about Glen's body?'

'We can do nothing now,' said Stephen. 'Let's go and shower and we'll meet in half an hour for breakfast.'

I tried to contain the burning rage in my chest. I was shaking, more with cold than with anger, so discarded my sodden clothes and pulled on long thermal underwear, jeans, T-shirt, shirt, sweater, coat and thick socks. The smugness of these people! Even when death was present, they cocooned themselves in platitudes. I was on my own here, I could see.

I crept out of the front door and braced myself against the icy wind. My plan was to find a path down to examine the body. But as soon as I stepped outside I could see how futile this was. Snow had blanketed the road and I could not see where to step. The edge of the cliff was treacherous, a sheer drop down the mountainside. I peered over the edge and the ground fell away into thick mist. If I was to climb down here, I would have to wait until the mist cleared. I could not even see the body. This was going to take a helicopter, paramedics, and it would be a dangerous operation. The snow flurries attacked me, the biting wind cut into me, and I began shivering violently. I tried to reassure myself that Glen was not lying alive and in pain, waiting for rescue – he must have died instantly, or if he was still alive after impact, after all that debris had smashed into him, he would have died from exposure.

I trudged back inside, discarded my sodden clothes, took a hot shower and dressed in dry clothes. This was not a simple accident. Not with Glen's belongings strewn all over the room. Someone had been in his room – a late-night visitor, and some struggle, a fight had occurred.

Pity I had not been at the scene first. I only had Stephen's word for what had happened. I had noted those glances between Reverend James and Stephen. Linda. Even Suzanne. This smelt of conspiracy.

A knock on the bathroom door interrupted my thoughts. I dressed quickly and opened the door to find Stephen's pale face staring at me. 'Rafe, Reverend James has some news. We need to all meet downstairs.'

Mike, Danny, Stephen and Reverend James stood in front of the crackling fire in the living room. I heard the women in the kitchen making breakfast.

Reverend James called me into the huddle. 'I have prayed about this, and God has given us an answer. We need to sit tight through the storm, and when the road can be made passable, the police will get to us.'

I stared at him. 'Have you contacted the police?'

'You don't need to worry about that, Rafe,' said Reverend James. 'During my prayers, a peace came upon me, a small, still voice telling me to trust God.'

'There's a body freezing over in our front yard–'

'Let us pray.' The men closed their eyes, bowed their heads, raised their hands up to the ceiling. I folded my arms, stared at them. 'All eyes closed, heads bowed,' said Reverend James. 'Be still and know that I am the Lord. Heavenly Father, help Rafe now accept Thy will.'

I slammed my fist against the wall. 'I can't believe this.

Excuse me, Reverend James, but a man has died and praying is not, in my view, going to help anyone at this point.'

Reverend James remained in prayer pose, ignoring me. Stephen opened his eyes, placed his hand on my shoulder. 'All things work together for good to those who love God.'

'He will take care of everything,' said Reverend James. 'We just need to stay put.'

'For fuck's sake,' I said under my breath.

Our prayer session counsel was interrupted by a scream from the dining area from one of the women. 'Reverend James, come here quick!'

We turned to see the four women hunched over Glen's place setting. Reverend James ran over to them. We followed. Alison stepped back to let Reverend James see. 'I was about to set the table for breakfast when...'

The envelope containing Glen's secret symbol was open. The slip of paper inside, a picture of two turtle doves, was torn right down the middle. Two words had been scribbled on each piece of torn paper: *Old Testament. New Testament.*

Alison looked up at the Reverend, who had gone grey. 'What does it mean, Reverend?'

Reverend James pressed his fingers into his eyes. 'Dear Lord, today is Boxing Day, the second day of Christmas.'

'I don't understand,' said Alison.

'On the second day of Christmas, my true love gave to me two turtle doves,' he reminded us. 'Two turtle doves signify the Old and New Testaments.'

Suzanne said what everyone was thinking. 'Did he... do this? Before he died?'

'He must have,' said Reverend James. 'He solved his riddle of the second day of Christmas.'

'Was he trying to tell us something?' Suzanne pressed her fingers to her lips. I could not help but feel that she was acting. Even if she was genuine, there was no way of telling.

This note had been staged. Premeditated.

Linda tugged on her husband's sleeve. He nodded. 'Let's eat.'

We took our allocated places, Reverend James mumbled grace, and we helped ourselves to bacon, eggs, sausages and toast. I ate without appetite, staring at each woman in turn.

Alison was crying. 'Poor Glen,' she kept saying.

Linda looked whiter than ever, and was stony silent with thin lips. 'My God, my God.'

Suzanne stared across at an empty chair and a torn envelope.

One of you was with Glen last night. One of you knows something.

Emily gave me a quick look. *We need to talk,* her eyes said.

'What do you make of it all, Reverend?' said Mike.

Reverend James finished his mouthful of egg and wiped his lips with a napkin. 'He was just doing what I wanted you all to do – solve the mystery of the twelve days of Christmas. Each of your designated days is a riddle. Glen solved his. It was unrelated to his death.'

I watched his trembling hands. His eyes. He was lying. And he could feel my scrutiny. He spoke to the group but kept glancing at me. 'I had planned on revealing each day of Christmas and talking about its significance, but this has made me stronger in my resolve to do it. To honour Glen, we will continue. Today, on the second day of Christmas, I was going to give a sermon on the two turtle doves, the significance of the Old and New Testaments. How the New Testament fulfils the Old–'

I clattered the knife and fork on the table. Pushed my plate away. 'This is unbelievable.'

He ignored me. The others listened intently. 'The centre of Christmas is Christ, and the second foundation on which our faith rests is the Bible, the two turtle doves, signifying the Holy Spirit descending on us, giving us understanding of its truths.

The Old and New Testaments are twin voices of truth from God, speaking of both his wrath and his love. Meditate on this truth. God has commanded it. He wants us to take this seriously.'

As the Reverend droned on, I watched Suzanne. She worried her bottom lip with her top teeth, as she had done when she was young. She fidgeted, threw worried looks at the Reverend, and when she caught my eye, made a silent plea with her lips.

Reverend James' sermons had always been absurd and illogical, but until I prised myself out of his narrow world view by taking philosophy at college, I had been under his spell. Everything is in God's hands, he was assuring us; He has a plan which we cannot understand, so all we have to do is trust and obey. *Happy the man who puts his trust in the Lord! Never fear! Not a doubt or a fear, not a sigh or a tear can abide while we trust and obey.* For twenty minutes I listened to the Reverend preach, watched the others sit meekly like sheep, as if our comrade's body was not lying stiff in the blizzard. No one had even suggested they try to get help. Although I wanted to walk out, I sat there, not to listen to his moralising but to watch everyone closely.

After the sermon, the women cleared the plates away and washed the dishes in the kitchen. I pulled Emily towards the corridor. 'Let's take a walk.'

'Good idea.'

'I want to show you something.'

She followed me up the steps and along the corridor in the men's quarters. 'I thought we were not– It's dangerous in the tower.'

'You can always go back.'

She squeezed my arm.

We climbed the short flight of steps, but found that Glen's door was locked.

'Didn't Reverend James lock it?' she said. 'Or Stephen?'

'Why would they lock it?'

'What did you want to see in there?'

'I wanted to look at that balcony again. And see if the cell phones are really all gone.'

'We can't now.'

I peered into the dimly lit corridor. I thought I saw something move in the shadows, but when I looked again I saw only a spidery corner. 'I saw Glen last night after you all went to bed. He was with a woman.'

'What?'

I nodded. 'Right here in the corridor outside his room. Exactly where we're standing now. They were talking, arguing even. They went into his room, he locked the door, and I waited for her to come out. She didn't. So I went to bed. She must have sneaked back to the women's side before he went out on the balcony and fell.'

Her eyes widened. 'Or she was here when he... fell.'

We both contemplated the possibilities. She left before the accident happened; she was there to witness it but then snuck out; or... or...

'Was anyone missing from the women's side when you went to bed?'

'Not that I know of.'

'Where were you?'

She punched my arm. 'Don't interrogate me. We're allies here, remember? If we're a team, we have to trust each other. No secrets.'

'Sorry. But the philosopher in me has to follow every argument. Examine every premise.'

'Yes, professor.'

She wrapped her pinkie around mine. 'Swear to tell me everything. Blood brother and sister.'

I pinched the bridge of my nose with my fingers, closing my eyes, trying to push a headache away. 'Sorry, Em, of course I trust you. But this is all a little weird.'

'More than weird. What do you think happened here?'

'Nothing makes sense. But my gut instinct tells me that this was not accidental.'

Gut instinct, intuition: shorthand for a very complex process that occurs in our brains. Intuition is not a mystical sixth sense but a computation of millions of bits of data our brain has received about a person or a situation, and the processing, calculations and sum of all this information gives us a 'feeling' about this person or situation that was as accurate as any mathematical calculation or tested scientific hypothesis. 'I mean, he calls us up into his room to specifically warn us about something. We stand on the balcony with him—'

'We all could have been killed.'

'He tears the two turtle doves card in half to show James that he gets his silly Christmas game. He meets some woman before he goes to bed. Argues with her. And then tragedy happens. An accident. But his shit is strewn all over the mountainside. The cell phones are conveniently gone.'

'Conveniently.'

'As if he threw them off himself. Or someone else did. The woman in his room.'

'Shhh!'

I heard the footsteps before I saw the silhouette in the corridor behind us.

'Rafe… and is that you, Emily?'

'Stephen!'

'What are you guys doing here?'

'Who locked Glen's door?' I asked him.

'I did. It's not safe to be here. If the balcony railing broke, who knows what else is going to give way. Reverend James' instructions.'

'We wanted to see if we could find any cell phones or devices.'

'I told you there are none. I checked.'

I wondered how much Stephen had heard of our conversation.

'Come, Rafe, Emily. Reverend James wants us all to stick together. And it's nearly lunchtime.'

No one had an appetite at lunch either. Glen's place at the table had been set, as if we were expecting him to show up. Reverend James launched into a sermon about bringing sheep back into the fold. The sermon was targeted at me. And Emily. And maybe Suzanne. The non-believers.

Suzanne nodded at some points he made, the whole time checking her reflection in the wall mirror. And the men stared too at her, gave furtive glances to hide the fact that Reverend James' words could not compete with the goddess in their midst. Even in the midst of a tragedy, she commanded everyone's attention. Linda and Alison were no better. Nostrils flared in high dudgeon as they examined her every move. Only Emily seemed immune, her eyes resting on me.

We were trapped by more than the blizzard. And in my case, also by my own curiosity. The ghoulish nature of the death, the rage and injustice of the cover-up. I should at least try to raise the alarm, as soon as the blizzard eases. For now I would stay and figure this out.

Reverend James persisted with his sermon. 'Nothing is accidental. Nothing happens without Him knowing. But Satan is prowling around like a lion, seeking whom he may devour.' And his gaze fell on me.

'Satan?' repeated Alison.

The Reverend's eyes narrowed. 'Don't fear, Alison. Satan has no power over us.' He laid his hand on his Bible.

'And what about those who don't believe in Satan?' I could not resist asking.

Alison shot me a look. I stared her down. Reverend James, however, locked eyes on me and smiled. But behind his smile was a dark threat. 'Unless you repent, you will all likewise perish,' he said. 'Luke 13, verse 1.'

I chewed on the leftover *pernice*. Mopped up the gravy with my roll, matched his stare.

Emily put a restraining hand on my arm. 'What are you saying, Reverend James?'

He kept his voice low, but I could tell he was losing his patience. He was not a man to be questioned. 'Not me, not what I am saying but what the Bible, God's word, is saying.' Reverend James reached into his pocket and retrieved a book that looked a thousand years old. The leather binding was raw and the edging had been eaten. Always the showman, he raised it in the air and waited until he had everyone's attention before continuing. '*Foxe's Book of Martyrs*.' He opened the book at a place mark. 'On the second day of Christmas, St Stephen was martyred.'

At his name, Stephen looked startled, as if caught in the act. Reverend James paused to measure the effect of his words.

'Martyrdom,' he repeated. 'Which is why we now call it the Feast of St Stephen. Like the carol—'

Emily cut in, singing the beginning of the carol. 'Good King Wenceslas looked out, on the feast of Stephen—'

I nudged her to stop, and the Reverend chose to ignore her intended impertinence. 'Correct. St Stephen was one of the first ordained deacons of the Church and the first Christian martyr.'

He brandished the book in the air, leaned on the table as if it were a pulpit. 'And if you have read Acts 7, you will know how he died.'

Danny raised his hand. 'He was stoned to death.'

'Yes. On the second day of Christmas, he was buried in rocks. Crushed to death.'

Alison held her hand over her mouth. Linda pushed back violently in her chair as if she had been shoved.

I refused to react to his histrionics. 'What are you saying? Logically.'

Reverend James placed the book on the table, rested his hand upon it. 'In God's world, nothing happens by chance.'

Utter bullshit, I wanted to say. Most things happen by chance. Yes, there is causal determinism, the idea that every event is caused by another, according to the laws of nature, but this was not what Reverend James meant. He meant that every event in the universe was approved of and orchestrated by God, be it a massacre, an earthquake or car accident. And now Glen's death. 'You're saying that God arranged some huge, meaningful coincidence here to match your *Foxe's Book of Martyrs?*'

Reverend James closed his eyes and placed his fingertips together. Spoke to the blackness. 'There are no accidents in God's world. All is foreseen, designed.'

I blew out of my mouth in exasperation. 'I don't believe I'm hearing this.' I appealed to the shocked faces around the table. 'Surely none of you believe this is part of some non-existent God's plan?'

But by their glazed look back at me, I gathered that they did. Reverend James' bald head gleamed in the light. 'God "worketh all things after the counsel of His own will: That we should be to the praise of his glory." Ephesians 1, 11 to 12.'

'Amen,' chorused Mike, Danny, Alison and Linda.

My words had fallen into an abyss. I stared out the far

window. The falling snow was relentless. By now Glen's body
would be completely buried, and impossible to find.

'Listen up, people,' said Reverend James, clapping his
hands together. 'It is time for us to meditate on our sins. Write
down your confession on the pieces of paper I gave you. Be
honest. No one will see them but God.'

There was no way I was spending my afternoon compiling a
list of my sins. I made a plan. I gathered my winter wear and
returned to the lounge. The weather had not cleared, but at
least there was enough light for me to find my way to the edge.
If we had no way of communicating with the outside world, I
should at least find my way down to the body. I didn't want to
be charged with gross negligence. Or not reporting a dead
body. Or obstruction of justice. But more than that, I didn't
want to be part of this God conspiracy, this lack of agency. I
had had enough of that.

Alison and Linda banged around in the kitchen, and Emily
joined them to sort out the evening meal. Danny sat crouched
over a Bible in one corner, while Mike scribbled on his sheet of
paper. Reverend James and Stephen were seated on the couch
by the fire, leaning forward with eyes closed, palms upwards to
God, praying. Suzanne sat on her own against the mirror.
Terror flashed across her face. But when she saw me looking at
her, she gave me a half-smile. 'Where are you going, Rafe?'

'A little walk. It's claustrophobic in here.'

'Outside? Are you crazy?'

I hauled on my heavy winter coat, pulled on a balaclava
and mittens, wrapped a scarf around my neck, and pulled
open the front door. Reverend James opened his mouth to
object, but I pushed open the door before he had a chance to
speak.

My plan was twofold: I would have another go at reaching Glen's body, but I would also hunt for the phones that had been blown out of the balcony window. The cold hit me like a wall, but this time I was well padded against the elements. The wind had picked up and the flurries had diminished, but the cold burrowed into every exposed chink of my armour. The moisture in my eyes felt as if it was going to freeze. The snowdrifts were deep, but I plodded my way around the castle until I could see the tower above me and the balcony with most of the railing missing. I stopped at the abyss of the valley where Glen had tumbled. The debris we had seen earlier was now blanketed in snow. No sign of phones anywhere. I shielded my eyes against the glare – the afternoon was surprisingly bright, and the snow was luminous. The mist had cleared, and I could see a shrouded shape in the snow metres below. The wind had blown snowdrifts around him. I put a boot out ahead of me and felt it give. No way I could climb down here. I needed equipment: ropes, other helpers.

I could see parts of his red jacket, his shoulder and arm, the heels of his boots. His head was haloed with a brown stain, and his limbs, positioned awkwardly, were broken.

And there indeed was his left hand, the wrist exposed, a sparkling object on his pinkie finger. Suzanne's ring. I wondered how she would feel about him dying with her ring on his finger. But she probably didn't even know he was wearing it.

Unless she was the one who had been in his room.

Some probable scenarios played out in my head. He had invited her to his room, shown her the ring, declared his eternal love for her. She had laughed, dismissed him, and he had threatened suicide. He had stood on the balcony and then an act of God or nature had intervened. He had slipped, plunged over, clutching the railing as it snapped off. He had tumbled down, smashing onto the rock. Suzanne had watched in horror, fled the room, terrified, and not said a word.

Or: he had threatened suicide and had hurled himself off the balcony, breaking the railing as he fell. She had fled, hiding her horrible secret.

Or…

No, that was too far-fetched.

I could not see her as a murderer. She had no motive. The snow flurried across Glen's body, hiding the blood. The spatter from his head wound had even stained his hand leaving a brownish mark. I felt an illogical need to reach him and clean it off. I wondered who would do him this service eventually. The snow flurried across Glen's body, and his body would soon be buried, so I hunted around and found two bricks, placed them at the edge of the chasm so that I would know where the body was.

Stamping my feet in the cold, of all people, I found Suzanne waiting for me in the hallway. 'Thank God you're okay, Rafe. What were you doing outside?'

Why would she be so interested in what I had found outside? I unpeeled the scarf and balaclava and worked my frozen lips. 'How okay can I feel when someone has just fallen to his death?'

I saw frailty in her now. And this was not acting. A sudden compassion for the girl in this larger-than-life actress's body welled up in me before suspicion took over. If she had been in his room, then only three possibilities remained. Accident. Suicide. Murder. And by keeping silent, she was implicated in whichever one it was.

She placed her hand on my arm to keep me here in the hallway a moment longer. 'What can we do?'

I spoke in a whisper. 'If Reverend James is not going to take responsibility for Glen's death, someone has to. Aren't you curious as to how Glen died?'

That moment of vulnerability was gone and the same old Suzanne was back. She took her hand away and shrank into herself again. 'Why are you asking me?'

I felt colder than I had outside. 'What were you doing last night when this all happened? Did you hear the banging doors?'

A flash of fear crossed her eyes. 'I was fast asleep. Emily woke me, said something was going on.'

She unfolded her arms, combed her hair with her finger – both signs if I could read them. You can tell the truth from someone's gestures, unless that person has been schooled in the art of lying. But her eyes told me everything. She knew more than she was telling me. I decided to push it. 'You know something more about this.'

Her hands were shaking. 'I'm not responsible here. I didn't– Why do people always think… Rafe, please.'

I stared into her eyes and she stared back. They were as green and unfathomable as I remembered them.

'Rafe, please,' she said. 'You're the only sane person around. Please get us out of here. Rafe, I…'

Reverend James walked into the hallway and her plea died in her throat. 'You two okay?'

Supper was a comforting ritual. Setting places, sitting at the table, routine. As if this was all normal. Chicken soup and hot rolls.

'Compliments to the chef!' said Reverend James.

'Thanks,' said Alison. 'Emily added her twelve secret ingredients. Linda made the rolls.'

'A blessing on the meal.'

We watched the darkness close in as we ate.

They wanted to avoid the subject, but I brought them back. I was not going to let them slip into denial. 'We have a legal responsibility to report a dead body.'

Alison and Linda looked down. The men turned their eyes to Reverend James. He was sole authority here. He stirred his soup, ignored my question.

'Reverend James, I'm worried about the body out there. And us carrying on as if it isn't.'

He gave me a withering look.

Mike gave a quick look at Reverend James that told me that they had already discussed this subject in private. 'Actually, it's the best place for it.'

I gave him a puzzled look. 'How?'

He dipped his bread roll in the soup and took a bite before answering. 'On Everest, there are at least two hundred dead bodies just lying in the ice.'

'And?'

'They can't carry them back. When I climbed up, there was a marker in one cave climbers used to tell them they were near the top. Mr Green Boots we called him. Just a frozen corpse lying there with green boots sticking out.'

Alison put her spoon down. 'Not while we're eating, please, Mike.'

Mike gave her a wounded look then opened his palms. 'But what I'm saying,' he said, 'is that it's the best place to preserve a dead body until the police get here.'

'We haven't even checked if he's dead,' said Suzanne. 'I have this terrible thought that he's alive, frozen, can't escape.' She was biting her lip, and hadn't touched her soup. Alison was holding her stomach and not eating anything either. Emily hadn't seemed to have lost her appetite and was sipping the hot soup slowly, all the while watching this exchange. Reverend

James too watched silently, his eyes flitting to me, to Mike, to Suzanne.

'C-can a b-body freeze and still be al-live?' asked Danny.

Mike nodded. 'Yes, but not for long. Once an Everest climber stopped in a cave to rest and his body froze. He couldn't move. Other climbers thought he was dead and passed by. But then someone heard him moan, realised he was still alive and rescued him.'

Suzanne's eyes widened as she put down her spoon. 'That's terrible, Mike. Is it possible?'

I shook my head. 'Glen fell twenty metres onto hard rock. His head was crushed. No one could survive that.'

We sat in silence. No one dared to eat for a few minutes.

'Poor Glen,' said Alison, still clutching her stomach.

'He died instantly,' said Reverend James. 'He's in peace now.'

I refrained from banging my fist on the table. Instead, I took it out on the bread roll, crumbling it into little pieces. 'Again, Reverend, how can you say that? Just to make us feel better?'

Reverend James placed a hand on his Bible, which was never far from him. *Damn! I had just precipitated another sermon.*

'We need not concern ourselves with the body, which is just flesh and earthly temple of the soul. At death, the soul leaves the body. Meditate on this.' He paused for effect. 'For we know that if our earthly house of this tabernacle were dissolved, we have a building of God, a house not made with hands, eternal in the heavens. For in this we groan, earnestly desiring to be clothed upon with our house which is from heaven.'

The Reverend was truly sealed off from this world, in a reality of his own, one walled in with Biblical quotes and plastered with smug self-righteousness. His neat answers were not rational, more to prop up his authority. Or else he was smudging things because he had something to hide.

After supper, Emily joined me by the window and we watched snow spatter against the pane.

'Any further thoughts?' she said. 'Suspicions?'

I nodded.

'Me too. I have something to tell you. But not here.'

I checked to see where everyone was. They were huddled around the fire. 'Come to my room, we can talk there. You wait here and sneak out a few minutes after I go, okay?' I walked quickly out of the room, making sure no one at the fire saw me, and then marched up to my room. I turned up the heat. Two minutes later, Emily creaked open my door. 'It's a better room than mine. But it's freezing.'

'Here.' I threw her my coat, and then bolted the door.

But as I turned she was in my arms. We held each other, as if we would fall if we didn't. Then she pushed me back so she could look into my eyes, still holding me at the waist. 'Good to see you again, Rafe. Really good.'

I brushed her hair out of her eyes with my fingers. 'You were a child last time I saw you. You were sixteen. You still look sixteen!'

'And you were always the rebel. The doubting Thomas of The Twelve. Are you still?'

I laughed. 'If God really existed, it would be necessary to abolish him. Of course. Maybe an anarchist now. Or a post-anarchist. Life is a proliferation of possibilities.'

She squeezed me tight at the waist, held me to her. 'Don't go all philosophical on me, Rafe. I'm just a nurse. The world is the world. That's my philosophy.'

'It worked out for you, Em. You're happily married. Rich husband. Children.'

She shook her head. 'Terrible things happened to me after you left.'

I looked into her green eyes again.

She let me go and we stood apart. 'Once I left the Church, I picked up my life, married. But I never forgave you for abandoning me. We were supposed to be blood siblings, but you never kept in contact. I wanted to tell you about my marriage, ask you about your life. You're still single, I hear.'

I laughed again. 'In a serial kind of way.'

She bit her lower lip. 'I always thought you would marry Suzanne.'

'Marriage is a prison I always managed to avoid.'

Emily raised her eyebrows. 'I see you staring at her in the mirror the whole time. Still under her spell.'

I shook my head. Took her hand again and warmed it with mine. 'To be honest, I think she knows more than she's letting on.'

Her eyes were wide. 'What?'

'Whoever I saw with him, in his room, knows what happened.'

'It's terrible,' she said.

'I have my suspicions. But nothing concrete. I spoke with Suzanne briefly before supper. She's acting guilty as hell.'

Emily pressed my fingers together. 'Still pursuing her, eh?'

I sighed. 'As a detective, yes.'

She made circles with her fingers and brought them to her eyes, to look like binoculars. 'Doing "research". Sure.'

'Seriously, she's terrified of something. And Reverend James and Stephen know more than they're letting on. How can Reverend James believe God let a balcony collapse to kill Glen? That it's part of His plan, which just happens to coincide with the second day of Christmas when St Stephen was buried in rocks?'

Emily rested her head on my shoulder. 'It's such bullshit. Exactly why I left his nutty Church of the Joyful Resurrection. Everything that happened – and some bad things happened in that church after you left, let me tell you – was "meant to be" and we were "not to question God's will". No question of how to try to put things right, or understand what was wrong. It was all God. Or Satan. Such crap.'

I brushed her hair away from her face again. 'So are you going to tell me now?'

She pulled my hand from her hair, grabbed it tight.

'Last night in Glen's room. You and Glen alluded to some secret. What was he going on about?'

She squeezed both of my hands. Sighed. Looked down. 'There's a lot.'

'Try me.'

She looked back to make sure the door was locked. 'I'm sure the woman you saw was Linda,' she said.

I wrinkled my brow. 'Linda? Not Suzanne?'

She held my hands even tighter. 'Glen and Linda were having an affair.'

It took a few minutes to take in. 'Glen? Linda?' I tried to imagine that ice queen, pallid skin, cold eyes, having passion for anything, anybody. 'You're absolutely kidding. The preacher's *wife* and Glen?'

Emily now wrapped both her pinkies around mine. The sign of truth. Double truth. Blood siblings. 'It was hushed up. But things still got very ugly and Glen left. I wondered how it would be, bringing Glen back into The Twelve. I knew they would have to at least meet to sort it out.'

I shook my head. Tried to remember the exchanges between Linda and Glen and Reverend James on the first day. I hadn't noticed anything. 'Last night, the people I saw were arguing. If it was Linda, it does make some sort of sense.' And here was the dangerous question. 'Do you think it had anything to do with his death a few hours later?'

Emily lowered her voice, barely audible above the wind rattling the window panes. 'No doubt.'

THREE

THREE FRENCH HENS

That evening, the wind howled, the snow fell and on that second day of Christmas, the Feast of St Stephen, the 26th of December, the nine remaining members of The Twelve huddled in the living room, their faces yellowed in the reflection of the leaping fire. The message was, according to God, to stay put, remain calm, and weather the storm. We had no way of contacting the outside world, so the police had no clue we were trapped. And here we were, playing silly games.

Old emotions bubbled up in me. She still held power over me. No matter how I denied it, Suzanne still burned inside my soul. I had spent my life pining and mourning, aching for her; no, not for her, for an idealised image of her. I had seen her everywhere and had fallen in love with a dozen copies of her. She had formed the shape of my desire and I was here to purge that. Suzanne had constructed herself with a series of stock images and the world, and I along with it, had fallen in love with a chimera.

She caught me staring at her in the mirror and I looked away. The fear in her eyes was unmistakable.

Reverend James held out a glass bowl, and one by one we placed our tightly folded pieces of paper holding our confessions. I had to admit it was a brilliant strategy, asking us to entrust our deepest darkest secrets to him. It was a matter of pure faith, because he could unfold them and read them. But he didn't. He held the bowl up to the chandelier and asked us to close our eyes and silently ask God for absolution. He waited until all eyes were closed. 'Emily. Rafe.'

I obliged. So did Emily. When I opened my eyes again, Reverend James had placed the bowl on the low coffee table by the fire. 'Amen.'

He lifted the bowl once more, and I watched him pour its contents straight into the fire. Some papers unfurled as they browned and crisped and lit up orange.

'May the Lord forgive us our trespasses, wash you all of our sins, and forgive those who trespass against us.'

Nothing new here – this was a sound psychological strategy used by therapists to detach patients from guilt, obsession, habit. But it turned Reverend James' flock into dependent, penitent sinners.

'What did you write?' whispered Emily, nudging me in the ribs. 'Yours must have been a long list.'

I grabbed her fingers to stop her doing it again. 'Not as long as yours.'

'I'd give anything to know what people wrote.'

I had watched each one place their folded piece of paper in the bowl. 'I doubt anyone would confess their real sins,' I said.

'Don't be so sure.'

And then Reverend James launched into another sermon. I tuned out and stared at Linda, fascinated by what Emily had told me. Linda sat tight-lipped as the papers burned. Now, every gesture of hers lit up with significance.

I had written a tongue-in-cheek 'confession'. I didn't believe in a God who kept a score of our sins and sent us to hell forever and ever to be tortured if we didn't repent of them. The universe did not work that way.

But now this confession scenario had taken on more significance. Was Reverend James trying to force out the truth here? Or hide the truth by focussing on others' sins?

"'Know ye not that the unrighteous shall not inherit the kingdom of God?'" Reverend James proclaimed with eyes closed (as he did when quoting the sacred scriptures).

It was an idle game at this stage. Whether Glen had been murdered or had ended his own life was an open question, but I for one suspected foul play. The obvious suspect was Reverend James himself. He finds his wife with Glen – again – calls on the wrath of God, God unleashes a lightning bolt which flings Glen onto the rocks. Adulterer!

Or Reverend James catches them at it, corners Glen on the balcony, and in his blind fury pushes him. Glen clutches the railing, it breaks, and he tumbles over the edge.

My gaze lingered on Linda and another scenario played out in my mind: Glen says he does not love her and refuses to rescue her from her unhappy marriage with this fanatical clergyman. She pushes Glen off the balcony, watches grimmouthed as he plummets to his death.

Somehow I could not believe any of the scenarios was true.

Stephen stared into the fire, sweat beading across his forehead. Maybe he punished Glen for his apostasy...

I shook my head, releasing these grim fantasies. According to the principle of Occam's razor, the simplest explanation is most likely to be the correct one. It was an accident, plain and simple.

But such an accident! It was no surprise that Reverend James could apply moral lessons. Adulterers were stoned to death in the Bible. No wonder this man of God saw this as fate, no, as moral retribution from above.

The sermon droned on. It seemed as if it was for Linda's benefit. Or it could apply to all. '"Be not deceived",' the Reverend intoned, still with eyes closed, '"neither fornicators, nor idolaters, nor adulterers, nor effeminate, nor abusers of themselves with mankind, nor thieves, nor covetous, nor drunkards, nor revilers, nor extortioners, shall inherit the kingdom of God."'

Emily nudged me in the ribs again. 'He's talking about you.'

I placed my hand over her mouth.

Reverend James' point was clear. He was more determined than ever to achieve the goals of the retreat, to help us find our way back to God. And if a gruesome death would help us flee into the arms of Jesus, then praise the Lord, so be it.

After the sermon, everyone retreated into their own meditative spaces. I stared into the fire where some pieces of paper, now ash, still retained their shape. I tried to make out the words, those dark squiggles against white ash.

'Rafe, I need to have a word with you.'

I turned to see Stephen's pallid face. 'Sure.'

With a sly glance at the others, Stephen escorted me to the entrance hall, out of earshot of the group sitting in a large circle discussing the sermon. Suzanne followed me with her eyes. Looked anxious. So did Emily.

Stephen led me upstairs with none of his usual diffidence. He did not hesitate for a moment, even when we passed through a stretch of darkened passageway where the lights had failed altogether. We came to a musty room across from the bedroom wings and next to the torture museum. He flicked the light switch and we stood in a library with heavy wooden shelves from floor to ceiling. I noted the ancient spines of the books tightly packed in rows, most of the titles in Italian or Latin.

Stephen stood by the window and stared at white mist, grainy flecks of snow and sleet battering the pane like a meteor shower pummelling a spaceship. He said nothing. I waited as he shuffled, shot a glance back at the open door and continued his silence. So I began the conversation. 'The police are not coming. Reverend James is going to keep us here day after day and subject us to sermons until we all repent. That is the plan. You're in on it, so please tell me.'

Stephen pushed his glasses back onto his nose, a nervous gesture from school days. 'Reverend James feels that we needed to reassure everyone, to calm them, make them feel that everything is under control.'

I stared at the blizzard. Snow had banked up the road, the walls, the hedges, unrecognisable as the place I had arrived at a day ago. 'But isn't it a little strange to do nothing about Glen's death. Doesn't that bother you?'

Stephen was sweating. His metabolism was all wrong. But then he was wearing a huge sweater with the McDonald's logo emblazoned on the front, a scarf wrapped around his throat and a balaclava on his head that covered his ears. He wiped sweat off his brow. 'What can we do? The police will be here soon enough. After the blizzard is over, I'm sure…'

'So why did you bring me here?' I gestured at the furniture shrouded in cloths, wishing to return to the warmth of the lounge.

He still spoke in a whisper. 'I made the arrangements for the twelve days. Rafe, I overheard you and Emily talking,' he nervously checked the doorway to make sure we were truly alone, 'about Linda and Glen. About whether this was an accident or not.'

My heart began to pound. Was I finally going to get some answers?

'I think I know what happened. And you're the only one I can tell.' Stephen licked his lips. Darted his eyes at me and away. He looked like a reptile at this moment, with his pock-marked skin, his plump jowls, his middle-aged spread – a reptile in winter clothes.

A floorboard outside the half-open library door gave a loud creak. Stephen turned white. He stood back, eyes wide in terror. 'I have to go.'

'It's just the wind,' I said.

We listened. My heart beat faster.

'Meet me in the guillotine room at dawn tomorrow morning. I have something I have to show you.'

He adjusted his scarf and peered into the dark corridor, up at the ceiling. 'And please, Rafe, don't tell anyone what I said.'

'You haven't said anything,' I hissed. 'Nothing that makes sense anyway.'

I chased after him, but Stephen had disappeared down the hallway. Returning to the library, I browsed the collection of books, shaken and puzzled.

The titles were not reassuring. *Medieval Torture. The History of the Inquisition. The Garrotte. French Executions.*

My mind stuck on the words Stephen had said. *I think I know what happened. ...made the arrangements for the twelve days.* The question was, what had he been asked to do? And, more to the point, who had asked him? What had frightened Stephen into silence?

A voice from the doorway called out, 'Hey, Rafe? That you?'

Startled, I turned to see Suzanne moving into the light cast by the window. Ghostly flecks of sleet reflected onto her face.

My heart picked up its pace. I checked the darkened

corridor where Stephen had fled. 'Were you... Did you just overhear my last conversation?'

Suzanne's hand fluttered to her cheek. 'What conversation?' She closed the door behind her and strolled towards me. Her hair was loose, falling over her shoulders and face. 'Rafe, you were always the confidante.' She placed a hand on my sleeve, so icy that I felt it through my clothes.

'You're cold,' I said, resisting the urge to rub warmth back into her hands.

In the light, she looked sly. 'Cold hands, warm heart.' Then her expression reverted to eyebrow-knitted fear. She pushed closer to me. 'Rafe, I'm scared.'

'Of what?' I said, stepping away from her.

'There is something you should know... about Glen. And me.'

'Glen and you?'

She nodded. 'When we arrived here, Glen said he needed to talk to me urgently.' She bit her lip.

'Go on.'

'He left the Church on a bad note. For years he didn't speak to me. I was sure he hated me.' She tossed her hair back out of her eyes. 'But then he... started sending me emails. Love letters. They were obsessive and I told him to stop. So I was pleased that when I arrived here he said we should talk. I came to this retreat partly because this would be a chance to get things sorted out.'

I had a sense she was lying. She looked uneasy when she said this. It didn't seem a good enough reason for a Hollywood star with multiple past lovers and global attention to spend time here in this isolated castle with people she obviously did not care for. I was inclined to think that the Hollywood scandal had driven her here into hiding more than any desire to repair old relationships. 'Glen was wearing your ring. He showed me.'

She glanced at her wedding ring, looking puzzled.

So she didn't even remember the cause of all our teenage heartache. 'No, that old ring you loaned out to us at school, that you used to hold poor boys in your power.'

'*That* ring?' She pouted, as if I had said something cruel about her. 'No, I didn't know that. He kept that old thing? I'd forgotten about it completely.'

Again, I did not quite believe her. 'He kept it for old time's sake,' I said, 'or at least that's what he told me.'

'Rafe…' She looked around, as if she now was wary of anyone hearing her, and drew me into the corner of the room by the end of the bookshelf. She looked fragile. She pushed close against me, so close I could feel her breath and her hair tickling my face. I had the absurd inkling we were about to become secret lovers, and she was going to kiss me. But no. She pulled a folded piece of paper out of her pocket and held it to her chest. 'Rafe, it's important that no one sees this.'

I stared at her quivering lip.

'Glen gave this to me before… he died.'

My head spun. I took a step back from her. 'So you're the one who met him last night.'

Her eyes were moons of fear. 'What?'

'Did you go to his room?'

'No.'

I scrutinised her carefully in the twilight. How can you ever tell if a good actor is lying? 'When did he give you this, then?'

'He left it under my door after dinner. Read it.' She thrust it at me and I held it towards the dim chandelier light.

Suzanne
Your life is in danger. In these twelve days of Christmas, I will do
*   all I can to protect you. I will prove my love for you.*
Forever
Glen

I folded the piece of paper in half again. My fingers were trembling. I looked into her eyes, which were gleaming with tears. 'Shit.'

She hugged herself, a gesture that reminded me of her as a teenager. 'I was going to talk to him today, but when he died, I was plunged into a spiral of terrible thoughts. I felt so awful. As if it was somehow my fault. I had to tell someone.'

'Suicide? You thought suicide?'

She wiped away a tear in a practised move I had seen in one of her movies. She was trembling. 'It was something to do with me. I know that. He was obsessed.'

'It was an accident. Don't take that upon yourself.' I didn't believe for a moment that it was an accident, but I had to hide my suspicions. If she was involved, accusing her would only drive her deeper into her acting self. But I was not sure this *was* her acting self. Her eyes were wide and moist. Her lips quivering. She took the note back but held my hand. Her fingers were ice cold and trembling. 'What did he mean? He said my life is in danger.'

I squeezed her fingers and looked into her moist eyes. Glen had told me the same thing last night. But I didn't want to tell Suzanne that. Not yet. It was cruel, maybe, but I did not trust anything she said. 'I might snoop around, see what I can find in his room. See if I can find any clues as to what happened and why.'

'Thanks, Rafe.' Suzanne took a deep breath and pulled away. She walked to the window and stared out. The pane was opaque with condensation. 'Is it just me,' she said, 'or does Reverend James seem just too comfortable with the fact that we hang around here, listening to sermons without doing anything about Glen?' She drew a line on the window, and then rubbed a small porthole to peer out. But there was nothing to see, only whiteness outside. 'I should have kept my goddamn cell phone.'

She was right. I should have smuggled it into my pocket. But I was not to know how badly I would need it. I stood next to her and wiped another patch of window. 'Well, if we're to believe Danny, there's no reception. But even so, there's always the possibility of making an international emergency call. The fact that they all went down the mountainside with Glen, along with all his stuff, is suspiciously ridiculous. I looked outside for the phones but didn't find any. Not one.'

'Stephen said the wind took them all down the mountain. But I think that he did it.'

I gave her a sharp look. 'Stephen?'

She pushed against me for warmth. Or consolation. 'No, Glen. If he... committed suicide, then maybe he took the phones with him. Maybe he wanted to take the whole world down with him.'

I put my arm around her and drew her close. She was shivering violently now. 'That's insane.'

She hugged me tighter. 'If I was still a believer, in their mindset, I'd also believe it was fate, or God. Or Satan.'

'But you're not a believer.'

'I always was a sceptic. Always doubted.' She stuffed the note back in her pocket. 'We'd better go back. Rafe, you have to make sure Reverend James doesn't do some mad thing.'

'Believe me, I'm trying. But there's much that doesn't add up here.'

She linked her arm through mine and we walked across the room, into the dim corridor and along to the women's wing. When we reached her door, she pulled away and disappeared into her room, closing the door, leaving me with my pulse elevated and a thin layer of sweat forming above my lip despite the cold. I made my way down the stairs and back into the living room.

After evening prayers, we made our way back to our individual cells, much like the monks and nuns of a bygone era.

As the men walked upstairs, I realised one of us was missing. 'Where's Stephen?'

Reverend James pointed to his closed door. 'He wasn't feeling too good and he went to bed early.'

'Suzanne's disappeared too,' said Mike.

I stilled the truth on my lips. 'I imagine, like everyone, she's gone to bed.'

I lay awake listening to the storm besieging the castle. The fluorescent reflection of the snow gleamed bright through the window. The darkness of the castle was shadowed with demons and fear. It must have felt like this in medieval times, grim and austere.

This fear, though, was real. A dead body lay crushed in the snow, left to freeze. Someone had written a note to Suzanne: *Your life is in danger.* Stephen had a confession to make. We were isolated with a mad preacher, coincidentally, or for more sinister unknown reasons. And his wife had had an affair with the man who'd just died.

I tossed and turned. Eventually, I walked to the window and squiggled in the condensation on the pane. I debated whether to tell Emily I was meeting Stephen in the torture museum at dawn. But no. Whatever Stephen had to say was best kept between us, for now.

Phrases replayed themselves in my head from the day before.

Your life is in danger.
Lock your doors.
Made the arrangements for the twelve days.
They were having an affair.

Night in this castle, in this blizzard, was an eerie fluorescence from the snow reflecting through the window. Eventually I fell into a fitful slumber. But around midnight, a thump shook the room and startled me awake. My heart drummed in my chest and I lay there contemplating my meeting with Stephen until I dozed off again. When I woke a second time, the dim glow of light on the horizon told me a new day had dawned.

Stephen had locked the door to the torture museum on the first day, but when I tried the handle, I found it open. The room was dark and cold and silent. A pungent, thick taste in the air mixed with a sick, sweet smell. Eight ghostly mannequins hung from the ceiling, the guillotine was silhouetted against the wall, and I could identify the various torture instruments by their shapes. Brazen bull. Catherine wheel. I shivered. It seemed a tad melodramatic of Stephen to want to meet here. Unless his intention was to frighten me.

'Stephen?' I called, my words echoing in the empty chamber.

Liquid sunlight trickled over the horizon, too feeble to much improve visibility in this room of dire consequences. I fumbled for the light switch, scraping my knuckle against the rough wall, and found it. No light turned on.

'Stephen?' I could hear in my voice annoyance tinged with a sense of foreboding.

In the pale dawn light, horror hit me like a freight train. There, in the shadows of the guillotine, lay a body. The head had rolled a metre or so away, leaving behind it a stream of congealed blood. Its glassy eyes were wide open, its mouth gaping as if in surprise. The guillotine blade was in its dock, having travelled the swift, deadly distance from the top.

Instinct sent me sliding back into the shadows. I listened to the thumping of my heart as I scanned the room for signs of life, for sight of the murderer.

The stench of blood made me want to retch.

I felt a black presence behind me about to envelop and smother me. The inky shadows were alive, advancing on me. Footsteps, the clink of a knife against a railing. But as soon as I faced the shadows, they raced away, revealing the dancing, mocking demons of my imagination. I sucked in a lungful of air to calm my nerves, and with it, a thick perfume of rose and musk assaulted my senses. And I knew.

A killer was in this castle.

All our lives were in danger.

I ran for the door, the dancing demons chasing me down the corridor.

When I reached the living room, breathless with fear, I saw Mike and Danny huddled around the table, their Bibles open. Quiet Time was a time of prayer, meditation and Bible reading that had been instilled in every Twelve member since childhood. Sensing my presence, they lifted their heads.

I clutched the door frame. 'Where's Reverend James?'

Mike frowned. 'He's in his room praying.'

'Rafe, you look w-white,' said Danny. 'Are you okay?'

'Fetch him now,' I demanded, ignoring his question. 'And Danny, bring your flashlight.'

The look on their faces declared their confusion, their innocence. But I trusted neither man. 'The museum room! And someone get Reverend James. Now.'

Under the twirling beam of the flashlight, the museum

revealed demons fleeing into the walls, growing into giants as they escaped into the ceiling vents and out of the windows.

'Rafe, tell us what you saw.'

I shuddered and pointed to the guillotine. The combined beams from the flashlights held by Reverend James, Mike and Danny zeroed in and alighted upon Stephen's severed head.

'My God.'

'Jesus.'

I studied their faces in turn, trying to read their expressions, searching for guilt, shock. But they looked bewildered, afraid, horrified. Reverend James gripped his chest, took shallow breaths. 'Lord Jesus,' he kept repeating. Mike was silent. Danny's mouth hung open.

'Look! Shine your flashlight on his left hand.' The body lay belly down and its outstretched hand clutched a card. Mike shone his flashlight on it and, though revolted, I stepped forward to study it in the light.

The third day of Christmas.

With a start, I realised that the thump I had heard last night had not been a slamming door; it had been the guillotine hitting the block of wood, severing the spinal cord, cutting through bone, in one clean movement. No screams. No struggles.

Reverend James shuffled from the corpse. 'Horrible. Hideous.'

A halo of blood surrounded Stephen's head. His eyes stared ahead, his mouth was open in a silent scream.

And now, in the light, I noticed his head lay on a large silver platter.

I recalled that in the French Revolution, the severed head of Charlotte Corday stared in anger at her executioner, and in more recent cases, the head reacted with shock at seeing its decapitated body. And even a case when the severed head reacted when his name was called. It meant Stephen may have been conscious long enough to realise what had happened to him, long enough to see his executioner.

The beam of Mike's flashlight wavered on the cobbled floor. 'How did you find him?' His question was infused with meaning.

Whatever suspicions I had of them, I realised the distrust was mutual. 'Last night he asked me to meet him here at dawn. He said he had something to tell me.' *About Glen's murder,* I wanted to add. I looked each man in the eye. Reverend James held my gaze, then broke it to reach for the card in Stephen's hand. 'Leave it!' I called, grabbing his arm. 'It's evidence.'

The Reverend shook me off, withdrawing his hand. 'Such a terrible accident. I told everyone this room was dangerous. The blade must have fallen…'

I was stunned at his continued denial of the obvious.

'Wait, what's this?' Danny's flashlight played across a Bible lying open in the corner of the room. I had missed it earlier in the pre-dawn light. The beam illuminated a passage marked in red.

Reverend James turned ashen. 'Corinthians 13. The third day of Christmas.'

I shook my head. 'Meaning?'

'Look.' Reverend James shone his flashlight onto the card between the dead man's fingers. 'The three hens stand for faith, hope and love. And the greatest of these is—'

'Love,' completed Mike.

As he spoke, we heard footsteps outside the room and a shadow loomed in the doorway. Emily, dishevelled, in her dressing gown, scratching her head. Behind her hovered Suzanne, Linda and Alison.

'Here you all are,' said Emily. 'We were worried. What's going on?'

I moved to block their line of sight. 'Please.' Reverend

James joined me, motioning to the women to move away. Too late. Linda screamed.

'Oh my God!' whispered Emily.

Alison hid in the corridor and began sobbing hysterically. Suzanne froze in the doorway, taking everything in.

The window rattled in the wind, the curtains blew like restless spirits, and if I didn't know any better, I would have thought I saw devils racing out of the windows. Primitive superstition still lives in our DNA.

Emily pushed past me, her eyes wide. She crouched by the corpse, pressed the flesh and let it go. Then she knelt by the head and opened one eyeball with the tip of her finger.

She knelt back on her haunches, wiping her hands on her dressing gown. 'Six to eight hours, I'd say.'

'Jesus Christ,' Suzanne moaned, standing in the doorway. Her horror seemed as real as mine.

I walked around Stephen's body, examining his limbs for any other injuries, and spied a small red dot, like a wasp sting in his neck. I crouched down next to Emily and pointed. She nodded.

'Time to get out of here,' I said. I waited until everyone had turned to leave before slipping my hand into Stephen's trouser pocket and palming what I found there into my own.

FOUR

FOUR CALLING BIRDS

No one had an appetite, but we sat dutifully at the dining room table and drank strong coffee, staring at one another. The thought was palpable: there was a murderer in this castle. Eight people sat around the dining room table in silence, and eight reflections imitated their despair. No one knew where to begin. Even Reverend James had nothing to say.

Linda had dressed and brushed her hair. Alison, also dressed, sat close to her, shivering. Suzanne, still in her dressing gown, positioned herself away from everyone at the far end of the table, her face the perfect mask of grief – tear-stained cheeks, red eyes, emotional restraint. Mike drained his coffee and stood. 'I'll go.'

'No,' said Reverend James, holding his arm.

Mike shook him off. 'There must be a way through. The road may be impassable for cars, but on foot I stand a better chance.'

Silence.

'Not now, surely?' Emily looked at the grey morning outside, the blizzard enveloping the castle like a shroud.

'And once you get into the village?' said Suzanne. 'No vehicle can get back here.'

'Helicopter,' said Mike, walking to the closet by the front door where all our jackets were kept. 'They can airlift us out. It's obvious we're not safe. None of us.'

Reverend James stood and followed him to the hall entrance. 'Maybe it will be safer if two of us go.'

Mike pulled his jacket on and zipped up the front. 'I'm a mountaineer, remember? This is what I do best.' He sat down to strap on his boots and then slipped on his gloves. 'If I leave now, we'll be out of here by lunchtime.'

Mike waved goodbye with his thick mitten as he opened the front door. I sensed relief in his stature, envied him escaping the confines of the castle. Emily and I stood by the window and watched him disappear into the whiteness of the courtyard. By my reckoning, it would take him three hours at least to plough through the snow, walk down that windy road and reach the village.

If all went well.

'God, keep him safe,' murmured Alison.

'"Trust in the Lord with all your heart",' intoned Reverend James, clasping his trembling hands, '"and lean not on your own understanding."'

'P-Proverbs 3, verse 5,' responded Danny with the eagerness of a child seeking approval.

I had learned this verse, and many others, back in the days when I was a believer, when life was predestined, ordered by God if you kept to His narrow path. Or Reverend James' narrow path. Now I trusted nothing but my own understanding to navigate the path ahead, my only moral compass.

And I would need all my understanding to figure this one out.

Back at the table, Suzanne chewed on one of her nails. 'What about Stephen's body?'

Emily answered for all of us. 'We leave it as it is. It's a crime scene.'

'Clearly an accident,' said Reverend James. 'But the police still need to determine how it happened.'

I bit back my words. No one accidentally got in the way of a guillotine or managed to have their head conveniently roll onto a silver platter. Plus there was the card.

'It's freezing in there,' explained Emily, 'so there's no chance of decay.'

'A natural morgue,' I added. 'Just like Glen's body in the snow.'

No one vocalised it, but despite what Reverend James said, we all knew the truth. Now there were two murders.

Linda stood. 'I'm going to make breakfast.'

Reverend James nodded. 'Good idea. I've locked the museum room. God willing, the police will be here this afternoon. Meanwhile, it is time for some spiritual reflection.'

I stifled a groan. This man who saw God's will in everything got ready to deliver yet another sermon. As he began, I watched him closely and listened for clues. Was his religious fervour, his piety, a façade concealing a ruthless murderer?

Once done, he clutched his Bible to his chest. 'Pray, and God will post an angel at the head of each of us. Everyone lock their doors when they are alone in their room.' He held his Bible aloft. 'We need to keep Satan at bay. Consider the frailty of life. The end can come like a thief in the night. We need to be vigilant, ready, at peace with God.'

Lock your doors: just as Glen had said.

The thoughts spun around me. Stephen had known something that had terrified him. He was going to tell me something in the library. Then he asked to meet me in the 'guillotine room'. Why?

He had some kind of evidence he was afraid to share.

Had he been killed because of what he knew about Glen's death?

But there was a worrying pattern beginning to emerge here that made me think there was more. On the second night of Christmas, the person holding the two turtle doves dies. On the third night, the man holding the three French hens card dies. And even my mind began playing tricks here and making patterns. French hens. The French Revolution. The guillotine. It reminded me of those people who apply numerological contortions to the Bible and use it to prove... well, anything they want.

Calmer now, Alison rose and announced she was going to help Linda make breakfast. 'Emily, Suzanne, want to join me?'

Neither woman looked keen, but food preparation had always been a gender thing in the Church, so they followed Alison into the kitchen. We men remained at the table and waited for our meal, no doubt some of us reflecting on the perniciousness of God's will.

A while later, Linda led the women out carrying trays of eggs, bacon, sausages and toast.

Linda served her husband, Alison the other two men, and Suzanne brought a plate for herself with meagre pickings – a tomato, lettuce leaves and a slice of toast.

Once all the women were seated, Reverend James began. 'What I have to say is going to be quite confronting. We will need the full armour of God to protect us here.'

He opened his Bible at a marked page, shuffled a sheaf of papers and read from his handwritten notes. 'On the 27th of December, the third day of Christmas, we traditionally recognise the martyrdom of John the Baptist. You all know the story. We have often used it in our sermons to warn about... adultery and sexual temptation.'

Danny's face lit up like an overeager schoolboy. 'S-Salome

was dancing before Herod and he offered her anything she w-wanted as long as she would keep d-dancing for him.'

Alison took a sharp breath. 'And she asked for the head of John the Baptist.'

'On a silver platter,' I finished.

'Christ,' said Suzanne, holding her hands up to her head.

Reverend James winced at the use of the Lord's name in vain and slammed his book shut. 'Yes. Only Christ can help us now. This is the work of the devil. Something I don't think even the police can help us with.'

I could not keep quiet. 'What are you saying?'

Reverend James pressed his fingers together in a prayerful (and I thought, sanctimonious) pose. 'After a lifetime of battling him, you come to recognise his tactics.'

I jumped to my feet. 'Come on. So Satan is prowling the castle killing people. Of course! Satan is the murderer.' I realised I was shouting. I sat down again, all eyes wide on me.

Linda glared, but her husband seemed unperturbed at my outburst. 'Yes, Rafe, yes,' he said, 'and I am not ashamed to say it. In the spiritual world, a battle rages between the forces of good and evil.'

'For fuck's sake.' I folded my arms.

I felt a deft kick on my shin. Emily leaned back in her chair and stared at the ceiling, her meaning clear. But I could not stop. The rage flowed out of me. All those years of repressed anger while listening to this man proselytising. I took a deep breath. Tried to restrain my temper. 'Let me get this clear: the world is controlled by darkness and light, God and Satan, each pulling strings, each intimately interested in human affairs, involved in the battle for our immortal souls. And if you, Reverend James, are correct, God and Satan are complicit in disrupting our reunion this Christmas by playing with symbols and numerology. Give me a break.' I flopped back in my chair. To think that as a teenager I had believed all this, had been gripped by the cult's powerful ideas. How easy it was to see the world this way! Angels of light. Demons of darkness. Satan, roaming like a lion seeking whom he may devour. My fingers found the object buried in my pocket. I needed to take matters into my own hands. Without the meddling of God or Satan.

As a group, our suspicions bred like fungus. I locked onto Reverend James; he locked onto me. Alison narrowed her eyes whenever I turned in her direction, and Linda shrank back into herself if she sensed my eyes upon her. Danny stuttered. Suzanne tried to hide she was biting her nails. Emily cat-stared, watching everyone.

The original plan for the day was meditation, prayer and sermons. But I was not going to stick around for that. We were all on edge, no doubt wondering who among us was the murderer, or whether a stranger lurked in the shadows. I pushed back in my chair, intent on returning to my room to order my thoughts.

'Where are you going, Rafe?' said Reverend James. 'I think we should all stick together so there's less chance of…' He trailed off.

'I'm not feeling well. I need to lie down for a while.'

I felt them watching me intently as I left. Every few steps, I checked to be sure no one was following me. I went directly to the tower, pulled out the key ring I had found in Stephen's back pocket. One key was for Stephen's room, I was sure; the other for the guillotine room. And my guess was that the third unlocked the door to Glen's room. The first key I tried fitted and Glen's door swung open.

I pulled it shut and locked it behind me. The room was ice cold, and the balcony doors rattled. I tested my step before peering over the balcony. Ran my finger along where the balcony railing had broken off. I expected rotten wood, an uneven crack, but instead I found a clean cut. I was not a builder nor an engineer, but even I knew enough to see that this was no act of God, or of nature, or of structural fatigue.

I looked below. The body was now completely buried in snow and I would not be able to tell where Glen had fallen if I hadn't made markers the day before.

I searched the room for the basket used to collect the cell phones. It lay on its side against the couch, empty. Not only had the killer murdered Glen, he − or she − had made sure no one could alert authorities.

Which suggested that someone in our midst was a brutal, cold, calculating murderer. But who?

Maybe Glen spurned Linda and this was revenge retaliation.

Maybe Reverend James planned all this to dispose of his wife's lover.

Or maybe they were working together.

Another suspect came to mind. It was hard to imagine how Suzanne had anything to do with this terrible crime. But she did. She too had been entangled with Glen's emotions. Letters and emails had been exchanged over time. And even though she had come to me in terror and shown me the note that said her life was in danger, this could have been a clever way to establish her alibi.

My philosophical training in healthy scepticism taught me to trust nothing, no one, and to be suspicious of appearances and hasty assumptions. To go against the grain of my emotional prejudices.

I scanned the room and noticed that everything of Glen's was gone. As if they wanted to obliterate him entirely. This was a carefully planned crime. And whoever it was had deliberately isolated us in the castle. Murdered Stephen. And would strike again.

The second key let me in to Stephen's room. The place was neatly ordered. All his clothes were folded neatly in the dresser. Nothing out of the ordinary here.

But he feared something, or someone. He knew something. He had been planning to show me something. The guillotine? But if his killer had gone to such dramatic lengths to silence him, he would have also cleaned out anything incriminating from his room. It was hard to imagine that the person who killed Glen was not the same person who killed Stephen. This was a serial murder, I was certain.

The only incongruity about this room was the bed. It was unmade, the duvet turned back, as if Stephen had just gone out for a pee, and meant to return soon.

I looked for signs of distress, for any preparation for what was to come. Did he have any forewarning? His Bible was in the torture museum, which meant he must have taken that with him. Perhaps the evidence was inside. He had gone there to name the killer, I was sure of it. There must have been evidence in the torture museum he was going to show me. I picked up his pillow to look underneath and noticed a spot of blood on the white cotton pillowcase. It could have been from a shaving cut or a scratch. But my thoughts raced to the small wound I had found on his neck.

He had been drugged, I surmised, before the execution. But how the killer had moved him from here to the torture museum was still a mystery.

Carefully locking the door to Stephen's room behind me, I checked for unwelcome followers before sneaking along the corridor to the museum. Once there, I was loath to go in. My stomach clenched as I opened the door and saw the dead body and severed head. But something in this room was a clue pointing to the killer's identity. I had to go through with this. The Bible lay where we had left it. I picked it up, leafed through it. Stephen's name was written on the inside cover and many pages had been dog-eared over the years. I looked again at I Corinthians, chapter 13, verse 13, which was circled with red pen: 'And now these three remain: faith, hope and love. But the greatest of these is love.'

What kind of a message was that?

A search of the room offered no further clues. What could he possibly have meant by 'evidence'? The only thing I could think of was that he had gone along with the killer's plans to rent this castle, to open the torture museum and to assign each of The Twelve one of the days of Christmas, without realising the killer's real intentions. Perhaps he had thought the elaborate plans were a game – until Glen's death.

I heard a thump in the corridor and the creak of a wooden floorboard. I quickly stepped into the shadows and stood still. Above me, the eight dummies swayed slightly in the draught. I waited for thirty seconds, and then squeezed out of the room into the corridor. There was no one there. But I could sense someone here, holding his breath, hiding in the shadows. I had to get back to the others. I locked the door, pocketed the keys, and walked briskly along the corridor, down the stairs and towards the living room, ready for the moment someone would pounce on me. The hair on the nape of my neck stood up. I was sure someone was behind me.

But when I entered the room, they were all present. Emily looked up. Suzanne also glanced up at me, as anxious as when she had met me at the front door the day before. Linda glared at me as she rose from the table and headed for the kitchen. Confused, I did a mental head count, looked behind me, as if the presence I had felt would reveal themselves. Nothing.

I joined Danny and Reverend James by the fire. Orange flames licked the charred stone fireplace. Danny threw on a new log and sparks flew. An ember spat out and landed on the rug, and Reverend James scooped it up and threw it back into the fire.

Linda returned with a pot of coffee and topped up everyone's mugs. She handed me mine, eyeing me suspiciously.

'Feeling better?' said Reverend James, his tone laced with irony.

'Do you think M-Mike's reached the village by now?' interrupted Danny, sharing the single thought that occupied us all.

By now, I hoped he was talking to the police. Soon they would be assembling an emergency team to fly a chopper to the castle. But in the deteriorating weather, the trek to the village might take much longer, even for an experienced mountaineer.

Linda collected the empty mugs on the tray and walked across the room. She pushed her backside against the closed kitchen door to open it, but found it jammed.

Danny rushed to her rescue. 'L-let me help you with that.' Brute force did not budge it. 'It's locked,' he said, peering into the keyhole.

I leaped up and tried the door handle. Locked. 'There's a way to the kitchen through the hallway. I'll just go through and open the door.'

But the hallway door was also jammed. I rattled the handle. 'But Linda just came through this door. Did anyone lock it?'

'No one,' said Reverend James. 'I didn't even know they locked.'

'B-but we l-left this door unl-locked?' said Danny, his stutter intensifying as the panic rose in him.

I thought back to the three keys I had found on Stephen's body. Each door in the castle had been fitted with the same brand of lock.

The only other exit from this room was the front door that led outside, the door through which we had farewelled Mike. It was fitted with the same mechanism. I tried the door handle but, as I suspected, it didn't budge.

'It's a smart lock. Electronically activated.'

'So you're saying we're locked in.' said Reverend James. He turned to Linda, and I could feel his anger at her. 'Linda, you were the last one in from the kitchen. How could you be so careless?'

She shook her head. 'I didn't lock the door. I…'

I walked down and stood between them. 'It's not her fault.'

Reverend James pushed past me, took out his room key and tried it on the front door, but of course it did not work.

Emily tried all the doors in turn, pushing her shoulder against each one. 'How long have we been locked in here? Linda brought in the coffee about ten, fifteen minutes ago, right?'

Not such a good detective, I thought: I should have been watching everyone. And surely I would have heard the click of the locks when they were activated. But you never know that something is suspicious until after it has been done. Classic magic trick technique: you do the switching or the sleight of hand before anyone knows what to expect.

Reverend James wiped his brow. Danny stared into the fire. Alison held her stomach, looking pale. Suzanne blinked back fear and kept staring at the doors, as if they would miraculously open by themselves. All of them were the very picture of innocence.

Into this scene came the crackle of a microphone being switched on. I looked up at the sound and noticed for the first time the two mounted Bose speakers on the wall, one in each corner.

'Greetings!' boomed a voice, echoing off the stone walls.

Linda screamed and jumped behind her husband, who

held her behind him. Danny pressed himself against the wall.
Suzanne let out a scream too. Emily looked at me, as if to say:
be alert here.

'You each have a secret.'

'Who is this?' Reverend James stepped forward toward the
speakers.

'Shh,' I said. 'Listen–'

'The Lord has brought you all together to confess. You
have transgressed the code of The Twelve.'

'I never... I swear, this is not me–' Reverend James wiped
his forehead. His wife flickered fearful eyes at him.

'Let your conscience find you out.'

'Wh-who-who is this?' Danny called out, staring up at the
ceiling.

'It's a recording,' I said, pointing to the speakers. The voice
had been distorted so that it sounded inhuman, with reverb
added to give a Hollywood god effect. 'Shhh,' said Emily. She
cupped her ear at the nearest speaker to her.

'The wages of sin is death. Judas was the one who betrayed
the twelve apostles. And just like Judas, you are each guilty of
betrayal. I have come to pass judgement and sentence on you.'

Suzanne had composed herself now and folded her arms.
'This is stupid. Who's behind this? Is this your doing,
Reverend?'

Reverend James appealed to everyone with his arms
outwards. 'It's not me.'

'No one will leave this castle alive. You cannot escape. I am
all around you, I can see you in your secret places, I can read
your thoughts, I am omnipresent, omniscient; wherever two or
three are gathered in my name there I will be also.'

At these words, Suzanne went rigid. She caught my
attention.

Reverend James also stiffened with indignation.
'Blasphemy!'

'Death has been visited already on four of The Twelve. These were no accidents. And in the past two days, death visited you twice again. And this is only the beginning.'

Reverend James was working himself into a lather. His face was red, and he shouted back at the speaker. 'Show yourself!' At the last statement, he picked up a knife from the table and hurled it at the speaker. It missed and twanged against the wall. He marched over to the kitchen door and rattled the handle. 'This is preposterous. Rafe, did you organise this?'

'Me?'

He lunged at me with an accusatory finger. 'While you were out of the room?'

I put out my hands to stop him attacking me. 'Steady on, Reverend.'

He turned to the others, shaking his fist. 'Who then? What sort of sick practical joke is this?'

I looked at everyone in turn too, gauging their reaction.

'Shut up, everyone,' said Emily, annoyed. 'Let's listen.'

But that was it. A crackle, and all we could hear was hissing.

At the same time the three door locks clicked simultaneously. Reverend James turned the handle and pushed the kitchen door open. He peered into the kitchen to see whoever was behind the door, but I already knew that he would find no one there. The locks had been electronically activated remotely and had been automatically released as the recording ended.

Now the speakers were silent.

Danny rushed into the hallway, banged open the now unlocked door and stared into the darkness. I tested the front door. It was also open. I examined the lock, turned the door handle. The metal knob that locked and unlocked the door from the inside now functioned as before. So, our keys could be overridden remotely. 'Lock your doors,' Glen had said, and it had been futile advice.

I looked around again at each person. I could hardly imagine that one of us twelve was a murderer. But someone was trying to set us up to suspect one another, knew us well enough to play us against one another. My thoughts returned to the two who had died in car accidents, accidents I had never heard about, until now.

'Search each room!' Reverend James called into the hallway. 'Danny? Rafe? The girls stay here.'

'Stop.' I blocked the passage door. 'Don't go anywhere,' I said, 'and don't let's split up.' I turned to Danny. 'Where is the sound system equipment in this place?'

He walked over to the other side of the living room and slid open a wooden door in a cabinet. We all followed and crowded over a Bose audio system inside.

The system was switched off, but when I placed my hand on the amplifier, it was warm. 'Someone thinks a cheap stunt like this will terrify us into repentance.' I looked straight at Reverend James and he stared back at me with venom.

'Some Judas thinks he can scare the Children of God with a threat like this.' He jutted his chin at me.

'Reverend James, Rafe, please.' Emily insinuated herself between us.

The Reverend shook her off. 'He said, "I am all around you. I can read your thoughts."'

'B-but we were all in here,' said Danny. 'He must have b-been here too, to put the recording on.'

Emily pointed to the amplifier. 'Any smartphone can activate a sound system. And a central locking system.'

'But we don't have our phones,' said Danny.

'What sort of sadistic creep would do such a thing?' said Alison.

Reverend James had not taken his eyes off me the whole time. 'It's sick,' he said. 'Blasphemous. Someone is mocking me. Mocking God.'

'But four deaths?' said Suzanne. She had been standing behind us, arms folded. 'He's talking about Sean and Jack?'

Danny turned to her. 'Th-they were accidents. He's p-playing with us.'

I clicked the on button, but the sound system remained mute. I had wanted to replay the recording and listen for other clues. Background noises, inflections perhaps, or speech patterns. I checked the power to the wall. Everything was in order. Whoever had set up this show had rigged it up to only play at his command.

Or her command. My gaze lingered on Linda and Alison, who were still clinging to each other. On Suzanne, who was standing aloof.

I reached in and checked the connections at the back of the amplifier. Emily touched my arm. 'What are you doing, Rafe?'

I stood up and shook my head. 'This is such a meticulously planned operation. Whoever did this has the technology, knows the castle. They must have made the recording a while ago and wanted to stage it, time it right. I'm just wondering why they went to all this trouble.'

I was careful to frame my thoughts as if we were talking about some ghostly third person, an outsider, and we were innocent victims. But one of us could have been lying. Maybe two of us. I watched all of their reactions. Surely if one of them had prior knowledge, there would be a change in them. They would show pallor, go red or avoid my gaze or I would see their throat tightening. I was searching for any of the classic symptoms of lying. Whatever you repressed emerged in unexpected ways. A Freudian slip. An unconscious compensation.

Emily frowned and touched her lips with her forefinger. 'How did he know we'd all be in the living room when he played the recording?'

I recited what I could remember of the recording: 'I am all

around you, I can see you in your secret places, I can read your thoughts, I am omnipresent, omniscient; wherever two or three are gathered in my name there I will be also…'

'That's Matthew 18, verse 20,' said Reverend James. 'He's playing God.'

Suzanne brought her hands up to both cheeks in shock. 'Rafe, I have a creepy horrible thought.'

I motioned her to come closer to the fire. 'What?'

'Did anyone see Mike leave the property?'

In the long silence that followed, Alison and Linda jolted upright as if they had both been struck by lightning. Danny shook his head from side to side, slowly trying to absorb the implications. Emily closed her eyes to think through the ramifications too. I tried to mentally retrace the steps Mike had taken before his departure.

'You're not suggesting–' said Reverend James.

'He could have doubled back,' said Suzanne.

'It's not true,' blurted out Alison. 'Not Mike!'

'Why M-Mike?' said Danny. 'It does-does-doesn't make sense.'

Emily began to pace the room, thinking hard. 'Just because the voice said all those things doesn't mean we have to believe him.'

'Or her,' I added.

Reverend James pointed his finger at Emily. 'I agree. This is just what the person wants us to do. It's a classic trick to sow suspicion. To make us turn on one another. We need to stick together.'

I could see that the others liked this idea better, that this meant an external enemy, not one of us. The thought that one of The Twelve, one of our own was doing this was too unbearable to conceive of. And they could be right. My mind immediately went to the concierge, even the owner of the castle. But

Suzanne stood by her suggestion. Folding her arms, staring them down. She could be right.

Linda glared at her. 'What have you got against Mike?'

'He could have come back to the castle,' she repeated.

'Let's search the c-castle, then,' said Danny, leaping up.

Reverend James stood, clapped his hands. Barked orders. 'Good idea, Danny. Guys, take the upstairs rooms, girls go together too. Go in pairs, no one must be alone. Be careful.'

'Mike would never…' said Linda.

I knew it was a waste of time. Whoever had organised this so smoothly would not be found easily. If this person was one of us, then they were sitting right in this room, acting afraid.

'We're not saying it's Mike,' I said. 'We're just looking at all possibilities. It could be any one of us here.'

Now they stared me down. I stared back. Danny averted his eyes, Alison shot angry daggers at me, and even Suzanne returned my gaze defiantly. Linda's eyes were wide, looking at each of her compatriots with fear. After that, no one wanted to separate, so the group combed the rooms as one large gang, clinging together. The men banged open cupboards, looked under beds; the women pulled open shower curtains, opened kitchen cupboards.

I watched them, scornful of such diversionary tactics. 'Aren't you missing the obvious?' They all looked at me. 'The first place we need to search is Mike's room.'

Mike's room was not locked, and so I walked in and the others followed.

Danny stood at the door. 'I feel b-bad going in here.'

Emily pushed past him. 'I don't.'

Mike's room was immaculate. I knew he was a neat freak, but there was some fanaticism here in the way he had made his bed, smoothed out the creases, tucked in the corners, as if ready for a military barracks inspection. He had squared his clothes into piles and centred his Bible on the bedside table. Reverend James picked it up and leafed through it.

'What do we know about Mike?' I said.

Emily shrugged. 'Who knows what fires burn in people's hearts, what poison grows.'

Reverend James turned on her. 'How dare you judge…?'

'Mike is strong in the Lord,' added Alison, looking daggers at Suzanne and Emily and me in quick succession. 'You should be ashamed of your accusations.'

'We're just being logical,' I said. 'Calm down.'

She pushed past me to follow Reverend James and Danny. We then swept from room to room, cell to cell, all determined not to acknowledge that this person was probably one of us, searching and doing a very good job of acting as scared as the rest of us. In a closet on the landing, I found a long coil of climbing rope behind some linen. Making sure the others were not watching, I pulled it out and took it downstairs, hiding it on the top shelf of the hallway cupboard with all the coats.

The search did little to settle our fears or suspicions. We returned to the living room, each of us at a loss as to what to do next. Suzanne drew herself into a foetal position and hugged her knees, rocking back in a big, comfy sofa chair. Alison and Linda closed their eyes in prayer, held each other's hands. I looked at the clock on the wall. It was not even midday. If Mike had indeed gone on his rescue mission, if he had no trouble getting through, he could possibly be getting help now. But if he was the murderer…?

Alison gaped out of the window, staring up at the skies.

'We'd hear a helicopter long before we'd see it,' said Reverend James, also peering out into the whiteness.

Alison clutched the windowsill, staring, staring for any trace of hope out there. 'We have to get out of here.'

The Reverend placed his arm around her. 'Have faith, Alison. Trust in the Lord. We have to believe Mike did go for help, and they'll be here soon.' Reverend James, I observed, seemed to be taking the course of events rather well in his stride.

Suzanne shook her head. 'I still have the horrible suspicion that Mike didn't go for help.'

Reverend James held Alison tighter. 'I know Mike,' he said. 'I think what you are saying is preposterous.'

'The whole thing is preposterous.' said Alison. 'I still don't believe it. It's the work of Satan. I know how he works. This is the work of Satan.'

'Or the scheme of a very fanatical mind who thinks we all need to repent,' I said, deliberately staring into the fireplace to hide where my suspicions lay.

Reverend James stormed over, red-faced. 'I have had enough of your insinuations. If I am to be honest, and I am sure I am not the only one in the room to think this, it looks like… very obviously that–'

I stood up to him, stretching myself to full height. 'That what, Reverend? What? Who set up this castle? Whose idea was it to come here? Who organised that each of the twelve days was to be a lesson for us?'

Again Emily put herself between us. 'Please, can't we just work together here?'

I stepped back. 'But if one of us is a murderer, we should be making sure we protect ourselves.' I stirred the fire with the poker. 'From one another.'

Reverend James bristled but did not move. He was no longer the centre of attention. Everyone was looking at me.

'What d-do you suggest we d-do?' said Danny.

I stared at each in turn. 'We stay together. And we ensure

that no doors lock behind us, and that no one is alone. If a helicopter is going to arrive, we need to prepare for an imminent departure.'

Alison glanced out the window, her face shining with hope. I walked up to her and peered out. 'The front courtyard, if I remember, is big enough, and clear enough for a chopper, and we can set up some landmarks easily visible from the air.'

The others murmured their agreement, except the Reverend who turned his back on me and fumbled at the dining room table for his Bible.

'Do we agree?' I asked, my question clearly directed at him.

He sighed, turned and held the Bible in the air. 'Bless those who curse you, pray for those who mistreat you,' he said. 'Come, Rafe.' Surprisingly, he opened his arms, walked over to me and gave me a bear hug. 'I'm sorry.'

I tried not to recoil, and was surprised at how small and frail the Rev now seemed.

We all wrapped ourselves with whatever scarves, coats, gloves, balaclavas we could find, and in a few minutes, seven of us ventured into the bleakness of the storm. I placed a wool hat in the doorjamb to stop an inadvertent lock, and realised as we went outside that I had again underestimated the weather. The wind had died down and it had stopped snowing, but it was way below zero, too cold to snow. The fallen snow had hardened to ice, like razors, treacherous to walk on. I was right: if a helicopter was to land anywhere, the courtyard would be the best place, clear of trees and large enough for manoeuvring. But maybe not on this ice.

I directed everyone to head for some benches half-buried in snow. These could be pulled out and placed in four obvious-from-the-air locations.

We wrestled with the outdoor furniture, but the cold became unmanageable. The benches were difficult to budge. Finally, we succeeded in moving one, and cleared a space large enough, I imagined, for a chopper to land.

'Come,' called Reverend James, his breath misting in the freezing air. 'Let's go in. At least we've made an effort.'

I saw his point. It was dangerous to stay outside any longer. Back inside, we rubbed numb hands and burning cold cheeks.

Danny began piling logs onto the already burning flames. 'Mike will get help.'

'Mike can be counted on,' said Reverend James.

I unwound my scarf, warmed my hands by the fire. Mike. Mike. Mike. The Mike I knew was a vain, narcissistic yet strangely compliant person, eager to please, brainwashed into parroting whatever Reverend James wanted him to say and think. He was not, in my opinion, capable of masterminding a stunt like the one we had just witnessed. But then the quiet ones are always the most dangerous, their poison seething below the surface. If Mike had murdered Glen and Stephen and was even now planning the next murder, then no help was coming.

The hours passed slowly. The afternoon light faded and with it any hope of a rescue. To pass the time, Danny and Reverend James played a game of chess by the fire, Linda took out her knitting and stared vacantly out of the window, Alison sat hunched over her Bible. Emily pretended to read a book on the couch with her feet up, but every time someone moved, she looked up, like a cat, watching for any suspicious movement. I took out my notebook and jotted down some thoughts in my journal. It looked like an ordinary, cosy winter's afternoon by the fire.

When it was time for supper, the women moved as one to prepare the meal in the kitchen. They jammed the door open with a chair so that we or they would not be locked out or separated. Tired of sitting, I walked around the room, checking for anything suspicious. I crouched by the cabinet and examined the audio system again.

I sensed Reverend James standing behind me. But I did not turn around.

'What do you think, Rafe?' he said.

'This was planned well before we got here. Before the deaths.' I turned and stared into his cold blue eyes. 'When did you plan this trip? And who knew about it?'

He rubbed his hand across his brow. 'Stephen. Glen. Myself. A few months back. The idea grew slowly. We booked the castle only last month, once you all accepted the invitations.'

This all sounded plausible. But only one of the three was still alive to tell. No one could verify his version of the truth. 'And who scouted out the castle beforehand?'

He moved closer to me, as if he didn't want Danny, who was still poring over the chessboard by the fire, to overhear. 'Stephen came here a week before to make sure it was all in order. I don't like your insinuations, Rafe.'

I shrugged off my irritation. 'No insinuations. Just trying to get as much information as I can.'

Reverend James again rubbed his brow with his hand. He was sweating. 'You're right, this was planned extremely well. How did he know we'd all be in the living room when he played the recording? Was he watching us?'

I recited the killer's phrase. 'I am all around you, I can see you in your secret places, I can read your thoughts, I am omnipresent, omniscient; wherever two or three are gathered in my name there I will be also.'

He looked afraid now. I had to try another tactic here. A

good detective should not alienate his suspects. 'Whoever it is,' I said, 'he – or she – knows exactly what they're doing. The thing is, Reverend James, we need to work together.'

It was clear from his expression that this idea offered him as little comfort as it did me. But it was a reconciliatory gesture and he welcomed it. 'You reassure the others,' I told him. 'Keep them safe and together at all times. I'll try to find out how "this person" is remotely accessing everything.'

The tactic seemed obvious, but Reverend James was buying it. By turning him into a co-detective, I removed any suspicions that the pious Reverend James was my prime suspect. Mike ran a close second. The horrifying third option was that they were collaborators. Hell, even Linda could be in on it. Alison? Danny? I doubted it.

And the most terrifying thought of all was that Suzanne was a suspect too.

Supper was a meagre affair. The conversation centred on Mike and whether he had managed to reach the village before nightfall. Maybe the emergency services had to wait until first light to begin their rescue operation. We consoled ourselves with the illusion that tonight would be our last in the castle. No need to panic.

I did not mention the very real alternative. If Mike was the killer, then we might have cause to be alarmed. We were sitting ducks.

'I l-lift my eyes up to the hills from whence c-cometh my help,' said Danny.

'Amen,' said Alison.

Reverend James interjected. 'Danny, let me point out something about that verse. The King James Bible is a mistranslation because of the lack of punctuation in the original. It's meant to be a question: "I lift my eyes up to the hills. From whence cometh my help?" And the answer is in the next verse: "My help cometh from the Lord". Not from the hills.'

Reverend James saw me staring quizzically at him. 'Hermeneutics, Rafe, hermeneutics. It's important.'

Emily yawned loudly. I could see she had no tolerance for Reverend James' interpretations. 'Let's go to bed,' she said, stretching her arms into the air.

Reverend James stood. 'Emily is right. It's late. And tomorrow we may have a long day. But please remember to lock your doors, pray, keep the angels around you, and no one wander off on their own. Stay safe.'

Lock your doors. I did not bother telling them how useless that would be.

'Are we going to be okay, Reverend?' said Alison, following behind him. 'I'm scared.'

'God's testing our faith,' said the Reverend, resting a hand on her shoulder. 'We must be strong.'

I tried not to be sceptical, but it was difficult to think he was being sincere. No one looked strong. The women huddled together, not wanting to go alone up into the dark corridor, so we accompanied them and made sure they were locked in their individual rooms before locking ourselves in ours.

At my room, I bade the Reverend goodnight. On closing my door, darkness fell like a heavy shroud. Shadowy figures leaped into corners. Then, as soon as I had locked it, I heard a tap at the door. I jumped, my heart racing like crazy.

'It's me.'

I opened the door. 'Em?'

Bundled in a blanket for warmth, she was worrying her bottom lip with her top teeth. 'I need to talk.'

She walked across the room and stood by the window, staring out at the void. Meanwhile, I made a cursory sweep-through of my room. I checked under the bed, in the cupboard.

She frowned at me. 'What are you looking for?'

I stood and dusted off my pants. 'I'm not entirely sure.' She left the window, closing the gap between us, and whispered, 'We both know Mike's not getting help.'

Mike was the obvious suspect, yes, but it also occurred to me that he had simply vamoosed, abandoning us to our fate. My philosophical training would not let me jump to any ready-made early conclusion. 'I suspect everyone.'

'Well, I'm not a murderer, Rafe,' she hissed, her hand flying to her chest. 'And I don't think you are.' She held out her pinkie and smiled. 'Blood siblings still?'

I twisted her pinkie in mine.

'Who has the next card,' she said, 'for the fourth day of Christmas?'

I saw where she was going with this, but asked anyway. 'Why?'

'We're not supposed to reveal our card until the day. So if we're murdered in the night, no one will have seen it coming. Someone must have the five golden rings.'

It couldn't be that easy. But she was right. The murderer's whole plan and the order in which he or she was going to kill The Twelve was all laid out in the cards given to us at the beginning.

'And another thing,' she said. 'Did you smell perfume in the guillotine room?'

I nodded. 'It was the same aroma I smelt in Glen's room after he died.'

'It's rose. I noticed it in our bathroom.'

'Everyone needs to reveal their cards. Ridiculous that we haven't thought of that.'

'Whoever has the five rings will be killed tonight. And we need to get the hell out of here before our cards are up.'

I gathered her in my arms, blanket and all. 'I swear I'm not going to let anything happen to us.'

'I'm not sleeping alone in my room,' she said, looking at me as she once had as a round-cheeked teenager. 'I'm staying with you.'

FIVE GOLDEN RINGS

I woke, pressed right on the edge of the king-size bed, tangled in blankets. It was still inky dark in the room, but the digital clock on the mantelpiece showed 07.04. I slid out on the left side, leaving Emily sprawled diagonally across the bed like a cat, and like a cat she opened one eye. 'Going somewhere without me?'

'I must make sure everyone is accounted for.'

She reached over to hold me back. 'Still alive, you mean.'

I dressed in the dark on my side of the bed, and she rolled over to her side, stood and dressed too. 'We've got to get out of here today,' she said.

I opened the door and peered out. 'Let me go first,' I said. 'Wait a while before you come out.'

She walked over to me and pushed the door closed again. 'You worried about what she will think?'

She hadn't changed one bit, knew how to stick the knife in. I shook my head. 'Emily?'

She folded her arms and smiled. 'Whatever you say, captain.'

Two could play at this game. I raised one eyebrow.

'Speaking of appearances, what will your husband think, you sleeping in another man's bed?'

She grabbed both of my hands. 'I don't know. I suppose his wife sleeping in another man's bed is no problem,' she said. 'It's what she does when she's not asleep that will upset him.'

I massaged her cold hands. 'Well, that's fine then,' I said. 'You were out like a light all night.'

She bit her lip and pulled her hands away. 'And to tell the truth, he wouldn't care. We're sort of separated.'

I scrutinised her face in the half-light. Sometimes I didn't know when she was pulling my leg or being serious. 'Oh? I'm sorry.'

'Don't be sorry. I'm relieved.'

The others were already up. Danny and Reverend James were hunched by the fireplace trying to revive the fire. I could hear Alison and Linda in the kitchen. The aroma wafting in through the open door told me they were making coffee. As I walked in, everyone paused for a fraction of a second then refocussed on their tasks. Suzanne sat alone by the window. I walked over, stood next to her chair and stared out at the clearing sky.

'How are you?'

'I hardly slept.'

It was an accusation. Or a seduction. The look she gave me would have melted me years ago. I wondered now, as I always had, how she managed to show all those expressions – hurting, seductive, pouting, vulnerable, pleading, sulking, standoffish – in one pose.

I had been in love with her since that first day I met her at school. My feelings hadn't changed; they were hard-wired into my DNA. I had come all this way to see if I had been cured, but now I suspected she had done permanent damage to my heart.

'I need to speak with you, Rafe.' She glanced around at the others.

Enter Emily. 'Good morning, everyone.' Her smile faded when she saw Suzanne and me in close proximity, heads together in a conspiratorial huddle.

'Breakfast will be ready soon,' said Alison, entering with a tray of steaming coffee. 'Come and sit at the table.'

I left Suzanne and headed for my seat, but Reverend James grabbed my arm. 'A word?'

'Sure.'

He made an urgent gesture towards the dark corridor, and I reluctantly followed him. 'This is meant to be a spiritual retreat.'

Puzzled, I looked back at Suzanne. But the Reverend's glance toward the kitchen where Emily had just disappeared told me what he was referring to.

Two people have died and all you are worried about is this? I said nothing, just gave him a look of disdain. *You puritan! Violence and murder are okay, but human intimacy is the ultimate crime?* I pushed past him and strode back to the table.

Emily came out of the kitchen carrying a plate of buttered toast and stood near me. I put an arm around her, hugged her close. He watched.

'You all right?'

'Of course.'

Reverend James took his place, looked anywhere but in our direction.

Linda brought in a plate of bacon and eggs and blackened tomatoes. 'Sorry, gentlemen,' she said, 'I'm not at my best today.'

Reverend James said grace and we ate. Well, the men ate. Suzanne pushed food around her plate, Linda pecked at her meal, Alison took small mouthfuls and chewed forever. Linda turned anxious eyes on her husband, and he reassured her that the food was fine.

All through breakfast, Suzanne kept glancing at me, nodding her head slightly as if to say, *please let's talk.* But there was no opportunity. Reverend James was determined to keep me away from both her and Emily.

After breakfast, Alison stood up first and took her almost full plate to the kitchen. 'Sorry, Linda, I'm not feeling too good. I need to go to the bathroom.'

Linda leaped up. 'You shouldn't go alone.'

Reverend James jabbed his fork in the direction of the women. 'All of you go with her. We'll hold the fort.' Linda followed Alison. Suzanne stood up to join them, wiping her mouth with a napkin and giving me a quick look.

'I think an equal number should go and stay,' said Emily, folding her arms, 'and I'll stay here, thanks.'

The Reverend glared at her and waved the other women through the doorway. As they passed through, I wedged the door open so it would not lock.

'Can we talk?' whispered Suzanne as she passed me. I nodded.

Reverend James motioned Danny to follow him to the fireside table, where he opened his Bible and read aloud a verse in Psalms: "'The Lord is my light and my salvation; I will fear no one. The Lord protects me from all danger; I will never be afraid."'

Emily leaned over to collect my plate. She spoke softly in my ear. 'That perfume we smelt in the torture museum, it's Suzanne's.' She passed her wrist under my nose and I inhaled

body was twenty metres away beyond a large void of snow. I uncoiled the rope, tied one end to the nearby fence post and the other end around my waist. Tested it for strength.

'You stay here,' I said. 'I'm going to climb down. Just make sure the rope holds, and let me know if it doesn't.'

'You're crazy.'

I reached over and grabbed a craggy rock to steady myself, but my foot plunged into a snowdrift immediately and I fell a few metres into the whiteness. I hit my shin on something hard underneath. She strained at the rope, holding me steady. But I could see this was not going to work. I could not gain purchase. I stretched my legs but could not find solid ground. I tried a little further along, hoisting myself over the edge. This time my foot found a rock jutting out, but as soon as I put my weight on it, it broke away and tumbled down into the snow. Emily held the rope tight and I hoisted myself back up onto level ground.

'Are you hurt?'

I shook my head. Just a bruised shin. It would be treacherous to attempt any climb down there now. I needed proper rock-climbing equipment. I untied the rope and coiled it on the ground.

Emily dusted the snow off my jacket. 'Let's go back.'

'Before we do,' I said, holding her by the shoulders, 'can you tell me what you and Glen were on about that night?'

She slumped. 'Hard to talk about. Let's walk.' She pressed into my side and linked her arm through mine as we walked behind the castle, hugging the hedges to shelter ourselves from the cold. The snow had stopped falling, but clouds hung low.

She took a breath. Another. She was shivering, and I held her tight. Finally, she spoke. 'It was on a camp. Reverend James called me in one night. His wife was away.'

I stopped walking to face her. 'My God. Are you going to say what I think you're going to say?'

She buried her face in my shoulder. 'I've never told anyone this. I would have told you back then, but you... deserted me.'

'I never—'

'You did. I needed you then, Rafe.'

'How old were you?'

'Old enough. It was a few months after you left.'

'It's okay, you can tell me,' I said.

She spoke so quietly that the wind carried away her words and I had to strain to hear her. I was trembling now too, and not just from the cold.

'I used to go to him for confession. At his house. We'd talk for hours. About you.'

'About me?'

'I was trying to get over you.'

'I don't know what you mean.'

'Come on, you must have known. Everyone knew about my obsessive crush on you.'

I looked into her eyes, but she turned away. 'I had no idea.'

She shrugged out of my tight grip. 'Don't worry. I'm totally over it now. Over it for years.'

'Wow.' This was the last thing I expected to hear from Emily. The past rearranged itself ever so slightly. 'So you told Reverend James about this?'

'Yes. Unrequited love and all that. And he gave me the "It is better to have loved and lost than never to have loved at all" sort of crap he told everyone.'

'I had no idea, Emily. Really. You should have told me.'

She shook her head. 'That would have just made me look like an idiot. I was no match for Suzanne's blinding light.'

I wanted to hold her tightly again, but she had pulled away and folded her arms.

'So anyway, when I told Reverend James all this, he— we—'

'Go on.'

'This is hard to say, Rafe. We… became close. He found a way to comfort me.'

The wind roared in my ears. My teeth chattered with the cold. But the ice in my heart was much worse. I dreaded what she was going to say next.

'Rafe, I was broken-hearted. You just left. There was no one to turn to.' She wiped her eyes. 'And then one thing led to another. He said I was a very satisfying young woman.'

I did not want to know what she meant.

She began walking again, away from me. I followed, straining to hear her. 'We met often. But I didn't care. It was my revenge on you for abandoning me. What was a girl supposed to do?'

'Emily, that's terrible. Please let me hold you–'

'No. It gets worse.'

'How can anything be worse than… him… he and you…?'

She said the words into the white sky. 'I fell pregnant.'

'The bastard.'

She shook her head. 'It was my fault. I wasn't using contraception. I hardly knew what contraception was. I thought he had it all under control. I thought, well I didn't think anything. I was confused. I was on the rebound. I was…'

I caught up with her, pressed her to me in a bear hug. 'Emily, I'm so sorry.'

'But he was very decent about it all.'

'Decent! He was a bastard.'

'No, I mean he took responsibility for it. He arranged the abortion. Paid for everything. Looked after me.'

We let the silence creep into us. Finally, I said, 'So that's your big secret.'

'And his.'

'This changes everything. Who else knows?'

'No one. Certainly not his wife. But I told Glen. And that

was a mistake. He was mad. He wanted to expose the Reverend.'

'Why didn't he?'

Emily entwined her gloved fingers clumsily around mine. 'Glen left the Church. He called Reverend James a hypocrite, he wanted nothing to do with The Twelve after that.'

'But he was having an affair too, with the Reverend's wife.'

'I think that was also revenge, but for what I don't know.'

'It all makes sense now,' I said. 'Well, more sense than it did before. But why then did Glen come back here?'

'I'm sure Glen wanted to expose him here. He wanted to have it out once and for all. That's what I was afraid of that night. That it would all come out.'

'And Reverend James wanted to have it out with him over Linda?'

She nodded. 'The perfectly entangled love triangle.'

'Or square,' I said, counting the people involved. James. Glen. Linda. Emily.

'Pentagon, if I add you to the mix.'

'Christ, what a mess.'

'But as you know, before Glen could do anything, he had an accident. Or someone wanted to silence him.'

'He was murdered.'

'And Stephen got wind of it and was bumped off too.'

Suddenly, it felt colder and darker and the wind more biting. We walked back in silence in the eerie stillness, crunching on frozen snow.

Now I was more confused than ever. After first suspecting Reverend James, I'd decided Mike was our man. His actions were the most suspicious. The conditions were so treacherous outside, yet he was quite happy to battle the elements to supposedly go and get help. But now Reverend James was back as number one suspect. He had motive here. A double motive – revenge for Linda's affair *and* covering up for his transgression with Emily. Means. Motive. Opportunity. All so obvious now.

I turned to Emily. 'We have to stop him. We have to watch Reverend James like a hawk. Observe… and stay alive.'

Emily clutched on to my arm. 'Just please don't let on that you know.'

'You know me. I will… humour him.'

She hugged me. Then stopped abruptly at the entrance door to the castle. 'Rafe.'

'What?'

'What the hell is that?'

A fluttering note was nailed to the front door. I recognised the same type of card from the dining table. The words: Four calling birds. The picture: four black birds cawing and flying in a circle around a Christ figure in a manger. Each one was labelled in a scrawling handwriting: Matthew, Mark, Luke, John. I pulled it off the door. On the other side was a map, drawn in pen. The castle, a path, the road, and a circle labelled X.

'This doesn't look good.'

We found the others huddled in a semicircle by the fire.

Suzanne stood up. 'We've been worried…'

'Thank God,' said Reverend James. 'Don't ever do that again.'

I pocketed the note. Looked at this man with new eyes. This was the man who had raped Emily – though she wouldn't call it rape – and had arranged an abortion to keep it quiet.

'I'll take your coat,' said Danny, but I shook my head, stretched my frozen hands towards the fire. Emily too pressed into the warmth, keeping coat, gloves and balaclava on.

Linda poured coffee for us, and I looked at her also with

new eyes. She didn't look as if she knew, but she was an indecipherable mask at the best of times, a thick coat of politeness and false courtesy. She played her role well. But I could guess what was underneath that veneer. Reverend James too played his pious puritan role so well. He stared at me as if he had heard everything Emily and I had said about him. But there was a more pressing matter to sort out.

'The four calling birds,' I said to him. 'In the carol. What do they mean?'

He saw my wild eyes. 'Sit, sit.' Reverend James made space for us between Suzanne and himself. 'Well, actually, calling birds may be a mistranslation. Originally it was four colley birds. Black birds.'

Emily and I exchanged glances.

'Colley means black. Blackbirds could sing and would make good presents.'

Everyone was listening now.

Reverend James sighed. 'I was hoping to make this a lesson every day. But the… mishaps have put paid to that.'

'No, Reverend,' said Danny. 'You said that n-nothing would stand in the way of God's message to us this week. We—'

I interrupted. 'No more moralising sermons, Reverend James. Just tell us the meaning of the four calling birds. Quickly. We need to know urgently.'

'My idea was that whoever has the four calling birds card must work it out for himself.' He looked around and drew blank stares from everyone.

'The four Gospels,' said Danny. 'Is that the meaning? Matthew, Mark, Luke, John.'

I nodded my head. 'I thought so.'

'What?' said Suzanne. 'What!'

'I think you'd all better see this.' I spread the note out on the table and they crowded around. I looked carefully at Reverend James' eyes. I saw fear. Did I see guilt?

'The four colley birds,' said Danny.

I turned over the card. 'And a map of sorts.'

I led the way, following the dotted line we were meant to take, out of the castle, down the road, between the tower and the barn, and veering to the right to the circle. The snowdrifts were deep in some parts and I had to skirt around them, keeping my bearing. 'Stop!'

I stood at the edge of a smoother patch of snow, which I now saw was a frozen body of water.

'The X is a small pond, a circular pond.' Emily pointed to a dark patch of ice, newly broken in the middle.

Everyone could see the dark shadow under the newly frozen veneer of ice, arms and legs spread out wide.

No way, I thought.

I ventured a foot forward on the lake surface, but my boot crunched through the ice into the freezing water.

'Stand back,' I said. 'It's thin ice.'

'He got this far and then... fell in the lake. Drowned. Froze to death.' Reverend James' explanation was more of a plea, his gesture of faith being the belief in things not seen.

To the senses, however, even in this dim light, the blue tinge of the ice was evidence of murder.

Danny crouched by the frozen lake, leaning forwards. 'Shall we tr-try to get him out?'

'How did he get under the ice?' said Alison.

Emily pointed to scars and lines on the ice. 'The ice froze on top of him. It was broken here. And refroze.'

Linda shuddered and hugged herself. 'How long do you think he's been here?'

I kicked at the ice with my boot. 'Overnight. Probably soon after he set out.'

'Are we sure it's Mike?' said Suzanne, leaning over the edge. 'We have to get him out of there.'

I shook my head. '*We* need to get out of here, or we'll all freeze.'

'And be careful not to slip,' said Reverend James. 'That's what happened. He slipped and fell and couldn't get out.'

He almost persuaded them – Danny and Alison and Linda, maybe, but not Suzanne or Emily. Suzanne's teeth were chattering loudly. 'Let's go back to the castle.'

'We can't just l-leave him here,' said Danny.

But it was below freezing, my lips and fingertips were numb, and my sinuses were pulsing with pain. No one else needed convincing. They followed me back to the castle, skirting the lake. Reverend James yelled: 'Stay together!'

Mike was a strong man, I thought. *Fit, athletic, and experienced at extreme outdoor conditions.* He couldn't have been stupid here. He would have avoided the frozen lake. And if anyone had attacked him, he would have fought back.

But now I could strike Mike off the suspect list. That only left my number one suspect. But how had Reverend James engineered this death? I had been watching him the whole time. No one had been out of sight long enough to do this. My suspicions began to focus on others now – the concierge, the owner of the castle. Perhaps as accomplices to do the Reverend's dirty work.

We thawed out by the fire, watched the sparks shooting out onto the hearth. There was nothing to say.

'It doesn't make sense,' Reverend James said at last. 'None of it.'

I shook my head. 'And the card on the door, the map, what was that? A suicide note?'

Alison spoke in a very quiet voice. 'Funny, Rafe and Emily went outside alone earlier. They went for a walk.'

Emily gave her a scornful look. 'The lake was frozen over long before we went for a walk.'

'People, people.' Reverend James clapped his hands. 'No divisions. That's what he wants.'

'Who?' said Linda, wide-eyed.

'Satan.'

Emily swore under her breath. 'The murderer, you mean. Let's say it. Own it. Admit it. The Murderer. Capital M.'

Reverend James glared. 'This is Satan's diabolical work. Whenever someone goes off on his own, he… disappears; he dies in a horrific way. We need to put on the full armour of God to protect us.'

'Reverend J-James is right,' said Danny, huddling by the fire. 'We should never have let Mike go alone.'

'He was going to get help,' said Linda. 'He…'

Reverend James nodded. 'Don't ever be alone. If you have to go to the bathroom, take a friend with you. Check out any hiding places before you enter a room.'

'We'll all help in the kitchen,' added Danny, 'so the girls are okay.'

Reverend James nodded. 'The men must sleep in one room from now on, and the women in another.'

'Surely someone will find us,' said Danny. 'At the village, they must know we're st-stranded here?'

'They won't know until the twelfth day,' I said. 'Unless the Reverend here sent some angels to tell them.'

Emily nudged me. 'Rafe.'

The Reverend's look was withering. 'Help will come.'

Alison's eyes darted to each person in the room. 'We should all be armed,' she said, her voice trembling.

Reverend James raised his Bible. 'This is the greatest weapon here. And I don't see why I shouldn't deliver the sermon I had prepared for today. It seems even more relevant.'

Much to my disbelief, the group settled around the fire ready to listen.

'I've already told you that the song, "The Twelve Days of Christmas" was sung by persecuted Christians. Well, it was written in 1780, and each verse is a code. The four colley birds, or calling birds, were a code for the four apostles, Matthew, Mark, Luke and John, carrying out "the Great Commission", spreading the gospel, the good news to the world.'

He peered at each of us in turn as we sat with unease around the fire.

I made an impatient exhale of breath. 'So what is your point, Reverend James?'

He picked up *Foxe's Book of Martyrs*. 'On the fourth day of Christmas, there was another martyr. In the fifth century, Steven of Constantinople died on this night, 28th December.'

'H… how did he die?'

'He was drowned.'

'Like Mike,' said Emily quietly.

'Stop,' said Suzanne. 'I don't want to hear it.'

'It's not what happened to Mike,' whined Alison. 'It isn't, it isn't, it isn't.'

Linda embraced her.

Reverend James thumped the book on the table. 'God wants us to hear this. There's a message in here for us. No point denying it.'

'The message,' I said, 'is that someone is out to kill us all. And very coincidentally is using your sermons, your book of martyrs, as a blueprint for the murders. I want to know why these murders correspond so tightly to your sermons on the *Foxe's Book of Martyrs*.'

'What are you saying?' A bead of sweat ran down Reverend James' brow. His face was red.

'If you want to stop incriminating yourself, you'd better stop with these sermons.'

'Shut up, Rafe,' said Alison, standing. 'How dare you say that about the Reverend?'

Danny stood too. 'Yes, Rafe, this is not app-appr-appropriate.'

'Fine.' Reverend James slammed the Bible shut and sat down, pulling his chair closer to the fire, his back to us. The sermon was over.

Suzanne stood too. 'Rafe and I will prepare supper,' she said. Emily looked up in surprise.

'We'll all help,' said Linda, also rising.

'No, you stay there,' said Suzanne. 'We'll be okay.'

'Well, what's it to be?'

'Lasagne,' she said, pulling a baking tray covered in tinfoil from the fridge.

'Courtesy of Signor Alfieri, the concierge. I know all these meals are ready-made. Don't try to pretend you prepared them from scratch.'

She turned the oven on to fan force, and the noise gave her the cover to speak to me. I knew that was the real reason she had brought me into the kitchen.

'Rafe, I need to ask your advice. Something has happened and–'

Too late. Linda and Alison entered the kitchen. 'Reverend James said we should come and help you,' said Alison. She looked smug.

'Excuse us, we're doing fine without you.' Suzanne indicated the oven. 'All done, see?'

But Linda and Alison would not leave. Linda took out lettuce and tomatoes from the fridge and began making a salad; Alison cut a French loaf down the middle and basted it with garlic paste from a jar she found in the cupboard. We were being policed.

We ate supper in silence. Emily watched Suzanne, and Suzanne watched me in distress that her efforts to communicate something to me had been thwarted. What did she want to say? I signalled to her that we could talk soon. But Reverend James had made sure there was no way this could happen. He stared at me, at her; he knew something was up. He also scrutinised Emily's every move. He was looking for signs of guilt. He was looking to see whether she had spilled the beans about him, I was sure.

After supper, Suzanne looked at me and yawned. 'It's late. I'm going to bed.'

Linda declared that she and Alison would chaperone Suzanne and Emily for toilet breaks and to prepare for the night ahead. It was a deliberate ploy to keep me away from them.

'Let's go then,' Alison said, and she and Linda stood. 'We'll make up beds in the same room.'

'Linda's room,' said the Reverend. 'And the boys will all sleep in my room.'

Emily shrugged her shoulders and nodded her agreement. With a look of resignation, Suzanne did the same.

Danny pushed back his chair. 'Gentlemen, let's s-sort out the rooms, move beds.'

As I left the table, I slid a butter knife up my sleeve. You never knew when you'd have to defend yourself.

Emily managed to push against me for a last word before we parted. We stared out at the snow-glowing night. 'I don't trust any of them,' she said. 'Not anyone.'

'Not even me?'

'What was going on in the kitchen there?'

'Detective work.'

She looked sceptical. 'Sure.'

I touched her cheek. 'Just watch Suzanne, okay? Something is up.'

She winked. 'Don't worry, Rafe. I'm onto it. I'll be all over her like a rash. But you'd better be onto the Reverend too.'

I laughed. 'Like a cheap suit.'

It was not pleasant sleeping with James and Danny. The thought that one of these men could be the murderer made it even more disconcerting. How safe was it to sleep in the same room? Whose idea was this anyway? The murderer's? And similarly, Emily could be sharing a room with a female serial killer.

Unless she was the female serial killer.

The rule – I had gleaned this from reading too many bad mystery novels – was that the murderer was always the one you least suspected. Not the obvious one.

Unless the obvious one was the one you least suspected.

The most suspicious: Reverend James.

The least suspicious: Emily.

Or Danny. His stammering bewilderment could be a ruse, hiding a dark lust for destruction.

Or myself.

I once saw a movie, *Hide and Seek*, where the investigator found, to his surprise, that he himself was the murderer.

But in the real world, the most obvious suspect was Reverend James Miller. Who else could have engineered this whole nightmare so perfectly, and made the deaths neatly correspond to his little *Foxe's Book of Martyrs*. And Linda could be his accomplice. Or Alison. Or all of them. But again, it felt more likely that he had worked with an invisible hand here – the concierge, the castle owner – to pick us off one by one.

There have been cases of cult leaders massacring their own flocks.

And so I lay awake, wired, vigilant. Feigned sleep. Watched Reverend James in the next bed. How had I found myself in this situation? Just like the old retreats at school when we were so terrified of not conforming, so eager to please, to get approval that we went along with this man's crazy ideas, burning our rock albums and 'secular' books, foregoing movies and TV as 'of the devil'. Aware that demons were always on our backs trying to get us to stumble and fall, tempting us with sexual desires, God watching our every move, frowning at our sins, wanting submission and obedience and worship. And behind it all was Reverend James, grooming us to be his sheep. It made me sick. I watched this man, his bald head full of secrets. I turned over in my mind Emily's revelations: Glen and Linda, James and Emily, and whoever else. This man's fanaticism may have been turned into an insatiable need for revenge and obliteration of all immorality.

Only when he was snoring deeply and Danny lying like a sack of stones on his mattress on the floor did I relax and begin to drift off to sleep myself.

But at around midnight, a creak of a floorboard brought me back to full consciousness. Out of the crinkled slits of my eyes, I watched a shadow rise out of the next bed. I reached my hand down the side of the mattress and felt for the butter knife, gripped its cold handle.

The shadow shuffled towards the door.

Danny.

Going to the toilet, I guessed. In the icy night, with that cold stone floor, he had wrapped his blanket around him and shuffled like a zombie in the dark. Turned the key in the lock slowly and carefully pulled open the door. Disappeared into the corridor.

I had to follow.

Reverend James was fast asleep, snoring lightly. I crept out of bed. My teeth were chattering. My bare feet stung with cold. I pulled the duvet from my bed and pulled it tightly around me, then put on my sneakers. I followed Danny into the corridor, hiding in the shadows.

No, he was not going to the toilet. Danny walked to the end of the corridor leading to the women's wing and paused by a window. The glow from snow on the ground gave me enough light to see his silhouette. He clutched a note in his hand, holding it tight as if it was guiding him. Then he walked down the corridor and hesitated outside the room where the women were sleeping. He touched the door handle, deliberating. My heart pounded. If he made any attempt to go in, I would tackle him and bring him to the ground. I clutched the knife and readied myself for attack. But no, he did not enter. He moved on, shuffling in his blanket like the ghost of a monk. I breathed out.

Danny turned and headed for the library. He pushed open the door and entered the darkness. I waited outside and listened.

Gotcha.

Danny had been the quiet one, the one least suspected. This was uncharacteristic behaviour for a follower, a sheep. Was Danny setting up a murder? Or going to commit one? And then I smelt the perfume.

Suzanne's perfume.

The thoughts spiralled in my head. He had lured her in here to murder her. She had tricked him into meeting her here so she could kill him. They were in league and were plotting to murder someone else.

I had been lured to my death. Or maybe this was nothing to do with murder. A tryst, a meeting of secret lovers.

But they knew how dangerous it would be to prowl this castle at night.

I peeked into the room.

There was no trace of Danny. The heavy shelves of books stood silently. The white gleam through the windows made a zebra pattern across the shelves on the floor. Danny was not in the room. But a cold wind blew and I saw a door ajar at the other end. I pressed myself against the wall and sidled towards it. I had not seen this door before, but I quickly discovered that it was another entrance to the torture museum.

We had left the window open in this room to keep Stephen's body cold. The torture museum was out of bounds, and we had locked it. But whoever could open and lock doors electronically had made sure this one was open. Now here was Danny going into a secret entrance in the dead of night. I saw only shapes cast in by the luminous snow outside the tall window. There was the guillotine. There was Stephen's body. Stephen's head. And I recognised other shapes too – the iron maiden standing there like a beast with mouth open, eight mannequins hanging from the ceiling, the brazen bull.

Danny could be hiding behind any of these objects, waiting for me. So I kept to the shadows, held the knife out. I expected some horrible thing – a spike through the neck, or two metal sprung doors to press me into a flesh sandwich. I experienced all the animal instincts of prey, the hackles rising, the beating heart, the blood draining from my extremities. *We're animals,* I thought. *Predators and prey.* And this was going to be survival of the fittest. My body was prepared for fight. Or flight. But not for silence, darkness and perfume.

No Danny anywhere.

Bewildered, I stood still as stone and listened. Heard nothing but the pounding of my own heart.

I returned to the library and scanned that room again in case I had missed something. But there was nothing.

I prowled the corridor, trying to sense by instinct, intuition. The perfume was turning my stomach. I tiptoed to the room where the women were sleeping. Listened outside for a moment and then turned the handle slowly. The door was locked. That was good.

Along the passage, the other women's rooms were empty.

Finally, I returned to the men's wing and entered our room. Reverend James was still asleep, in exactly the same position I had left him, on his back, snoring. Danny's bed too was occupied. Danny had pulled the blanket he had been wrapped in over his entire body and was asleep. I stood by the man's bed, knife at the ready, listening.

SIX

SIX GEESE A-LAYING

I must have fallen asleep shortly afterwards, because it was dawn when I awoke, the knife slack in my hand.

And now Reverend James was gone. I knew that he rose early to pray every morning, but we were not supposed to be out of one another's sight.

At least Danny was still asleep in his bed.

In the rosy light, I spied a note on Danny's bedside table. I reached for it. Danny did not move. I unfolded it, squinted at it. Handwritten in pencil, in soft loopy writing, it said:

Danny, be there, please. Library midnight. I have to speak to you.
Life or death.

The note reeked of perfume. I was sick with nausea as I placed it back on the table. Suzanne was playing a game here, but what?

'Danny!' I whispered.

No response.

I threw back the bedclothes, reached over to shake him

awake. But he was not there. The pillows and blanket had been rolled into a ball.

'Shit.'

I ran to the door and pounded along the corridor, then leaped down the stairs and into the living room. 'Reverend James!'

Reverend James was on his knees, bowed in prayer, facing the window. On the floor in front of him sat his open Bible and the *Foxe's Book of Martyrs*. Nothing unusual. Reverend James had done this every day of his life for as long as I had known him, and had exhorted his flock to have their own 'Quiet Time' every morning at dawn, to pray to God and let Him speak to them through His Word. 'How long have you been here?' was my first question.

Reverend James opened his eyes. 'Rafe, you don't disturb someone's Quiet Time with God. You know that.'

I restrained a violent urge to lash out at him. 'Where's Danny?'

He breathed out in annoyance. 'I left him asleep. And you too. Both of you snoring away.'

'He's not in our bedroom.'

He did not react. 'Maybe he's having a Quiet Time somewhere. As we all should be doing.'

I shook my head. 'His blanket was plumped up to look like he was in it, but he's gone.'

Reverend James closed his Bible. 'Maybe he's in the loo.'

'I'm going to find him.' I strode into the dining area and stood by the breakfast table. Stopped dead. 'Look!'

Five plastic golden rings lay on Danny's placemat, arranged in the Olympic design. I knew what that meant.

'Five golden rings,' said Reverend James. He picked one up, examined it, weighed it with a shaking hand. 'The fifth day of Christmas.'

I scrutinised his reaction. He acted unsurprised, unemotional, as if he knew exactly what this meant. I hid the dread I felt in my own stomach. 'Danny?' I crouched down to examine something on the floor, 'Look.' Under Danny's chair, in the semi-darkness, lay a Bible, or what was left of a Bible. Pages had been ripped out and lay scattered all over the floor.

Reverend James bent down and picked up the vandalised tome. His fingers trembled. 'The first five books of the Bible. Ripped out.'

He gathered the torn pages, peered at them. It was too dark to read, but he seemed to know exactly what pages they were. 'The five golden rings. That's what these are. The Pentateuch. The books of the law.'

I stared directly at Reverend James. 'Who would even know what the five golden rings mean, except you?'

Reverend James blinked at me and dropped the pages. 'It means that none of us are safe. It means–' He turned and ran for the door.

I ran after him. 'Wait!'

He climbed the stairs and bounded along the corridor, and I followed in hot pursuit. Ignoring me, he stopped outside the women's bedroom and pounded on the door. 'Are you okay in there? Linda? Ali?'

A sleepy Suzanne in pink marshmallow dressing gown, gossamer hair like a spider web all over her face, opened the door. 'Reverend James.'

She barred the door, the ghost of an ironic smile on her face. 'Sorry, Reverend, Rafe, you can't come in here. We're still in a state of... undress.'

I smelt that perfume on her and it made me want to retch. 'Danny's missing,' I said.

I looked unblinking into her eyes to ensure I could see beyond the façade. The first reaction is always the honest one. Her eyes flooded with terror. Affirmation of some fear, but not surprise. 'But Danny was with you.'

Emily pushed past Suzanne, wrapping her dressing gown around her. 'Danny's missing?'

I peered past her into the dark bedroom. 'Has anyone seen him?'

'He's certainly not in here,' said Emily.

Linda and Alison crowded the door too.

Emily pointed down the corridor. 'Maybe he's in the bathroom.'

'I'll check the men's bathroom and bedrooms.'

But Danny was nowhere to be seen.

'Let's check the women's bathroom,' Suzanne said. 'Together.'

I led the way, banged open the door, inspected the toilet stalls, the storage closet. Emily pointed to a row of bottles on the shelf. Shampoo, conditioner and a small rose-coloured bottle with a stopper. 'Suzanne's perfume,' she mouthed. I picked up the bottle, sniffed it and winced.

'Excuse me!' I turned to see Suzanne frowning at me. 'That's mine.' I had no time to think of an excuse for why I was sniffing her perfume. She looked panicked.

'Danny!' Reverend James' trembling voice multiplied in the echoing corridors. Stone-cold walls bounced the voice back. He beckoned us all out of the bathroom. 'We have to go room to room. But all together.'

'Knowing Danny, he's praying somewhere,' said Alison. 'He always has a Quiet Time when he wakes up.' But she said this without conviction.

'I hope so.'

'Where are we going, Rafe?' asked Emily.

I led them into the library and past the rows of shelves. Perhaps I had missed something in the dark last night. Perhaps Danny was still here. But the room was empty. I tried the door handle at the end of the room. It was locked. 'We have to get in here.'

Reverend James frowned. 'Where does that door lead?'

'The torture museum.'

'No, the door to the museum is on the other side of the corridor.'

'Just trust me.' I took out the bunch of keys I had filched from Stephen's corpse and tried one key after another. No luck. What chance did I have against a remote electronic locking mechanism? 'We'll have to go around to the torture museum door.'

Reverend James' eyes were wide. 'You think he's in there. He couldn't get in. I have the key.'

'Doors open electronically in this castle,' I said. I rattled the door again. 'He came through here. Anyway, we've got to go around the other side.'

Reverend James led us around to the entrance through the corridor and unlocked the door. I pushed past him into the room.

'I don't think this is a good idea,' he said. 'The ladies should stay behind. After all—'

'I'm not staying on my own outside,' said Linda.

The first thing I smelt was the faint trace of perfume. Ice-cold air blew in through the open window. Nothing else was amiss. But instinct had pulled me here, and a sense of dread.

'You sure he came in here?' asked Emily.

I nodded. 'That library door was open in the middle of the night. Wide open. Every door can be controlled electronically, remember?' I scanned the room again. Something was different. I just couldn't figure out what.

Then Alison screamed. 'Ugh, I stood on something sticky.' She lifted her feet, and I squinted to see what it was. 'A flashlight, please.'

'Oh my God,' said Emily as she shone the light on the floor.

'Come away from there.' My heart thumped insistently.

Alison had been standing next to the iron maiden. And that was what was different. The iron maiden, the sarcophagus with spikes, had been open, upright and on display the last time I had seen it, like a crocodile displaying its teeth. Even at midnight, I distinctly remembered seeing it open at a ninety-degree angle. Now it was shut. And from the bottom of the rectangular-shaped coffin oozed a pool of viscous gleaming liquid. Alison had stood in this patch of what looked like oil or glue. She left footprints as she walked away.

Linda screamed. 'It's blood.'

I shone the flashlight on the sealed iron maiden casket. The maiden engraved on its lid screamed in silent terror, her naked, steel-black torso gleaming in the reflected light.

'Don't,' said Reverend James as I reached for the coffin handle to open it. 'Everyone back.'

Linda and Alison hid behind Reverend James. He shielded them with his arms as if I was going to unleash some terrible attack on them. Suzanne stepped backwards out into the doorway.

We all knew what we were going to find. I yanked on the two metal clasps on the lid and pulled the iron maiden open, slowly. My feet stuck to the floor. I wanted to retch. I could smell death.

It was jammed. I pulled with two hands at the lid. 'Someone give me a hand!'

Emily wrapped her dressing gown tight around her and stood on one side. Her slippers stuck to the floor as she positioned herself to pull on the handle. 'Slowly now, on the count of three.'

It gave reluctantly, as if it had been glued shut. It made a ghastly sucking noise as the two sides parted. I had steeled myself for what was inside, but even so, I stepped back in shock. Emily gasped and let go of the handle.

The iron maiden was occupied. What had been a polished

casket of gleaming spikes was now a mess of bloodied flesh impaled front and back. The lid which we had just pulled open tore away the flesh on its five spikes.

Danny's dead eyes stared out at us in sullen terror. One spike had pierced his throat, another had gone straight through his heart. The third spike had impaled his back. Of the remaining two, one had pierced his left thigh and one his right arm. Blood had drained out of the bottom of the casket onto the floor and had congealed around the casket.

Reverend James shielded his eyes and prayed. 'Please, God. No.'

Alison doubled over, clutching her stomach and dry retching. Linda embraced her, trembling violently. Emily stared, wide-eyed, silent. 'We have got to get out of here – and get hold of the police,' said Suzanne.

'I'm not staying here a second longer,' said Alison to Reverend James. She wiped her slippers on the floor, as though wiping off mud. 'You have to get us out of here. Now.'

I stared at the body, and then at the sarcophagus that had enshrined Danny. The spikes had been strategically placed to penetrate his body from both sides. There was no way anyone could live once trapped inside this coffin.

'Close it,' called Reverend James.

I ignored him. Instead, I reached into the casket and touched Danny's face, felt for the pulse in his neck. His skin was cold. He had been dead a while. His eyes gazed out at the room. *Danny, Danny, what were you doing here at midnight? Why didn't I see you? Why couldn't I save you? Who did this to you?*

On Danny's neck, I found the same little red dot I had seen on Stephen. I stepped away, my feet sticky on the blood. Emily peered over and saw the red dot too. Alison and Linda hid behind Reverend James, and Suzanne stood by the door with arms folded, hugging herself tightly. She fixed her eyes on me.

'Didn't you sleep in the same room?' Emily whispered. 'I mean, how did he… get separated?'

Reverend James answered. 'He was gone when we woke in the morning.'

'He got up in the middle of the night,' I said. 'I saw him.'

'No!' said Suzanne from the doorway. Her reaction was so unexpected, I stared at her. She reddened. Her lips quivered. 'No! No! No!'

'Rafe, you should have stopped him,' said Reverend James. 'At least you should have woken me up.' He stared hard at me.

'I thought he was going to the loo. I followed him.'

All eyes were on me. Prime suspect. 'Wait a minute. Listen to me.'

'You followed him where?' said Suzanne.

'To the library.'

'Oh God,' said Suzanne, looking so pale I thought she might faint. Alison and Linda held her. I stared at her, suspicion and nausea mounting inside me to breaking point. The note. Of course. She had lured him there with her note.

'And,' said Reverend James. 'You saw him in the library.'

I shook my head. 'I saw him go through the open door between the library and this room. Last night this door was open. But when I followed him, I couldn't see him anywhere.'

Alison stepped out from behind Reverend James to face me, her eyes full of hatred and accusation. 'You were here in the middle of the night?'

'I was. The iron maiden was open and empty when I searched this room. I'm sure of that. I went back to the men's bedroom, and there he was, or so I thought. So I went to sleep. But in the morning, I realised he hadn't returned. It was just his bedclothes, arranged to look as if he was still there.'

I said nothing about the note. An instinct, a hunch. Suzanne's terrified eyes fixed on me. She had just moved into number one spot for prime suspect. Or maybe tied with Reverend James.

But for the others, the air was frigid with judgement against me.

A murderer, I wanted to say, *would not confess to following the victim out to his death.*

Alison's face was cold and judgemental.

Reverend James frowned. 'Come.' He ushered the women out of the room and into the corridor. 'It's freezing. Close the door.'

'Poor Danny,' said Alison.

'And Stephen...' said Linda.

'And Glen,' said Emily.

'And Mike,' I said.

Reverend James closed the door. We stood in the corridor, suspicion our closest companion.

Emily wrapped her dressing gown tightly across her chest. 'This is beyond terrible. We can't just passively...'

I turned to leave but felt the Reverend clutch at my arm. 'Where are you going, Rafe?'

I shook free of his grasp. 'I'll meet you in the living room.'

He grabbed at me, but I ducked past him. 'You're not going anywhere on your own!'

I marched past him and bolted along the corridor to the men's bedroom, ignoring the footsteps I could hear behind me. I rushed to Danny's bedside table to get the note, but it was gone. I searched the floor in case it had blown off, flapped the blanket and pillows in case it was in Danny's bed. But it had vanished.

'Rafe?'

Suzanne stood, out of breath, at the doorway. 'I have to talk to you urgently.' She closed the door behind her and locked it. She had a mad look about her, as if she might do anything, and for a second I felt a sudden sharp fear that here was the killer and she was coming after me. To silence me. To get her incriminating note.

But no.

'I can't believe I did it again,' she said, bursting into tears and throwing herself against me. Her pink dressing gown was soft. Her hair smelt of green apple shampoo. Her perfume revolted me now.

I tried to hold her away from me. 'Tell me…'

Sniffing, she pulled out a piece of paper from her pocket and passed it to me. 'Danny gave me this last night.'

I stared at the childish block letters, unevenly spaced and aligned.

Meet me at midnight. Library. Urgent. Life or death. Please, Suzanne, I need to speak with you, or I will die. Don't fail me this time.

Suzanne gripped my shirt. 'I didn't go. I got this note and I thought, *It's a set-up. He's trying to lure me away.*'

I held her hand tight. 'So this is what you have been trying to tell me.'

She held me tighter. Spoke into my chest. 'I locked the door and made sure no one could get in. I was waiting all night for Danny to come and get me.'

Now I was confused. I had steeled myself off from her, suspected terrible things of her, but with her in my arms, all I could feel was compassion. 'You thought he was the killer?'

She nodded. 'And then when he died, I first thought he killed himself. Like Glen. Like Stephen. Like Mike. Because of me. The note says he will die if he doesn't speak with me, and so I killed him.'

I tried to pry her from me, not trusting her, not wanting to feel what I was feeling, but she held on. 'Suzanne, get a grip, calm down. They didn't kill themselves. None of them.'

'I'm scared, Rafe.' She grabbed my shirt and pulled.

I steadied her hand. 'Danny had the five golden rings card.

Not you.' I took a breath. 'Suzanne, I have to ask you something–'

But she pulled away and cocked her head towards the door. 'Shh!'

Outside I heard the troop coming along the corridor to find us, calling our names.

'It's okay,' I shouted out. 'We'll be right there.'

I held her shoulder and stared into her eyes. I wanted to see how she reacted. 'Danny had a note. In your handwriting. I read it. It was by his bed and now it's gone.' I gestured to the table. 'I came back to get it.'

Her eyes widely innocent, her lip quivering, like a scene from one of her movies, she asked, 'What did it say?'

'The same as yours. Meet me at midnight.' I hesitated. 'A secret tryst.'

She gripped my collar tighter, until our faces were inches from each other. 'I never wrote a note to him. Never.'

Her eyes were teary, beseeching. My heart was racing. How could I not believe her? 'You sure?'

'Why would I write him a note?'

The door shook as someone hammered on it. Reverend James. 'Rafe?'

She tensed up against me.

'Just give us a minute,' I called.

'So you never wrote him a note?'

She detached herself from me and walked up and down the room, as if she was performing a soliloquy. I could see she was distressed. Or was playing the part of someone distressed. And overacting. She grabbed her hair; she wrung her hands.

I pointed to the chest of drawers where I had found the note.

'I never wrote to him. Ever.'

I stared into her eyes again. She looked sincere, but then again, if she could cry on demand, she was capable of faking any emotion. More hammering at the door. Linda's voice. 'You okay, Suzanne?'

'She's fine,' I called back. 'Give us a minute, please.' I pushed Suzanne towards the window, away from the door. 'So if you are right, someone set you up. Or set him up.'

'You don't believe me?'

I stared at her pouting lips but did not say what I really thought. If I was going to play to win, I knew enough to keep some cards to myself. 'But if the note I saw was fake, then the letter from Glen might be fake too. Maybe someone is using you as bait to lure them to their deaths.'

She looked afraid. Stood back from me.

'Cat and mouse. Fisherman and fish.'

The hammering on the door continued. Reverend James yelled, 'Open this door. Now.'

I crumpled her note and stuffed it in my pocket. 'Not a word about the notes. I want to get to the bottom of this. Find whoever wrote them.'

In response, she touched my lips with her fingers. I unlocked the door. Reverend James stood in the entrance, red-faced. 'How dare you—'

Linda and Alison pushed past me and embraced Suzanne, escorted her out into the corridor as if rescuing her from my evil clutches. 'You okay?' Alison said to her, shooting me an accusing look.

I glared back. 'She's fine. Everything's fine,' I said.

Reverend James narrowed his eyes. 'It's not fine, Rafe. It is definitely not fine.'

Emily stood, arms folded, shaking her head at me.

No one felt like eating, but that is what we did. Anything to feign a sense of normalcy after seeing Danny impaled like a chicken kebab. Linda poured trembling mugs of strong coffee for each of us, and Alison brought in a plate of pancakes. Thank goodness. I could not stomach more bacon and sausages. I dripped maple syrup on my pancakes and wolfed down three to quell my queasy stomach, then burnt the disgust down my throat with black coffee. I stared at Danny's place-mat, at the five plastic rings, at the torn books of the Bible piled up on the floor.

I expected that Emily, being a nurse, was the only one of us who had seen a dead body before. I had never seen heads decapitated or bodies drowned, or splattered on rocks, or pierced through with thirty-centimetre-long swords in an enclosed space. And never had I been so helpless as to have to leave them in that state and to sit in the same house, eating pancakes and staring at their possible murderers. This had a surreal quality about it, thinking of Stephen and Danny as if they were exhibits in the museum, their blood pooled around their bodies in halos of stickiness.

I should move them, for dignity's sake.

No, we should get the police.

No, just get the hell out of here. Escape this madhouse.

But we were snowed in, buried in an icy morgue.

And now the notes. I didn't know if I could trust Suzanne's account of things. I sifted through the new evidence in my mind. It seemed… childish. Exchanging notes as if we were teenagers. Someone was playing games here, dabbing Suzanne's perfume everywhere. And, if she was to be believed, someone was forging her handwriting, playing a silly – but very deadly – game.

1)Suzanne receives a love note from Glen. Glen dies that night.

2)Danny receives a note from Suzanne. Suzanne receives a love note from Danny. Danny dies that night.

3)Glen warns me to lock my door. He dies before explaining why.

4)Stephen tells me he has evidence. He dies before he can explain.

5)Suzanne's perfume is found at the scene of every murder (except maybe Mike's).

Suzanne. Suzanne. Suzanne. I stared at her in critical fascination. Tried to separate the facts from the feel of her embrace, her pleading eyes.

'More coffee for you all,' said Linda. 'It will help.'

Reverend James' face was ashen as he held out his cup. 'I knew this would happen,' he said.

I looked up at him sharply.

'Satan was ready to pounce. He saw it as a challenge. The Twelve getting together again. I thought we were strong, but we were divided.'

He is mad, I thought, *or else presenting a cunning smokescreen.* 'What are you talking about?'

'I should never have invited you all here. Face our sins, confess our iniquities. He's mocking me.'

Now was the time to confront him, with all the others present so he could not squirm away. 'Reverend James, you planned all this. We need to talk about what was supposed to happen.'

He looked frightened. Cornered. 'I planned for each of us to consider our sins on the day chosen for us... but only to purify ourselves. Not murder. I didn't foresee this cruel mockery of my intentions.'

I stared into those eyes. Saw delusion, saw fundamentalist truth, pain, heartache, righteous stubbornness. But did I see a murderer? 'Well, let's hear it then, Reverend.' He looked like a cornered rabbit. 'The sermon. You said you had one prepared for each day of Christmas. A lesson for each of us. So, let's hear it.'

'Don't mock the Lord,' said Alison, staring at me with such hatred I could feel it as a physical force.

'He's not the Lord,' I said. I sipped my coffee slowly. 'We have a killer playing cat and mouse with us. They may be one of us.' I stared at Alison until she dropped her gaze.

'Or,' she said, her voice full of ice, 'he may have followed Danny out into the corridor last night and killed him.'

'Or,' I said, looking directly at the Reverend, 'he may have planned this to coincide with his *Foxe's Book of Martyrs*. Each death suspiciously follows the pattern laid out by Reverend James' sermons.'

Reverend James clapped his hands as if to kill an annoying mosquito. 'Enough!'

Linda placed her hand on her husband's shoulders, hid behind him, stared at me.

'Okay, okay,' said Emily, clattering her cup on the table. 'Let's all take it easy. For all we know, it has nothing to do with any of us. It may be someone hiding in the castle, such as the concierge or the owner. That's what we need to consider. Be alert, stick together – for now.' She stabbed a look at me. 'Every time someone wanders off on their own, they get killed. Never, ever go off on your own, anyone.'

'You can talk,' said Alison, pointing her nose contemptuously at Emily. 'You and Rafe are going off all the time.'

Linda added her protest. 'And Rafe ran off with Suzanne to his room.'

Suzanne turned on Linda, angry. 'He didn't run off with me.'

Reverend James raised his hands. 'Please, please, girls.'

Alison pressed her hand to her head. 'We have to get out of here. Today. We're rats in a cage.'

I did not want my request side-tracked. 'Go ahead, Reverend James,' I said. 'I'm not being facetious. I really want to hear today's sermon.'

Reverend James opened his *Foxe's Book of Martyrs* and looked at each member of the group in turn. He licked his lips and began: 'Who was martyred on the 29th December, the fifth day of Christmas?'

Blank stares. He found the dog-eared page and pointed to an underlined passage. 'St Thomas à Becket.'

'The Archbishop of Canterbury?' said Alison, her curiosity piqued in spite of her terror.

He nodded to her. 'In 1170, on the fifth day of Christmas, four of King Henry II's knights burst into Canterbury Cathedral after the Archbishop had given his Christmas sermon on the true meaning of Christmas. They stabbed him with their swords. Five times. Five wounds.'

'Five sword wounds,' said Emily. 'Just like Danny.'

Reverend James scanned the sermon he was meant to give on the sixth day, then hesitated. I could see what he was thinking. This would incriminate him. He shook his head and slammed the book closed. 'I don't know what to make of this. Every time. Satan is mocking us.'

'It makes sense to me,' I said, counting on my fingers. 'Glen stoned to death, Stephen beheaded, Mike drowned, and now Danny impaled on five swords. Just like the martyrs on each of the days of Christmas. Very coincidentally like the book, and very much in line with the sermons you planned to hit us with.' I let the ideas sink in. The others flicked their stares from me to him. 'You can't seriously believe this is the work of supernatural agents.'

Reverend James placed his trembling hand over his heart. 'That's exactly what I'm saying. It's the work of Satan.'

I could tell by the expression on Emily's face that we shared the same thought. Only a madman would do this. A meticulous, Biblical fanatic with intimate knowledge of torture, martyrdom and the religious meanings of the twelve days of

Christmas. And there was only one madman present with that knowledge.

Alison and Linda whispered together, and then called Emily and Suzanne over. 'Excuse us, Reverend,' said Alison, 'we need to go to the loo.'

Reverend James frowned. 'Not alone. All together.'

'I'll go with them,' I said.

'No,' said Alison. 'Not you. We're fine, thank you.'

'At least take a weapon of some sort,' I said. I still had a niggling fear that the concierge, or the castle owner, in cahoots with Reverend James, was hiding somewhere in the castle.

The women took kitchen knives and moved as one organism out of the room. That left us two men together alone, me and the killer. Surely it was I who needed protection. I also drew a knife from the kitchen drawer. 'Just in case the killer attacks while they're gone,' I said.

Not to be outdone, Reverend James also took a knife from the drawer. He placed it on the table in front of him. A truce, of sorts; a mini nuclear cold war.

We stared down each other, two adversaries making no pretence of the hostility between us. If Reverend James was innocent, then he would no doubt suspect me. He pulled up his chair close to me so he could speak in his low, God-like voice. 'I want to be honest with you, Rafe. You need God back in your life. That is what this is all about. You need to repent. God can forgive, even at this late stage.'

I could not believe what I was hearing. I gripped the knife tight in my hand. 'What do you mean, what this is all about? You mean the murders?'

He pressed his fingers together, looked at me through them like he had done all those years ago when he'd summon me to his rectory office as a school kid. 'You backslid, Rafe. I held the most promise for you. You were a leader in the Church. Why did you lose faith?'

I shook my head. 'I lost my delusions, my prison bars.'

Reverend James bunched his fingers into a fist. 'Will nothing bring you back to the Lord? Not murder, not fear of death? That is what is happening here. God is using Satan's handiwork to get us to repent, recommit ourselves. The Bible—'

But I was not going to be preached at by this man with his archaic beliefs. Not now. 'The Bible was written by men, not God. It is largely plagiarised from other religions. I refuse to let this conglomerate of jumbled stories from primitive patriarchal cultures dictate my life.'

He leaned back, smiled. He was not listening to a word I said, I could tell. 'Fancy words, Rafe. Fancy academic words, but the Word of God remains—'

I rolled my eyes. 'Your word.'

He tensed up. 'There is only one God.'

'Yes, yours. And people who don't believe in your God are cast into hell. Or persecuted. Or killed.'

He stood. 'What are you saying?'

I had to be careful here. I kept close to the table in case he lunged for the knife. I would not have put that past him, he looked so angry. 'Religious zealots kill for their beliefs. I think we're seeing it here. Some madman who thinks he can execute us one by one,' I said.

He jabbed his finger in the air to emphasise every word. 'Satan is the destroyer of life, not God. You want to destroy my faith? Never. Satan is inside you and you don't even know it.'

I retreated to the fireplace. Staring into the flames, I kept my eye on the poker in case he tried any tricks. 'So there we have it. I'm Satan, you're a religious fanatic.'

Silence.

I turned and he was sitting again, his face in his hands.

When he spoke, his voice was cracked. 'Rafe, I wanted us all to gather here for Christmas to put Christ back into Christmas. To renew our faith. I'm not a murderer.' He stared at the Christmas tree, which twinkled and flashed and glittered, seeming to mock him.

'Hold on!' I stiffened. 'Wait, did you hear that?'

'Jesus save us!' Reverend James reached for his knife and brandished it at the doorway. I heard a thump then a bang down the corridor. Thump, thump, thump. It sounded, in my state of fear, like someone dragging a dead body down the stairs. I reached for my knife too and dashed into the corridor.

Only to find Alison, Linda, Emily and Suzanne coming down in a long troop, dressed in mittens, scarves and hats. Emily wore a satchel on her back and Suzanne's bag was slung over her shoulder. Alison was dragging a large suitcase behind her. I lowered my knife.

'What is this?' said Reverend James over my shoulder, still grasping his knife.

Alison zipped up her jacket. 'We're not staying a minute longer. We're leaving. You too, Reverend.'

Open mouthed, Reverend James stared at Linda, and she shrank back, hiding behind Alison. 'Linda? What are you going to do?' he thundered. 'Order a cab? Walk out of here? You can't take a suitcase!'

'We've had enough,' said Alison. 'Enough.' She pulled her suitcase past me towards the front door as if she fully intended to drag it outside through the snow.

Emily looked determined too. 'If the men don't, we women have a plan – walk to the town. There is a road. We can do it.'

'Or die trying,' added Suzanne, joining the two other women at the front entrance.

Reverend James lunged ahead of them and barred the front door. 'It's dangerous.'

'Dangerous?' echoed Suzanne, with a laugh. 'And staying here is not?'

He stood with arms crossed. 'Ye of little faith—'

'Faith has nothing to do with it, Reverend,' said Suzanne, her face taut. 'Someone has died here every single night. I'm not staying here to find out when it's my turn. You heard that recording. You said it was a hoax, but after four horrible deaths, it ain't no hoax.'

I pushed past the women. 'I'm coming too, then.'

Alison stiffened. 'You weren't invited.'

'I'm not letting you go alone,' I said. 'We all go. No one splits up.'

Reverend James stood resolute at the front door. Linda, Alison and Suzanne now turned and made for the kitchen where we could hear them gathering supplies. Then he marched into the kitchen and we heard raised voices.

I caught Emily's arm. 'You can't just walk into ice and snow.'

She shook me off, her expression cool. 'The way I figure it is this – Mike didn't even leave the castle grounds. The roads might be totally walkable. We're just assuming we're snowed in, but what if we're not?'

I held her arm. 'Mike was murdered out there.'

She stopped, and her resolute expression softened. 'But if we go in a group, we'll be safe. You coming then?'

I nodded. 'Let me bundle up too and I'm out of here.'

I stared at Alison's suitcase. 'She really thinks she's going to take that?'

Emily shook her head. 'She's beside herself with fear, Rafe. She can't think straight.'

Reverend James walked through the kitchen door, Linda and Alison following him. 'I'm staying. And my wife is staying too.'

Emily glowered at him. 'Why are you so stubborn, Reverend James?'

'Having faith in God is being stubborn? Yes, it is, Emily. Haven't I taught you anything? Abraham wrestled with God until he got what he wanted. He didn't take no for an answer. God wants us to be stubborn, steadfast, resolute.'

Linda took off her coat and sat next to her husband. 'I'm staying.'

Suzanne gave her an incredulous look. 'You really are staying? In the loo, we all agreed to go.'

Linda linked arms with her husband, looking brave. 'We're staying.' But her terrified eyes told a different story.

There was a reason I did not insist that Reverend James and his wife follow. I wanted to test a hypothesis. I watched them as the other women prepared to brave the weather. Emily had pushed Alison's suitcase behind the door.

The Reverend did not show any fear. Anger, betrayal, self-righteousness, yes, but no fear. Either he was truly a man of great faith, or he had no need to be afraid because... well, he was the killer.

Suzanne peered back at the couple in the living room. 'I can't believe they're going to stay behind.'

I shrugged my shoulders. 'We can't force them.'

I opened the front door, steeled myself against the cold and took the lead. My plan was to follow where I believed the road lay, all the way down the mountain, stop for rests, keep everyone warm and get to the village. But as soon as I stepped outside, I knew it was a mistake, that we would never make it. The weather had deteriorated again. The wind gusted sideways, and a sudden squall of sleet reduced visibility to almost zero. The road I wanted to naïvely follow was gone – a blanket of grey and white amorphous landscape. Snow in the court-yard had banked up and in corners the drifts looked deep. As a test, I crunched onto the frozen pathway from the front entrance towards the road. My leg sank into an icy drift that threatened to swallow me.

'Hang on,' I yelled to the women behind me.

Alison waded past me. 'I'm going.'

'Be careful!' Emily edged forward.

Alison took one step past me, slipped and disappeared in the whiteness.

'Shit!' I waded after her, pulled her up. 'You okay?'

She shook me off. 'Don't touch me!' She tried to go forward again. 'You were not meant to come.'

Mist swirled up from the valley, sleet attacked us, wind roared in my ears. My face was already numb. I watched her fall again. Reaching forward, I pulled her up and we stumbled back to the entrance.

'Leave me alone!' She wriggled out of my grasp.

'No way we can make the journey,' I told the others.

Suzanne peered over the edge. 'Is there any other way down?'

Alison brushed the snow off her and glared at me. 'You don't want us to go. You want us all killed. You're the one who wants us dead. I know it.' She thrust her finger in my face. 'You and your heathen friend Emily always whispering together, sneering at us, undermining our faith. You just came here to mock us.'

Emily tried to put an arm around her, but she violently pushed her away. 'Calm down, Ali, you're hysterical.'

But she let Suzanne embrace her. 'Let's go back to the castle. You're freezing.'

'I'm not going back in there with him.' She pointed at me, covered her face, and began sobbing and convulsing. 'Just keep him away from me.'

Suzanne led her away. 'Come.'

She let Suzanne support her as she stood and stumbled back towards the front door.

Emily and I watched them open the door. My nose and mouth were numb, my sinuses crackling, a headache pulsing in my right temple. I turned to Emily. 'I'm the suspect, then.'

'Yes, of course. It was her idea, Ali's, to get away. She wanted to leave you behind. She hates you. She hates me. She doesn't know where to turn.'

'Poor Ali.'

She stopped. 'Now tell me what's going on between you and Suzanne.'

'Not here in this freezing wind.' I began leading her to the castle where Ali and Suzanne were already opening the front door. We found a sheltered portico and huddled against the wall out of the wind.

Emily pointed to the front door where Suzanne had just gone through. 'She's playing you so well. Don't you see? It's just like old times.'

I wrapped my arms around her. 'I have something to tell you.'

She leaned into me for warmth. 'What?'

'When I last saw him alive, Danny had a note in his hand... from Suzanne.'

She jabbed me in the stomach. 'I knew it. She's guilty as sin. Tell me more.'

I glanced at the closed front door, making sure no one was about. 'He was carrying it when he wandered into the library, then it was on his bedside table when I returned, which is why I thought he was back in his bed. I read it, but when I rushed up later to retrieve it, it was gone. Reverend James was the only one who could have taken it. And put it there in the first place.'

Emily whistled. 'What did it say?'

'It invited Danny to a secret tryst. And it reeked of her perfume.'

She slapped her thigh. 'I knew it!' But then she gave me a suspicious look. 'And what was she doing in the room with you? Trying to seduce you out of putting her down as a suspect? You're falling for it, you know.'

I shook my head. My face was numb with cold. 'She came to tell me that she had a note too. She claimed Danny had given it to her, asking her to meet at midnight.'

She frowned. 'Wait, I'm confused. There were two notes?'

I pulled the note out of my pocket, but it was hard to read in the freezing sleet and my hands were shaking – from the cold and from the accusation. Emily's scorn was not something to brush off lightly.

Emily's teeth chattered. 'She set up a secret tryst with Danny?'

'I think she's being set up.'

She smiled at me. 'Sure, sure. She's innocent. And you're not biased at all.'

'Emily…'

'Maybe. Or, as I said before, she wants you to think she's being set up.' She gave a sigh of exasperation. 'She manipulates people. She's an actor. She's playing us all. Including you.'

I turned her face towards mine so I could look in her eyes. I saw the scorn there, but a dancing merriment too. 'I don't know if it's play-acting or not, but she's in as much distress as the rest of us. We're all scared.'

'You fall for it every time.'

'You underestimate me.'

She smiled, as much as you could smile in this cold. 'Nothing has changed, has it? Amazing how it still gives me the shits. It's sickening and yes, disconcerting to watch every man dissolve when she's in the room, and every woman go mad with envy.'

I held her face, saw that she was never going to let this go. It must hurt her more deeply than I thought. 'Was Suzanne in the room with you last night? The whole time?'

She nodded. 'Yes. And I should know, I was awake the whole frigging night. Scared the others would do me in. So I locked the door. Kept the key. No one could have got out.'

She shivered. 'Come on, let's get back inside. I'm freezing.'

We crunched on the hard snow towards the front door. 'My prime suspect is still Reverend James.'

'But he was with you the whole time last night.'

'Snoring. But I fell asleep and when I woke in the morning, he was gone.'

We had reached the front door. We stopped again, and Emily turned to me. 'I have to agree with you: much as I suspect Suzanne, I think Reverend James set the whole thing up. He arranged the venue, the twelve days, and he said every day would reveal something. Each of us destined to die on a certain day, in a particular way.'

'But Suzanne is still acting very weird for a supposed innocent victim.'

'The women think it's you. You were the last person to see Danny alive. We only have your word. You led him to the torture museum, trapped him in the coffin thing, and then set up his pillow to look as if he was still asleep, then raised the alarm. You met Stephen in the torture museum. If we weren't blood brother and sister, I would think it looks pretty suspicious.'

I nodded. It was suspicious. If I was them, I'd suspect me too. 'Then Ali must suspect you too. We met Glen in his room before he died. We were outside when we found Mike drowned.'

'I don't blame Ali. Motive – we're heathens. Motive, means, opportunity, all boxes ticked.'

I reached for the door handle. 'Can we go inside now? I'm freezing my arse off.'

'Just keep an eye on the Reverend. And,' she added, 'the actress. Or rather, stop keeping an eye on her. It's nauseating.'

I spent the rest of the day watching each of them. Observing, making sure no one slipped away. They in turn watched one another... and me, all of us wary, resigned to being imprisoned here.

'Supper is served!' Linda called out, as if this was an ordinary day and nothing was amiss. It was something she had to hold on to, I could see – the semblance of normal domestic life when all was crumbling around her. And I was sure her faith too was crumbling. I had been watching her carefully ever since I found out she'd had an affair with Glen. So she was not the meek wife I had always believed her to be.

Her husband's faith was certainly not crumbling, or else he was using it as a smokescreen. But he had one of those unchangeable fixed minds. I found him as rigid, intolerant, unbending and impenetrable as ever. All the signs of a sociopath, a murderer even.

Alison? Alison had lost it.

Suzanne was still a mystery to me, and my feelings wavered between sympathy and suspicion. She was either a victim or a very good actor. Could she be the black widow spider in the centre of this web? I did not know. I had no grounds for motive here. But instinct told me not to trust her. Not to trust myself.

The food was still abundant, having been rationed into twelve daily portions, and all Linda had to do was heat it up. Chicken biryani tonight, with rice and vegetables. Reverend James was already in his usual place at the head of the table. Suzanne brought out a steaming bowl of white rice, and Linda

the curry. But no one touched it. The ghosts of form and cere-
mony were all that held us together. We sat in our usual places,
opposite the empty places of the murdered, and avoided
staring at the macabre display of their death mementos on
their place settings.

Alison refused to sit with us at the table. She sat by the fire
on the carpet, her legs up to her chin, her arms clasped around
her knees.

Suzanne called to her. 'Come and join us, Ali.'

She did not respond. Although she was crouched with her
back to the group, I could see her in the mirror. She was shivering, likely from the cold terror inside her. She had been pushed
too far, I could see that. Linda walked over and tried to put an
arm around Alison's shoulder, but she pushed her away.

'It's a test,' said Reverend James to all of us, but directed at
Alison. 'A test of our faith. Like Job in the Old Testament. He
lost everything, and still clung to his faith. Satan tried to make
him renounce his God. He threw everything at him – death of
his family, pestilence, wild weather, disease, and still he
remained steadfast. This is the same. We have to withstand
Satan's fiery darts, keep faith and then everything will be
restored tenfold as it was to Job.'

'Amen,' said Linda, filling each plate and passing it around
the table.

I snorted. 'Restored tenfold? So Glen, Stephen, Mike and
Danny are going to miraculously rise from the dead on your
command?'

Emily nudged me under the table. 'Okay,' I said. 'Sorry.
But we need to talk about what's really going on here. What
are the remaining days of Christmas?'

Reverend James recited them. 'Six geese a-laying, seven
swans a-swimming, eight maids a-milking, nine ladies dancing,
ten lords a-leaping, eleven pipers piping and twelve drummers
drumming.'

'So each of us was assigned a different day, and we've been targeted in that order. We need to know who is next.'

He gave me a dirty look. 'No one is next,' he said.

I glared back at him. 'I meant, who was assigned the sixth day of Christmas? I know I'm the eight maids a-milking. So if the murderer continues his plan to eliminate us all, I can expect an attempt on my life in two days' time. Who's today?'

'I am,' called Alison. 'I'm six geese a-laying.' She pulled the card from her pocket and threw it into the fire.

Reverend James called across to her. 'No one else is going to die, Ali,' he said. 'I will make sure of that. We'll stick together.'

She ignored him. He turned back to me and I pointed my fork at him. 'Nevertheless, the killer is playing by some strict mathematical logic. He or she has assigned a death for each of us corresponding not only to "The Twelve Days of Christmas" but to saints martyred on those days.'

Emily nodded. 'So if we want to stay one step ahead, we have to think like the murderer.'

Suzanne turned the curry and rice on her plate with her fork. 'But there are only… were only ten of us.'

Linda, who had been silent, now could not contain her fear. 'He said he had murdered Sean and Jack before we arrived here. He's out to get all of us, the entire Twelve.'

Reverend James patted his wife's arm. 'Then he's lying. They each died in a car accident.'

I took a mouthful of curry and regretted it. My stomach turned. I chewed and swallowed. 'Let's assume the murderer was speaking the truth. That he, or she, killed Sean and Jack. That he is out to get us all. The question is, who is next?'

'I'd rather die in the snow out there than… here in that torture museum,' said Alison.

'We'll look after you,' I said. 'Even if the killer is among us, we'll make an arrangement so we're all safe. From one another.'

'The only way to do that,' said Reverend James, 'is if we stay up all night.'

'Or one of us keeps guard,' said Emily.

'But who?' said Suzanne, looking around. 'Who can we trust?'

We stared at one another.

I shook my head. 'Let's abandon trust and faith. I propose mutual mistrust. This is how the world works. Expect the worst of people. It's an ugly principle, but one that works. Why do we have disclaimers and preventative measures in place in almost every aspect of our lives? Why the rule of law? To stop us doing harm to one another. We're all monsters and it's only the rule of law that keeps us from each other's throats. So I propose we go back to each sleeping in separate rooms. Barricade ourselves in. No one goes out or in. Trust no one. How does that sound, Ali?'

'He can open the doors electronically,' said Linda. 'There's nowhere safe.'

This made everyone stop eating. She was right. Alison crumpled into a ball. Suzanne swallowed hard. Even Emily did not know what to say here. The curry burned down my throat. No one else ate, but I forced it all down. I wanted strength to fight this killer. I needed clear thinking. Logic.

'I feel sick,' said Suzanne. 'Sorry, Linda, I can't eat anything.'

'At least drink. Keep hydrated.' I poured glasses of juice for everyone.

Alison took the glass of fruit juice Linda passed to her and drank it in painful gulps.

Suzanne turned to the Reverend. 'Six geese a-laying. What does that mean, Reverend James?'

He took a deep breath. 'The six days of creation. God

created the heavens and the earth and on the seventh he rested.'

'And?' I said.

Linda answered for him. 'He made man in his own image and gave him dominion over the other creatures.'

I mulled over the word dominion, scrambling for a sinister interpretation, one involving murder.

'He also created the creatures that creepeth upon the earth,' she added. The Reverend nudged her to be silent.

I was thinking furiously. The murder was always connected to martyrdom. 'Reverend James, perhaps you can tell us who was martyred on the sixth day of Christmas, and how. This may give us a clue.'

Reverend James furrowed his brows. Picked up the *Foxe's Book of Martyrs*. 'I prepared a sermon here on steadfastness in the face of persecution. But don't think, please, that I had any intention–'

I tried to hide my impatience. 'Just tell us what you found out.'

He swallowed. Darted his eyes about the room. 'Let's see. Christmas Day is the first day of Christmas, so the sixth day of Christmas is…' He leafed through the book. 'December 30th, the sixth day of Christmas, the year AD 304.'

All eyes were on the Reverend now.

'St Anysia was a wealthy woman from Thessaly, Greece, who was martyred by a soldier who tried to drag her to a pagan sacrifice.'

'How did she die?'

He shook his head. Looked across at Alison.

'Tell us, Reverend,' said Alison. 'I need to know this.'

He swallowed. We all waited. He closed his eyes as he spoke as if the words were painful to get out. 'A Roman soldier stabbed her in her face six times with his sword.'

The silence was punctuated with the crackling of embers

exploding in the fire. Alison sat rigid, her back to everyone. Suzanne held her throat with her hand as if she was choking, and Linda pressed herself against her husband, who sat rigid in his seat. Emily mouthed a silent 'wow'.

I stood. 'It's not going to happen. So here's my plan. We lock ourselves away, barricade the door, trust no one, and meanwhile I will interview everyone in turn. Look for motive, means and opportunity. I have a few clues, but none of them make sense. I need more information. If I can talk to each of you, get a picture of this–'

'Yes, Mr Poirot,' said Suzanne.

Alison now turned, her face red. 'Why you? Why not our pastor? He's the leader. He should do the investigation. We don't trust you.'

Reverend James nodded. 'I have already taken this on. I have prayed and God has told me–'

'No,' I said. '*I* don't trust *you*.'

His eyebrows knitted in thunderous disdain. Linda wrapped her arms around her husband's shoulders. 'Who do you think you are?'

I walked around the table as I spoke. 'A philosopher, a rational thinker. I'm trained in logic and rational thinking. Philosophy is a systematic discipline. It deals with evidence. Fact. Not faith. Not prayer.'

'Faith,' said Reverend James, 'is the substance of things hoped for, the evidence of things not seen.'

'How can faith provide evidence?' I said. 'The things unseen here we find out by deductive logic.'

'We've all read your blasphemous book,' said Linda, still holding on to her husband as if she would fall over if she didn't.

'*God is Dead*,' said Alison, using air quotes. She stood now and joined the group, behind Linda and the Reverend. Together they formed one faction, the anti-Rafe faction, I realised. I was flanked by Suzanne and Emily, but whether they were the pro-Rafe faction, I did not know. I certainly did not trust Suzanne, but at least she sat in solidarity with me.

Alison continued. 'We examined it at Bible study one week. And in many sermons. Reverend James showed us the folly of your depraved arguments.'

Reverend James pulled Alison into a bear hug with his left hand. Linda still clung to his right shoulder. 'We had to meet it head on,' he said. 'We couldn't let it fester in the minds of our congregation.'

'I'm flattered!' I said. 'I should have been there to listen to what you had to say.'

Alison jabbed her finger at me, emphasising every word she said: 'The fool hath said in his heart there is no God. That's what God says about you in the Psalms. You're the fool. We made a big mistake inviting you here. Inviting the serpent into paradise.'

Reverend James made a motion to quieten her. Linda joined the chorus. 'I can't believe you wrote that book, Rafe. You said some terrible, unforgivable things against the Church. I didn't want to read it.'

'Some members of the congregation suggested burning it,' added Alison.

'Girls, please,' said the Reverend, but his attempt to stop their outpouring of vitriol against me was half-hearted. I could see these were his words, his hatred, echoed back now.

Linda clung to him for support. 'Reverend James said we needed to gird our loins against the fiery darts of Satan.'

I held up my hands in mock surrender. 'Oh, so you think I'm Satan too now?'

'An agent of–' said Alison, glowering.

Reverend James raised a hand. 'You attacked me personally in that book, Rafe. Personally. But I forgave you. I am wearing the armour of God. The belt of truth, the breastplate of righteousness, the shield of faith which can extinguish all the flaming arrows of the evil one, the helmet of salvation and the sword of the Spirit.'

Linda could not hold herself back now. 'Rafe, you made many enemies with that book. It was hard to forgive you, hard to be with you at this retreat, and we know that you have brought evil among us. You did this. You brought on this terrible situation. Demons trailed behind you, and we let you all in.'

'You want to destroy us, and our faith,' said Alison, again jabbing her finger in the air at me from the safety of her Reverend's embrace. 'It's obvious you came here to destroy us.'

I walked over to their side of the table. Both women shrank back as if I was going to attack. 'Wait a minute. I was invited here by Reverend James. It was someone else's agenda, not mine. If what you say is true, then let's look at who organised this retreat. The obvious suspect is Reverend James.'

'You're still accusing me?' Reverend James let go of the two women and walked over to face me. We stood a metre apart, sizing each other up.

I stared down at him and spoke as calmly as I could. 'You planned this trip. You're the one using the song and *Foxe's Book of Martyrs* to structure each day. Ergo, you are the killer.'

Alison slapped her palms on the table. 'No.' Her face was so red she looked as if she might explode. 'You, Rafe, saw the opportunity, knowing we were all gathered together and you could pick us off, one by one. That's how much you hate us.'

I spread my arms out. 'I don't hate anyone—'

'Stop it!' shouted Suzanne. 'Enough! This is ridiculous. We need to calm down.'

Alison slumped into her chair. 'I'm feeling so sick, I need to go to bed. But I'm too terrified to be on my own.'

I spoke softly. 'Well, let's stick to our plan, okay? Lock your door. Barricade yourself in. And if you hear someone trying to push the door open, you yell out. Make sure the window is closed tight. If you want me to check out your room to make sure it's safe before you go to bed, I will.'

But this did little to soothe her. She pressed her hand against her chest. I feared she was having heart palpitations. 'Asking a murderer to check my room?' she said. 'Like asking a fox to look after a henhouse.'

Reverend James, who had stood his ground against me, now turned to the door. 'Please excuse me too.'

'Where are you going?' I said.

He pushed the door open. 'I don't have to account to you for everything I do.'

'We should stay together. The plan—'

'You obviously don't think we do. You do as you please.' Reverend James walked through to the hallway, and then I heard him stomping to his room.

Linda guided Alison out of the room too.

I checked around at the others, who looked stunned. 'So much for sticking together.'

Emily shrugged. 'So much for your philosophical investigations. We have two factions now. Us and them.'

Suzanne put on a brave smile. 'I'll make coffee.'

'Hot chocolate would be nice. But let me help,' I said.

I left Emily warming herself by the fire and followed Suzanne into the kitchen, propping the door open so we could all still see one another. I rummaged through the kitchen drawers while she boiled the kettle and poured boiling water into three cups. She emptied sachets of chocolate powder into each and stirred. 'What are you looking for?' she said. 'Sugar is over here.'

I said nothing. But I found what I was looking for in a high kitchen cabinet, a box that contained a sewing kit. I pulled out a black cotton reel and pocketed it.

Back in the living room, we sipped hot chocolate and stared

at the fire. I heard the toilet flushing upstairs. Linda returned a few minutes later, but not with Alison. Suzanne made her a hot chocolate and she sipped it gratefully. 'How is she?' said Emily.

Linda shook her head. 'She's feverish. She's lying down in her room. Don't worry, I locked the door behind me. She's safe.' She showed us the key.

I looked sceptically at it.

'I'll check on her in a few minutes.' Linda directed the blame at me. 'She's having a bit of a breakdown.'

'She's not the only one.' Emily invited Linda over to a seat by the fire. 'You okay, Linda? You look worn down.'

Linda wiped her eyes. 'Fine, fine.' Emily reached out and held her hand. 'Thanks,' she said. 'It's okay, it's okay.'

So we waited. Listened to Reverend James rumbling around upstairs. 'What is he doing?' I said.

'He's praying in his room,' said Linda. But after we heard a crash, she corrected herself. 'He's upset. He's only always got our best interests at heart. He brought us here for good reasons. And he blames himself. He was so excited about this reunion.'

'I think we'd all better go to sleep,' said Suzanne, draining her cup.

'Given the mistrust among us,' I said, 'it seems that everyone has tacitly agreed to go back to sleeping in their own room. Just make sure you lock your door.'

Linda pointed at the electronic lock on the hallway door. 'But if he can unlock and lock doors electronically...'

'Wedge a chair behind your door, pull a chest of drawers against it, block anyone coming in.'

They followed me upstairs and along the dark corridor. I stopped at Reverend James' door and called to him. 'We're all going to bed now. Make sure you lock your door and push something heavy against it.'

No response.

'Reverend?'

A grunt.

Then we went further along the corridor, all together, to Alison's room.

'Ali,' called Suzanne through the keyhole. 'It's us.'

No response. My blood went cold. 'Open it. Quickly.'

Linda unlocked her door with the key she had shown us earlier. I peered in. Alison was lying motionless in a ball on the bed in her dressing gown, but it was twisted around her as if it had been used to wring her neck.

I rushed over. Saw she was staring into space, had twisted the sleeve and was sucking on it. She took it out of her mouth. 'Go away.'

'Phew,' said Emily. 'You're safe.'

I took the key from Linda and pressed it into Alison's palm. 'Lock your door, Alison.' I spied the heavy dresser and pushed it towards the door. 'Push this against the door when you lock it, and then you can make sure no one can come in.'

I checked the window and made sure it was fastened tight. No one could get in that way. I checked for any doors that might lead out of this room, but like the others, it was a solid-brick, four-cornered square of a cell. No way in or out except by the door.

Suzanne placed her arm around Alison's shoulders. 'Ali?'

Alison nodded. 'God bless,' said Linda, squeezing Alison's hands with her own. 'Stay safe, Ali.'

She closed the door and we waited outside.

I heard Alison turn the key and scrape the chest of drawers across. I tried the door. It was locked, barricaded.

'Good girl,' called Suzanne. 'Sleep well.'

At her door, Suzanne hugged me. The hug was longer than it should have been, and tighter. I was aware of Emily watching us. I made sure Suzanne locked her door, and heard her pulling a piece of furniture against it. We then entered

Emily's room, where she gathered her pyjamas and pointed along the corridor towards my room. I nodded. 'I'll be there in a minute.'

I pulled the reel of black cotton from my pocket and tied it at ankle level across each doorway. If anyone left their room in the night, I would know about it. Or if anyone entered anyone's room, I would know about it too.

Back in my room I did the same. Strung cotton across the entry, locked and bolted the door, and pushed the dresser against it. Emily was already in her pyjamas and sitting up in my bed. 'What are you doing?'

'Making sure the murderer can't get into this room, or any other, without me knowing it.'

'*She* may already be inside the room,' she said, pointing to herself.

'*He* may already be inside the room.'

'We have to trust that neither of us is the murderer.'

'Faith is the belief in things unseen…'

Lying in bed, I doubted my strategy, leaving everyone alone and isolated. But I did not trust us all together either.

'That was a very long hug,' she said after a long silence. 'What game is she playing?'

I lay back on the bed and stared up at the ceiling. 'Maybe she's just scared.'

'Maybe she wants you to think she's scared.'

'By the way, it's New Year's Eve tomorrow,' she said.

'It is?'

'The seventh day of Christmas. I've been keeping track.'

'Great way to start the new year, then. Hope it's a happy one.'

SEVEN SWANS A-SWIMMING

New Year's Eve: the seventh day of Christmas. I woke up with Emily whispering in my ear. 'Wake up, sleepy head. I've been watching you for ages. Wondering how you sleep so peacefully, like a baby.'

I leaped up and checked the room. The door was still barricaded and locked, the windows shut tight.

'I don't know how you slept through the night,' she said. 'Don't you ever feel afraid?'

I combed the hair out of her eyes with my fingers. 'Fear is an external imaginary, like pain. You can respond to it, or you can put it at arm's length, observe it at a distance. Or reason your way out of its grip.'

'Easy for you to say. I was so restless all night. My mind couldn't let go of those images of Danny, and Stephen, and Mike.'

'You're a nurse, you must be used to gore and body parts.'

'True. I usually can disassociate. But the horror gets into your veins, like the cold. Just seeps in. I felt so safe with you, though. I pity the others all on their own. Funny, Linda should be with Reverend James, but they insist on sleeping apart, even at a time like this.'

'Maybe she's wise not to trust him,' I said. I moved the dresser, unlocked the door, and felt for the cotton thread outside. It was intact. 'Better see how they all are.'

I checked each door in turn along the corridor and nodded with satisfaction as each cotton line was also intact. No one had been in or out of these doors last night.

'They're all still asleep,' whispered Emily, tiptoeing so the board would not creak so loud. 'Why did we have to get up so early?'

'Just doing my job.'

'Let's go and make some coffee.'

I followed her downstairs and into the living room. While she blew the fire into life, I went into the kitchen to find clean cups and put the kettle on. Then I heard her cry out. 'My God.'

I found her staring at Alison's place at the table. On the mat was a bowl of six large eggs.

Emily clung to me. 'What does it mean?'

'Ali?'

'We'd better get to her room, quick.'

We bounded up the stairs and along the corridor. I rapped on the door, shouting Alison's name.

Emily knocked on the other doors, raising the other women.

Linda and Suzanne were the first to unlock their doors and step out into the corridor. Then Reverend James appeared at the end of the corridor, wearing only a towel and holding a razor. His chin was nicked and blood oozed down his neck.

'Six geese a-laying,' I said. 'Six eggs on Ali's plate.'

'Ali, open the door!' Suzanne rattled the door handle, turned it to get Alison to come and open it. But to her surprise the door opened a little. 'She didn't lock it!'

I felt the thread across the doorway; it was intact. 'It was locked last night. I checked it.'

The dresser was still in place against the doorway, and I had to shove it away to get into the room. Suzanne stumbled as she broke the thread, but caught herself as she rushed in after me. The room stank of Suzanne's perfume. There, on the bed, lay Alison covered in blood. She wore an iron mask with a devil's face etched on the front. 'The heretic's mask,' I said, recognising it from the display cabinet in the torture museum. Blood seeped from her chin onto the floor. Suzanne's screams filled the room.

'Help me with this, she may still be alive.'

Emily checked her pulse. Shook her head. I checked Alison's body for other wounds, and found the telltale little red puncture wound in her neck. I crumpled, defeated. I had tried to ensure her safety. She had feared for her life, and had predicted this. And I had reassured her that she would be okay. How hideous.

I held the mask lightly with both hands. 'Ready?'

'I think you shouldn't watch this,' Emily said to Suzanne and Linda. Linda hid behind her husband, and Reverend James closed his eyes in prayer, but Suzanne watched, steely-eyed. Emily held one side of the mask, me the other, and we pulled upwards. My stomach turned at the sucking sound, the resistance as the spikes pulled out of her eyes, nose and mouth and the blood flowed onto my hands.

'What are you doing to her?' started Reverend James. 'Please—'

'A cloth, a towel, please.'

Suzanne grabbed a towel that was draped over the back of the chair and flung it at Emily, who dabbed the eye cavities, nose and mouth. Alison was dead. Had been dead for hours.

'Look!' Emily whispered. There, gouged into her forehead, were the numbers six six six.

Reverend James fell back. 'Satan be gone!'

Emily dabbed the cuts with the cloth. 'Superficial wounds, cut with a sharp knife,' she murmured to me. She turned to the others. 'I think the mask would have killed her, suffocated her.'

Reverend James closed his eyes. 'Jesus, help us.'

Emily gave a small cry when she noticed the note Alison was concealing in her clenched fist. She pulled it out from between the dead woman's fingers and unfolded it.

I immediately recognised the handwriting. It was the same as that of the letter I had found by Danny's bed, the same as the note in my pocket. Suzanne's handwriting.

But it was Reverend James who said it aloud. 'Another note!'

I stared hard at him. Only Emily and Suzanne knew about the note, and I doubted either of them would have told the Reverend.

Suzanne stepped back against the door frame to the hall-way, eyes wide. 'I didn't write it.'

It was an odd thing to say. She hadn't seen the note. 'It's in your handwriting.'

Her eyes pleaded with mine. 'You know it's a set-up. You know that, Rafe.'

I snatched the note from Emily's fingers, but she held it tight. 'Read the damn thing,' I snapped.

Emily read aloud: 'On the Sixth day, God commanded us to subdue our vile base nature and have dominion over every living lustful thing that moveth upon the earth. The sixth commandment is Thou Shalt not Kill. The mark of the beast is six six six. The number six symbolises the frailty of human weakness. Man was created on the sixth day. Men are appointed six days to labour. The sixth day of Christmas. One short of perfection.'

The air was heavy with the smell of death. Linda was shaking violently. Reverend James looked about him with arms up in defence as if demons were swooping on him. No one spoke for a long time. Emily folded up the note.

Finally, Suzanne said in a trembling small voice, 'Who would do such a thing? What sick mind?'

'Ali,' wailed Linda. 'Poor Ali.'

Suzanne put her arms around Linda.

'Dear Lord Jesus,' said Reverend James. 'Help us.'

I helped Emily wrap Alison in some towels and blankets we found in the cupboard.

'Now what do we do?' said Emily.

I looked from the window to the room. 'The door was locked. I heard her push the dresser against the door.'

'So how did the monster get in?' said Suzanne. 'Did she let him in?'

'I thought you said you had made the rooms safe,' wailed Linda to me.

Emily checked the window, which was locked tight. 'So she must have known him,' she said, looking directly at Reverend James. 'Or her.' And she looked straight at Suzanne.

Suzanne gave Emily a scornful look. 'I had nothing to do with these stupid notes.'

I played with the lock, turning the key. If this was electronically activated, the killer could easily have remotely opened the door. But then the dresser was in place. The cotton thread too.

Reverend James looked pointedly at me. 'She knew not to trust Rafe. So much for your plan to keep us safe.' He dabbed the blood on his chin.

I resisted the urge to retaliate. I knew I had failed Alison, had failed the others. 'I don't need to be reminded how terrible

I should feel, especially by some sanctimonious, holier-than-thou preacher.'

'Now you look here,' said Reverend James, once again stepping towards me. He lifted his chin and clenched his fists. What, was he going to punch me?

'Save it for later,' said Emily. 'Right now we need to move Alison to our makeshift morgue.' With that, she placed a towel over Alison's face, and then the women followed this funeral procession as Reverend James and I carried her to the torture museum. It was a struggle for us to carry Alison across the corridor. She smelt of blood. Here was another death I had been unable to prevent. She had tried to run away, would rather have died in the snow outside than like this, and I had made her stay and face the most horrible execution imaginable. The only consolation was the murderer's *modus operandi*. He killed them, or at least rendered them unconscious before he applied the torture instrument to them, I was sure. But it was little consolation: he had done this not in mercy but practicality. It was easier to affix the heretic's mask to an unconscious or dead victim than to one who would scream herself to death.

Emily walked ahead, pushed open the door, I went ahead to check it was safe, and we placed Alison gently on the floor near the window. Linda unwrapped the towels and blankets. 'We have to keep her cold.'

Reverend James inspected the line of torture implements in the open cabinet. 'I remember the mask being over here.' Sure enough, the tag was still on display on an empty cabinet: 'Heretic's mask'.

Such irony, I thought: Alison was faithful to the end, and died in a heretic's mask.

I quickly scanned the room. It looked as if nothing else had been touched. The three other corpses kept guard over the remaining torture instruments, frozen in position like trophies collected by some sick serial killer. Emily checked each corpse to make sure the cadavers were being kept cold enough to avoid any deterioration setting in. Snow had blown in the open window. It had gathered in corners like ghost cobwebs as well as behind Stephen's head and body, making an icy cushion. The blood that had pooled around Danny's sarcophagus was ice-purple.

While the others were engaged, I looked across the room and spied a set of medieval handcuffs and two sets of keys in a display cabinet. The handcuffs were shaped like horseshoes; the iron was dull with rust, but they looked serviceable. I slipped them into my coat pocket along with one of the key sets. I also pocketed a small dagger.

Just in case.

'Please, can we go,' said Linda to her husband. 'Now can we leave this despicable place?'

'We meet in the living room,' I said. 'The Truth Session begins in fifteen minutes.'

They all knew what I meant. In the old days, Reverend James used to conduct what he called Truth Sessions. He would gather the kids into his office in a big circle and demand public confessions, interrogate them about their transgressions. Kids would end up crying, baring their souls, humiliating themselves, purging their secrets.

In the living room, as they sat in a semicircle around the fire, I stood before them and outlined what was going to happen.

'You know the rules. We question one another and we have to answer honestly, no matter how confronting. We must get to the bottom of this.'

'Who are you to do this?' said Linda. 'Reverend James should conduct this session—'

I ignored her. 'You will all have a turn at asking questions.'

Reverend James nodded. 'It's okay, Linda. I agree, we need to talk. I have nothing to hide.'

Linda sulked beside her husband, throwing me resentful glances. I faced the group. All eyes were on me. Now was the moment of reckoning.

'Reverend James, tell us the precise meaning of the note in Ali's hand. Earlier, you mentioned the six days of creation.'

He sighed. 'Yes, that's right. On the sixth day, God made man and gave him dominion over the earth.'

'So how would you say this connects to Ali's death?'

'Why ask me? I have nothing to do with Ali's death.'

'You have explained every death so far.'

'I have no idea.' His face was red in the reflection of the firelight.

'I do,' said Emily quietly. Everyone turned to her. 'The heretic's mask inflicts six wounds on the face. It has six prongs. That's the first thing I noticed when I was examining her.'

I had seen it too. I could see the others working out which six wounds in their minds.

Emily continued: 'Whoever did this planned it well in advance, setting us up in this deserted castle, in the middle of winter, with an array of torture weapons to use against us, to make his point. Each torture weapon numerically corresponds to the day.'

'I don't understand,' said Suzanne.

'She's saying,' I said, 'that this had to be planned so well in advance that only Reverend James could have known the plans.'

'That's ridiculous,' said Reverend James. 'I was always here with you.'

Linda held her waist tight as if she had a stomach cramp. 'How could any of us have carried out these hideous deaths? We were always together.'

Emily shook her head. 'Were we? Maybe this person, one of us, had an accomplice. Maybe even the concierge, or the person who owns the torture museum. Did anyone actually see the concierge leave?'

'You mean he could be hiding in the castle somewhere?' Suzanne looked over her shoulder at the dark passage.

The Reverend suddenly lunged past me and picked up the poker. He stirred the logs violently in the fire, making sparks fly. 'So, Rafe, what gives you the right to question everyone first?'

'Because I know something you don't know. About Glen. The night he was killed, that first night, he called me urgently to speak to him. It was the first thing he said when we met.' I looked at Emily and she widened her eyes in feigned surprise, looked grateful that I had decided not to involve her with this... yet. 'So I went to his room and we stood on the balcony. Yes, the one that he fell from later. And Glen said he was scared of something about to happen, and told me to be careful. To lock my door. What was he afraid of? He knew. But what did he know? I never found out.'

'Whoa,' said Reverend James.

Linda looked terrified. Bit her lip.

'Why didn't you tell us?' said Suzanne. 'He knew about all this?'

'I didn't know what he meant then. I thought Reverend James had trapped us here to reconvert us, to expose our past sins.'

Reverend James nodded. 'Partly true, yes. God called me to bring you together for a recommitment of our faith.'

'There's more,' I continued. 'I saw him with someone, a woman, arguing with him, and she went into his room that night. Who was that?'

Linda would not meet my eye, but her face reddened. Reverend James looked visibly shaken.

'One of you women went to see Glen that night. Who?'

'I don't think any of us would admit it if we did,' said Emily. 'And why would we meet him?'

'To sort out old wrongs, maybe.'

Linda stood up. 'I'll go make coffee.'

'Sit down,' I said. 'I think that person was you, Linda.'

'What?' said Reverend James. 'How dare you accuse my wife?'

'I saw you. I heard you arguing. Then you went into his room. I want to know what happened in that room.'

'I never left my room,' said Linda, her face pale now, her eyes wide. 'Why would I visit Glen?'

'Because you were still having an affair with him.'

Reverend James turned from the fire to face me, the poker red hot in his hand. 'Rafe, I'm warning you. These baseless accusations—'

'Put that poker down. Let me continue.'

The Reverend lowered his hand, as if only now realising he was brandishing a weapon, and placed the poker back in its stand.

My heart was beating loudly, but I stood my ground and continued speaking calmly. 'Some unfinished business, Linda. You were having an affair with Glen, and you visited him that night. I want to know what you were doing and how long you were with him. You're the key to everything.'

I had never felt such hatred directed at me as at that moment. Linda's eyes. Reverend James' frown. 'Rafe, I'm warning you.'

'Reverend, this is a Truth Session. You will have your turn.'

The others stared. No one had crossed the Reverend in public before without retribution. I had been waiting to do this for twenty years. It felt good. I returned my gaze to Linda. 'Let me assume that your visit had something to do with his death later on. You were the last person to see him alive. Did you kill him? Or did your visit make your husband jealous enough to go and kill him?'

'You're mad,' said Reverend James, smothering his wife in an embrace that was meant to shield her from me rather than show any affection.

I stared past him into her eyes 'Let Linda answer. You don't always have to answer for her.'

But Linda would not speak.

'Rafe, are you sure you saw someone with him?' said Suzanne, moving closer to Linda and touching her arm.

I looked at her closely. Suzanne was also someone I suspected of visiting Glen that night.

'And what were you doing prowling around late at night?' said Reverend James.

'I heard a noise.'

'So you say.'

'And then Glen is stoned to death for adultery. You, Reverend James, said so yourself.'

He let Linda go and stood at the fire again, avoiding my gaze. He stuttered a little as he spoke. 'I said nothing of the sort.'

'You stoned him to death for adultery. You passed judgement. And then you gave a sanctimonious sermon the next day justifying his murder.'

'It's not true. I never even spoke to Glen.' Linda was weeping now. Suzanne put her arm around her.

'It was an act of God,' said Reverend James to the fire. 'A rotten railing.'

'It was no accident. It had been sawn so that whoever leaned on it would fall.'

'What?' said Emily. 'You never told me that.'

I nodded. 'Linda, tell me where your husband was that night.'

Reverend James picked up a log and hurled it in the fire.

'Look at me, Reverend.'

He turned and looked directly into my eyes. 'Are you implying that I, Reverend James…?'

'Not implying. Deducing. And there's more. Stephen. Your henchman who helped you organise this retreat came to me, terrified out of his mind after Glen's death. Wanted to speak to me, said he knew everything and wanted to tell me. Then he conveniently died before he could tell me about your treachery.'

Reverend James continued staring into my eyes, unblinking. 'This is preposterous and you know it.'

'Not if you then preach a sermon neatly explaining how his death fits into the third day of Christmas martyrdom. So planned. So organised. Did you really think we'd believe it was an act of God… or Satan?'

He suddenly closed his eyes, muttered a few inaudible words as if he was praying, then stared at me again. 'Rafe, stop playing your silly philosophical games. You hate us, you hate me and you've come back to exact your revenge on everyone. If anyone set up and committed these murders, it's you.'

I opened my arms wide. Now we were getting somewhere. I welcomed a rational, logical, coherent argument. This was my territory. 'Then please interrogate me. We need the truth. But while we're being frank, let me pull no punches. We have a murderer using Reverend James' sermons, his schemes and his book of martyrs to carry out hideous crimes. You brought us here to teach us a lesson. Did that plan include murder?'

He waved his hands at the remaining Twelve in the room. 'You're accusing me of murdering my own flock.'

'The evidence points directly to you,' I said.

He shook his head. 'What evidence?'

I pointed to his neck. 'The blood on your collar after Ali's death.'

'I was shaving.'

'You knew about the note left on Danny's table, but I had told no one about it.'

Reverend James' eyes darted to each member of the group. He couldn't get out of this one. He looked at the doorway now as if he was about to bolt. 'I saw the note when I rose for my Quiet Time and pocketed it.'

'It was the ruse you used to lure him to his death, and so you had to rid yourself of the evidence. But I saw it.'

'Here.' He pulled the note out of his pocket. 'I was not going to show anyone this, but seeing as you are accusing me—'

'Please don't,' said Suzanne. 'Why does everyone insist on dragging me through the mud? I didn't write it.'

Now everyone stared at her.

'It's in your handwriting,' I reminded her.

Reverend James folded it over. 'Yes, it's in her handwriting.'

'Tell everyone what it says.'

He darted a quick nervous glance at her. 'It's an arrangement for her to meet Danny at midnight in the library,' he said.

Suzanne shot me a venomous look. She would never forgive me for this. 'First you accuse Linda then Reverend James, and now me? Rafe, I told you everything... about the notes. Someone is setting me up.'

I shook my head. 'That's the weird thing, Suzanne. You're at the heart of this. Glen was talking about you to me before he died, and he also wrote you a note.'

'What note? Another note?' said Reverend James.

Suzanne's face was fiery red. She sure was not acting this time. She was furious. 'I showed you that note in confidence, Rafe.'

'It's the truth game. Tell us what was in that note.'

She stood and paced the floor. Speaking to the fire rather than to us, she said, 'He was declaring his love for me.'

'Every time I stumbled on the scene of a murder,' I said, 'I smelt your perfume. Emily can bear me out. Every time.

Except of course when we found Mike outside. Can you explain that?'

Suzanne stopped pacing and stared at me, tears forming in her eyes. 'No.'

'The note,' I said, 'says you planned to meet him at midnight.'

She wiped one eye with her sleeve. 'Of course I didn't. I wouldn't arrange a meeting with him at midnight. Or any other time. Why would I do that? I was trying to avoid him.'

'And you say you didn't write this note, even though it looks like your handwriting?'

'How do you know what my handwriting is like?'

'You're kidding. At school we all received your "I just want to be friends" letters. We all kept them like precious artefacts.'

Reverend James held up his hand. 'Leave her alone. First you attack Linda, then me, now Suzanne. Come on, Rafe. Enough of this word sorcery.'

'I'm just trying to fit the clues into the jigsaw puzzle to get a picture. Trying out hypotheses. I want to find out the truth.'

Now the Reverend took his place at the front of the gathering. 'Maybe I can also play this game, Rafe,' he said and began a torrent of questions. 'Where were you when Glen was killed? Why were you in the corridor snooping around? You say he was with a woman, but why should we believe you? He was with you and you killed him. You were the last to see Stephen too, and you lured him into the torture museum. You lured Danny there too. And then you conveniently discovered Mike's corpse and came back to tell us. How do we know you didn't drown him?'

'Because I was here with you eating breakfast when Mike drowned.'

James shook his head.

'At least it's out in the open,' said Suzanne. 'We know exactly what we think of one another. And it's ugly.'

'We all stand accused,' I said. 'Any of us could be the killer. Linda, Suzanne, Reverend James, me…'

'Emily's getting off lightly here,' said Suzanne. She's the only one not accused of being a serial killer.'

I smiled. 'It's always the least suspected who is the murderer.'

Emily shook her head. 'We've opened up some pretty big wounds here today.'

'I haven't finished yet,' I said. 'She's not unscathed, you know.'

'Let's not go there,' said Emily. 'Really not.' She gave me a hurtful look. This was betraying our trust, our blood brother–sister relationship. I knew that, and I felt terrible. But I had to flush out the murderer. Our lives were at stake. And she was key. I took a deep breath. *Forgive me, Emily.* 'Yes,' I said,' I am going there. I think it's directly relevant to the motivation of the killer.'

Emily stood, fuming. 'No, Rafe.' She walked towards the kitchen. 'Truth Session officially over. Who wants some coffee? I'm making.'

Reverend James moved closer to the fire, turning his back on the rest of us. Linda joined him.

'Reverend James,' I called. 'This is a Truth Session. Come back here and face the truth.'

'What's going on?' said Suzanne.

Emily closed the kitchen door behind her.

Suzanne walked to the window, stared out at the whiteness. I stood next to her. 'You had to bring up the notes,' she said, under her breath. 'I thought I could trust you.'

I had made enemies of my friends now. But I had my

reasons. 'Sorry, Suzanne. I wanted to see everyone's reactions and what they knew.'

She cast a look back at the fireplace. 'Reverend James, you mean.'

I nodded.

'What was all that about with Emily?' she whispered.

I shook my head. 'Everyone has some hidden secret, some skeleton in the closet. But there are so many missing pieces here. Tell me what you know. Why you think you're being framed?'

She shook her head. 'Jealousy. Revenge. I don't know. I feel it's me this killer is getting at.'

'Or maybe that's just your narcissistic way of thinking.'

She gave me a hurt look.

'Truth Session still on. Tell me about the skeletons in your closet, Suzanne.' I don't know how long I had been standing there with her, mesmerised by the snow outside, and having a conversation that was on the verge of flirting, bantering, teasing, but I felt uncomfortable, as if I was fraternising with the enemy somehow. I was getting information, interviewing suspects, I told myself, but it felt more like making peace with old wounds.

I looked back at the fire and was concerned to see that Reverend James was not there. Linda was crouched on the settee, warming herself. I strode over. 'Where's the Reverend?'

She looked up. She had tears in her eyes. 'He went to the kitchen to help Emily, I think. I don't know. Had to go to the toilet.'

'Jesus, we're not meant to wander around alone.'

I walked into the kitchen. 'Em, how's that coffee coming along?'

No Emily.

No Reverend James.

The pantry section of the kitchen hid another door. I

pushed through it and saw that it led into the corridor and up the stairs. 'Emily!'

Now I panicked. I climbed the stairs to the first floor, raced along the corridor and barged into the library. The door from the library to the torture museum was open, and inside I heard thumping. 'Emily!'

Hackles rose on my neck, and my heart beat double time. I really didn't want to go in alone, but I pushed through into the room. Icy wind blew onto my face. The first thing I smelt was Suzanne's perfume.

'Emily?'

The decapitated body of Stephen on the guillotine; his head still on the floor, towelled and cushioned. Danny's body impaled on five spikes in the iron maiden. Alison lying shrouded in a blanket. And in the corner, the Catherine wheel weighed down by a body lashed to its seven struts, tangled red hair, and a face covered with a blindfold, her mouth gagged by some hideous metal device. The perfume made me feel sick.

EIGHT MAIDS A-MILKING

I t took three steps to reach her and another two seconds to remove the blindfold. She blinked at me.

'Emily, you're alive? Thank God.'

She made an impatient noise.

I recognised the device in her mouth as the pear of anguish. I had seen it on display on the table on the first day – a metal prong with four metal spiked petals that sprung open and tore a victim's mouth, or other orifice. For some reason – some miracle – this torture instrument's spring had not been released and I could remove it from her mouth. Gingerly, I pulled back her lips to avoid the sharp spike at the end of each flange tearing into her flesh. 'Ugh,' she said.

'Don't talk!' I pushed down her tongue as I pulled the flange out of her mouth.

I held her head. Checked for other injuries.

She licked her lips. 'I'm okay, except for that hideous sweet perfume.'

I examined the ropes tying her to the wheel. She was only loosely tied. I grabbed the dagger and sliced through the strands, careful not to nick her skin. The ropes were supporting her, so I held her to stop her falling as I gently lifted her up. She stretched. 'Ow, it hurts like hell.'

'There's a small tear in your cheek.'

'Let's get that bastard.'

I stared at her. 'You saw who it was?'

She tried to sit up but then fell down again, holding her mouth. She nodded.

I eased her gently back to a lying position. Then I took off my sweater and placed it under her head. 'Reverend James?'

The words echoed in the room. She nodded again. 'I was in the kitchen and he grabbed me around the neck.'

The rage bubbled in me. 'And look here!' I picked up the card attached to the top of the wheel. Seven swans a-swimming. 'His calling card.' She craned her neck to see. I showed her.

'You sure it was him?' I knew it was, but I wanted her confirmation. I tasted bile in my throat. Pure hatred. How dare he do this to Emily! But then she was alive. He had botched it somehow. Maybe he had been disturbed.

'He came from behind, jabbed some dart into my neck. Then he stuffed some horribly sweet-tasting rag in my mouth.'

I smelt the air. 'Chloroform? Mixed with Suzanne's perfume. I'm going to get him.' I gripped the dagger tight.

'I woke up here, tied on the wheel, this hideous thing in my mouth. Ugh. I thought I was a goner.'

I raised the dagger, slashed at the Catherine wheel. 'I'm going to kill him.'

She clutched on to my arm. 'Rafe, be careful.'

I pulled the handcuffs out of my pocket, checked they were in working order, stuffed them back. 'Can you walk? We have to get you out of here.'

Her eyes were blazing.

I led the way out of the room, dagger first, shielding Emily from any would-be attackers in the corridor. With her hobbling a little, we walked to her room, and I made sure it was safe. 'Lock the door and I'll find him.'

'Rafe…?' She held my hand, drew me close and hugged me tight. 'Thanks.'

I had to contain my rage. I was a logical thinker. But seeing Emily trussed and suffocated like that tipped me over the edge. I charged into the living room, dagger aloft. And there he was, sitting by the fire, warming himself, as if nothing had happened. Suzanne sat on his right, Linda on his left. Blind rage flooded me. 'Reverend James!'

Before he realised what I was doing, I lunged at him, clicked one handcuff on his right wrist, held the dagger at his gullet. My hands were trembling.

He tried to stand, but I pressed him down again into his chair with the blade of the dagger. His eyes were wide with fear. Linda jumped up. 'Rafe, what are you doing?'

I pressed the blade under his chin, and my hand was so unsteady that it nicked his skin and drew blood. 'Give me your other hand.'

'Get away from me!' His voice quivered as he pushed back into the chair to avoid the tip of the blade. I grabbed his left hand and clicked the second handcuff on him. 'You bastard.'

Linda rushed to her husband, but I blocked her with my arm. 'Stay away, Linda, I'm warning you.'

'Are you mad?' Reverend James raised his handcuffed hands in the air. 'You can't do this.'

'Suzanne and Linda.' I pointed into the corridor. 'Go and tend to Emily, quick. She survived an attack on her life.'

Suzanne stared at me. 'But Emily's in the kitchen.'

'She's in her room. She's lucky to be alive.' And to Reverend James, 'I am taking charge, as I should have when I first suspected you. Now you will talk!' I laid the flat edge of the blade against his neck.

Reverend James squirmed in the chair to try to get away from me. 'I have no idea what you're talking about. What's happened to Emily? I went to look for her in the kitchen but—'

The dagger nicked his skin again and a line of blood oozed onto the blade. 'You know bloody well. You did it!'

Linda watched me in horror as I roughed up her husband. Yet he was still acting innocent. Terrified, but indignantly feigning innocence.

'Come.' I hauled him to his feet by his coat. 'Up to my room.' He stood, ready to make a bolt for it, but I grabbed his handcuffs so his arms were pulled in front of him. Then I frog-marched the protesting Reverend upstairs. He stumbled, cursing at me. 'There's a place in hell for you, Rafe,' he spat. 'God will make sure of that. At least spare the women.'

I shoved him forward. 'You still act out the charade that it was me? I saw with my own eyes what you did! You're despicable.'

When we reached my room, I pushed him inside and he fell onto the floor.

I locked the door, pocketed the key. I spied a heavy chest in the corridor and pushed it across the doorway. Tied cotton thread across the doorway.

Two bewildered women were cowering at the bottom of the stairs. 'What are you waiting for?' I shouted at them. 'Emily needs help urgently.'

I raced along the corridor and knocked on Emily's door. 'It's Rafe. I have the bastard all tied up.' I heard her scrambling to unlock her door and open it.

Suzanne rushed to her. 'My God, Emily.'

Linda stared from the doorway, dazed. As if she could not believe what had just happened.

'Sure there's nothing broken?'

Emily shook her head. 'Where is he?'

'He's handcuffed, don't you worry,' I said. 'All safe. You need a nice strong cup of coffee.'

She nodded. We walked to the living room.

'I'll do it.' Linda looked grateful to get away and into the kitchen. Once she was out of the room, I whispered to Suzanne. 'He tried to murder her.'

'Reverend James? You saw him, Emily?'

'No, he grabbed me from behind. Jabbed some paralytic drug into my neck, and then smothered me with chloroform.'

'We didn't even hear it,' said Suzanne, 'and we were right here.'

'There's a back door from the kitchen to the hallway.'

Emily touched her face gingerly. 'I can't believe I let him do that to me. I feel so... powerless. So stupid.'

Suzanne was trembling. 'So what do we do now?'

I paced the room. 'We make a citizen's arrest until we can get hold of the goddamn police. No wonder he didn't want to try to contact them. No wonder he hid all the cell phones. No wonder.' I punched my fist into my palm.

Suzanne looked up at the window. Snow spattered the pane, and beyond the frame all we could see was white fuzziness. Her eyes were wet. 'We'll never get out of here.'

'We will now. We have the murderer. Or at least the mastermind behind the murders. Meanwhile I'll keep him locked up, and we sit tight. Until tomorrow. Or until I throttle him with my bare hands.'

Suzanne stared at me in alarm. 'You'd do that?'

'I swear, I could.' I hit my palm again with my fist.

Emily held her head. 'Such a throbbing headache. Mouth hurts like hell. Nausea, headache. He must have used fentanyl, or maybe even etorphine. Midazolam, maybe.'

I helped her sit comfortably on the sofa. 'Speak English, please.'

'Etorphine is what they use to dart wild animals. But this feels more like fentanyl, which is an opioid, used for pain medication. It's about seventy-five times stronger than morphine and can induce unconsciousness, or if in high enough doses, coma or death. But for some reason he didn't give me a strong dose, thank God.'

'You're a walking medical journal,' I said. 'I think I'll call you *Lancet* from now on.'

'It's my job. Side effects are... nausea, yes, dry mouth, yes, confusion, amen to that, asthenia or weakness, double amen.'

'What can we do to help?' said Suzanne.

'There should be a first-aid kit in the kitchen.'

'I'll check,' said Suzanne.

Emily pulled me closer and squeezed my hands. 'He revolts me. He's always revolted me. The thought of his hands on me... that he would stick that thing on my face. I want to stick it on his face. Squish it into his holier-than-thou lying face.'

Another night to get through. We had the killer, but I could not rest. My heart was still beating fast, and rage flowed through me. I paced Emily's room, restraining myself from bursting into my own room and confronting him again. *How dare you? Who do you think you are?* And like Emily, I wanted to torture him, impale him, box him into one of those torture instruments and watch him suffer while his blood ran over my feet. I wanted him to know how it feels. Then I'd lie him on the guillotine, keep him alive so he could watch the blade come down on his neck. I, who prided myself on logic and deductive reasoning, on a cool head, was burning for revenge. It scared me.

The horrible suspicion that he was not alone nagged at me. He had to have an accomplice. One person alone could not have achieved all this, given the gruesome circumstances of the murders and attempted murder. The concierge. The owner. And Linda must have been complicit in some way, so, despite her distress, I locked her in her room and took the key.

I would leave the Reverend in my room to ponder his sins tonight.

I made sure Emily's door was locked, and then pushed her wardrobe against it. But I felt too wired to sleep. Emily fell into a deep slumber in my arms and I lay awake, recalling the details of the events of the last seven nights. Knowing now who was behind it all, it had been obvious from the start. The Reverend had planned every move, down to which torture instrument was appropriate for each person and which day was appropriate for each person to die, and had engineered each person to be isolated each night. Cold-hearted, scheming bastard. But I was puzzled still about many things. How had he known Mike would be outside on the fourth day? How did he get into Ali's room? And he must have forged those notes from Suzanne in order to lure the male victims away from the others. He had made a classic faux pas by admitting knowledge of Danny's note, and he had been absent at exactly the time some of the murders occurred. But I believed now he could not have done any of this without an accomplice. That was my next mission, to find out who, and stop him… or her.

I fell asleep late, and woke early with a fright. Emily woke too and clutched my arm.

We listened to the scraping and thumping coming from the corridor. I leapt up and pulled on my shoes and dressing gown. 'Someone's moving the dresser in the hallway.'

Emily was wide-eyed. 'Reverend James?'

I pulled the wardrobe away from Emily's door. I opened

the door to see Suzanne across the hallway. She was peering out of her doorway and looked flustered. 'Suzanne, what's going on? Did you make that noise?'

She indicated the heavy wardrobe behind her. 'That was a mother to move,' she said. 'But I felt a little claustrophobic in there.'

Emily in her pyjamas peered out of the door, and Suzanne gave a double-take, realising only then that I had slept in Emily's room. 'You two?'

Emily nodded. 'Platonic,' she said, 'in case you're wondering.'

Suzanne gave me a dubious look.

'Oh,' said Emily, 'by the way, guys, happy New Year!'

'It's New Year's Day today?' said Suzanne.

She nodded. 'Eighth day of Christmas. Happy New Year.'

'What a way to spend New Year,' I said. 'But at least we're safe.' I peered up the corridor. 'I have to go and check on him.'

They followed me to my room. The wardrobe was still barricading the door. Cotton thread unbroken. Door locked. I listened at the keyhole.

'Reverend?'

Not a sound. I was about to enter, then decided to let him stew in his own juices a little while longer. I wanted to interrogate Linda first.

The three of us marched back down the corridor to Linda's room. I took out the key and unlocked her door. Knocked gently. She did not respond. My heart beat faster. I pushed open the door and – thankfully – found Linda awake, praying by the side of her bed.

Linda glowered at us and did not get up off her knees.

Suzanne walked over to her and squeezed her shoulder. 'Glad you're okay. I'll make us some breakfast.'

I turned to Emily and Suzanne. 'Yes, breakfast would be good. Meanwhile, I need to speak with Linda in private.'

'Sure, boss,' said Emily.

Suzanne shrugged her shoulders. 'Okay.'

I waited until they were gone. I had planned this interrogation in the night. She must have known something about her husband's intentions. She must be in a tortured state, knowing that he had murdered her lover, as well as her brothers and sisters in the Lord. Maybe she had been covering for him. Or else she was in on it. 'Let me tell you where I'm at, okay, Linda, and you can help me, help us, help your husband even.'

She did not look up at me. She had her finger on a passage in the Bible open on her bed.

'Linda?'

In response, she began reading the passage aloud, tracing each word with a trembling finger: 'When the Lord Jesus is revealed from heaven with his mighty angels in flaming fire, inflicting vengeance on those who do not know God and on those who do not obey the gospel of our Lord Jesus. They will suffer the punishment of eternal destruction, away from the presence of the Lord and from the glory of his might.' Then she stared up at me. Her eyes were red-rimmed.

'Linda, I'm not accusing you of anything, I just want to know how this all happened.'

She closed the Bible. I imagined the hatred she must feel towards me. 'We should have known,' She said.

'Maybe it all began with your affair with Glen.'

She covered her face with her hands. Wiped tears away. A different Linda looked back at me. A defiant Linda, one who had the strength to stop being the meek pastor's wife and have an affair. I was expecting denial, but to my surprise, she admitted it. 'It was in the past. It was a terrible mistake. I paid for it so many times over.' She pointed to her Bible. 'As you can see. How do you think I feel? Can you know the pain of what you took such delight in exposing here?'

I felt sorry for her. I wanted to show compassion. I reached out my hand. 'I did not take delight in this.'

She shrank away from my touch. 'God made sure the wages of sin were paid long before you came along with your judgemental prying.'

'The wages of sin is death.' I recalled the verse we had memorised as teens. It had haunted me then. It must be haunting her now.

She shuddered. 'I had to earn my right to be a good wife again. I had to be ten times the helpmeet. But he forgave me. It was all going so well. Until this retreat.'

'How did you feel about meeting Glen here again?'

She gritted her teeth. Looked up at me. Wiped a tear that was running down her cheek. 'I didn't want to ever see him again. But he emailed me, told me it would be good, that seeing each other again would give us all closure, that he would not bring it up or embarrass me. He swore this. But Jay was tense. When I knew Glen was coming, I was afraid. Jay had been so angry with him, and this was the first time they would see each other since that time. Ten years. No, more. I was so afraid he would do something.'

'Kill him, you mean?'

She shuddered. 'No. Confront him. And that's exactly what he planned. I dreaded it. When I saw what he was doing that first night, I was terrified.'

'You mean asking us all to write our sins on paper?'

'Yes. He wanted Glen to confess. He wanted me to confess. Jay wanted repentance, apologies, and then forgiveness, reconciliation. He wanted to purge the demons that had been attacking us all. Clear the way. Restore The Twelve to its former glory. He would never, ever harm the hair on anyone's head. I know what you're thinking, but it isn't true. Vengeance is mine, I will repay, says the Lord. Jay would never take it into his own hands. Never. True, we did pray for justice, for truth, but when people started dying, we knew it was Satan… or an agent of Satan.'

This was longest speech I had ever heard her make. Normally quiet, submissive, now she was shaken and angry. And clearly she hated me. 'So you went to see Glen in the night. You knew this would make things worse. Were you still having an affair?'

Her eyes were wide. 'I never went to see Glen.'

'You swear?'

'On this Bible.' She placed her hand on it.

'Then who did I see in the corridor with him?'

'I have no idea.' But she looked pointedly towards the door. 'Suzanne?'

She nodded.

'You think Suzanne had something to do with all this?'

She nodded. 'You and Suzanne and Emily.'

I stepped back. 'That's ridiculous. Delusional. Linda, your husband just tried to kill Emily.'

She threw herself on the bed, pushed the open Bible away. 'I don't believe her. Or you. She… she's pure evil. Like you. She made it up.' Linda backed herself up against the head-board of the bed. 'I hate you. I try not to, but I hate you.'

'Blame the messenger, is that it?'

She narrowed her eyes at me. 'No. That horrible book you wrote. You destroyed our reputation with that book. I wanted him to confront you about that book. He wanted you to repent.'

'*God is Dead*? My book destroyed the Church?'

'And so when you agreed to come here, he wanted to sort everything out. Then you bring all the dirt into the open. It's all your doing.'

'Or maybe he came here to get revenge on Glen, punish me. You know it's the eighth day. If I hadn't locked him up, my life would be in danger. You've just told me his motives now for killing Glen, Emily, me. Any more? Why did he want to kill Ali, Mike, Danny, Stephen?'

I was not expecting it. She sprang to her feet and lunged at me. Slapped my face hard. I gripped her hand to restrain her, but she fought and struggled. 'You– You monster!'

'Knock, knock!' Suzanne was at the door with a tray of coffee and toast.

'Whoa!' Emily rushed in to hold Linda back. She pulled her off me and sat her down again on the bed. Linda buried her face in her hands.

Suzanne frowned at me. 'What did you say to her?'

Linda spat the words at us. 'Just leave me alone, all of you.'

Suzanne placed Linda's coffee and her plate of toast on a bedside table. 'Here, Linda. We'll leave it here, okay?' And to me, 'Let's have ours in the living room.'

I held my burning cheek. 'We're finished here anyway. After breakfast, I want to interrogate the Reverend.'

'Interrogate?' said Linda.

'Interview, then. Find out exactly what happened. And if he has any accomplices. We're not out of the woods yet.'

We ate toast and sipped coffee in the living room. Then I hunted around and found what I was looking for on the dining room table – the Reverend's Bible, his sermon notes, his anno-tated *Foxe's Book of Martyrs*, his diary. This was evidence indeed. I snatched it up and sat by the window to read.

The leather-bound Scofield's Bible was worn, and I remembered it from those early years when Reverend James brought it out every Sunday and pored over it. Inside the Bible I found scraps of paper, dog-eared pages, and handwritten notes labelled one through twelve. His sermons for each day! The sermons began with a diagram of the twelve days of Christmas. Ten of the days had been marked with the name of a member of The Twelve present at the beginning of the retreat. *And in order of their murder – so far.* Furthermore, each name was cross-referenced with pages referring to passages in *Foxe's Book of Martyrs*.

The bastard! He had planned it all so neatly, just as I thought. And right in front of us, outlined in this book. I turned the page and gave a start. For today, the eighth day, January 1st, I found my name scrawled next to a heading:

The 8 Beatitudes – Matthew 5:3–10.

I slammed the Bible shut. As predicted by the card I'd received on day one, I was to be the New Year victim. Today was my day of doom. I had caught him just in time.

But what was this? In a pocket at the back of the Bible, I discovered eight folded notes. I opened one and read: *Did not tithe the full amount.* Another one read: *I cannot control my impure thoughts.*

On each note, a name had been written with a query after it. Stephen? Danny?

Then I understood. On that first night we had written our transgressions on scraps of paper, and Reverend James had burned them. Or said he burned them. But when our eyes were closed in prayer, he must have switched them for a fake set of notes ready to toss into the fire, and kept the originals so that he could read each and every Twelve member's secret confessions.

And then he had planned an appropriate punishment for each.

No, he had this planned well in advance of that.

I felt bad: I should not read people's secret confessions.

Did not tithe the full amount.

The Reverend had guessed this brief confession had come from Stephen. To Danny he had assigned:

Impure thoughts. Lust. I self-pollute every night, and hate myself for doing it. I fantasise about women, even married women. Lord help me.

Mike was:

Pride. I feel I am better than everyone else. I am so impatient at other people's weaknesses and follies. Arrogant. Yes. Proud. Yes.

On a scrap smaller than the others he had written 'Alison':

I talk about people behind their back. Back-biting. Then smile and act all false when they are around. I'm a hypocrite. I pretend well. But I'm a mess inside.

Linda's matched the account she had given to me:

You know me, Lord. You know everything. I have tried to be all you want me to be but I cannot be, I cannot. I fail. Every day. I doubt. I need faith, I need to trust you more, but I don't.

The Reverend had written Suzanne's name confidently on her scrap, and the writing was similar to those on the notes I had found:

I never really believed. There was a time I went along with all this. But I never believed in sin, in confessing sins. Maybe I am just so far astray that I don't even know I am in sin. You want confession – here goes: I don't love my husband. I don't love my kids. I am self-obsessed. I know that. I use people. But is that sin? Or just smart?

And here was Emily's confession.

I am an adulterer, a liar, cheater, philanderer, back-biter, sexually immoral, an idolater, have sex with other women, a thief, greedy, a drunkard, a slanderer, a swindler and much more.

And finally, mine.

There is no god.

Emily and Suzanne walked into the room. I quickly stuffed the notes back into the pocket and snapped the Bible closed again.

'Linda wants us to take up some food for her husband and see if he's all right,' said Suzanne.

Emily reached over. 'Reading your Bible, Rafe?'

I brandished it in the air. 'He set this whole thing up, for revenge. To teach us all a lesson. Accused us of the seven deadly sins. He's deranged. He had plans for each day, exactly as we said. And he almost got away with it. But with you, Emily, he bungled it.'

'It was weird. He didn't tighten that face pear thing, whatever it was. That would have suffocated me.'

'I wonder why. Was it a bungle or did he relent?' I did not say what I was thinking with Suzanne present. Reverend James had had an affair with Emily. Maybe, just maybe, he had relented. At the last minute, found he still loved her and couldn't go through with it. 'And I'm next.' I waved the Bible. 'He had plans for the eighth day of Christmas, wrote my name next to the date, something about the beatitudes.'

Suzanne lowered her voice. 'And Linda. Where is she in all this?'

'We have to watch her carefully,' I said.

'You think she's involved?' said Emily.

I lowered my voice. 'I'm sure she must have known something. After all, it began with revenge against her ex-lover Glen. But she's on the hit list. He means– meant to get rid of her too.'

'Okay, so we have motive,' said Emily. 'But how did he commit all these murders? He couldn't have done them on his own.'

'What we have been suspecting all along. He must have had an accomplice. And I'm thinking–'

'Linda.'

I shook my head.

'The concierge!' said Emily.

I nodded. 'But we haven't seen him anywhere.'

'Or maybe the owner of the castle, the crazy man who is obsessed with all these torture instruments. Maybe he wanted to try his devices out on people. His ultimate fantasy, and Reverend James and he came up with a plan, a medieval plan, to punish the sinners in his flock, the adulterers and apostates and blasphemers.'

Suzanne shuddered. 'So it isn't safe, even if we have Reverend James locked up.'

'I need to speak to him, find out exactly what is going on. Maybe use him as guarantor of our safety, if there are others.'

Suzanne brightened. 'Like a hostage.'

'Exactly.'

'We shouldn't leave Linda on her own,' said Emily.

Suzanne stood. 'I'll get her.'

Linda and Suzanne sat in the living room opposite Emily and me. I stared at her, still not knowing how implicated she was in her husband's transgressions. She looked nervous, entwining her fingers together, and kept shooting glances out of the door. 'I think I should get him some breakfast and coffee,' she whispered, not to me but to Suzanne.

Suzanne raised her eyebrows to me. 'Should we?'

I shook my head. 'Maybe you're not quite getting it, Linda. Your husband just tried to murder Emily. Has most likely murdered all the others. And you're concerned that he's hungry?'

Linda bit her lip. 'I want to see him. You can't lock him up.'

I held out the Reverend's Bible. 'He wants to kill us.'

'Give me that.' She made a lunge for it, but I held it away from her and she stumbled.

'It's evidence, sorry, for the police. Criminal material.'

'You ruined everything. Everything.'

I had never seen Linda like this – red-faced, wild, angry. I liked this woman better than the passive, pale-eyed, submissive woman I had known her as. I deliberated. 'All right, you can see him, but we're not letting him out of that room. If you want to be with him, we'll have to lock you in there too.'

'Better than being in here with you snakes. Let me take him some food and drink.'

'Not just yet. I want to talk to him first. All of you stay here.'

I took the dagger in case Reverend James still had tricks up his sleeve, but as I listened at the locked and barricaded door, I heard only silence. No one had disturbed the thread I had placed across the doorway. I moved the dresser away, knocked, and waited. Then I turned the key.

I stepped inside, dagger at the ready.

'Reverend James?'

I had many questions, but the first was paramount: how to ensure our safety. Where was his accomplice, if indeed he had one? How could we negotiate safe passage out of here? Were we still in any danger? But I was met with silence and cold.

The handcuffs were lying on the bedside table, open, a key in the lock.

Shit!

I looked desperately around the room. I poked under the bed, pulled open the closet, ran to the window and tried the handle. It was tightly closed. I looked at the doorway. He couldn't have got out that way. My heart pounded. 'Reverend James!'

I checked my pockets. I still had the key to the cuffs. This must be the duplicate I had foolishly left on the torture museum display cabinet. Maybe Linda had sneaked in and given him the key while we were downstairs. Anger rose in my throat. Rage at this man. And my foolishness to think I had safely locked him away. How stupid of me!

I had to think of the women's safety first. I ran down the stairs, calling out, 'Suzanne, Emily, Linda. Are you okay? Stay together.'

Emily and Suzanne stood by the fire, staring at the dagger in my hand. I lowered it. 'Where's Linda?'

'Isn't she with you?' said Suzanne. 'She said she was going to get some food for the Reverend. We told her to wait, but she wouldn't.'

I jangled the handcuff key in the air. 'He's gone.'

'What?' said Suzanne and Emily together.

'How?' said Emily. 'You said you had locked him up in your room.'

'And Linda?' said Suzanne. 'She said she—'

I ran into the kitchen. No sign of Linda. 'Shit.'

'They could be anywhere,' said Emily.

Suzanne frowned. 'She did help him, then.'

Emily nodded. 'Yes. She was playing with us. It was all an act.'

I sat by the fire, turning the dagger in my hand. All the pieces fell into place. 'Let's face it, we're the only non-believers here. Alive, that is. We were all inside that cult, we all know how it felt, that fanatical view that the world was against us, that we were right and they were all evil followers of Satan. Who knows what madness lives in people? He called us heretics, apostates, enemies of God. She called on God to smite us, prayed for vengeance. She threw some verse at me when I talked to her, about Jesus casting us into hell for our sins.'

Emily nodded. 'So they planned to eliminate us. He and Linda. I can see it now. Such hatred. And self-righteousness. And delusion.'

'I can understand Glen's murder. That was jealousy. A way to purge the Reverend's pain and his wife's unfaithfulness. But

Stephen, Mike, Danny and Ali were innocents. They were his closest followers.'

'He tried to kill me too,' said Emily.

'You're an apostate. Me too. You too, Suzanne. It's obvious why we should be on the hit list.'

Suzanne crinkled her nose. 'Forgive my ignorance, but what is an apostate?'

'Someone who renounces their faith,' said Emily. 'In some religions, like some extreme forms of Islam, it invites the death penalty. Medieval Christianity tortured people for apostasy.'

'Hence the torture museum,' said Emily.

'It's a bigger threat than atheism,' I said. 'For someone to de-convert, to reject the true teachings of God (whatever they are), threatens the very foundations of that religion. Undermines faith. You have to eliminate apostates or shut them up.'

Emily whistled. 'And we were conned into coming here. Into this trap. Shit. I should have followed my instincts. I was never going to come. But I wanted to see you guys.'

'Me too,' I said. 'I knew it was a mistake to come, but I felt there was something to resolve.'

'With Reverend James?'

'No,' I said, looking at Suzanne.

'Shall I leave now?' said Emily.

Suzanne looked at Emily, almost kindly. 'No. So, Rafe, have you resolved whatever it was you came to resolve?'

'I'm not sure yet,' I said.

Suzanne shook her head. 'We all had things we needed to resolve. But I felt I was being set up. I feel like Reverend James is trying to pin those murders on me. All those fake notes, using my perfume.'

'Who knows the mind of a deluded religious fanatic?' I said. 'He sees sin everywhere. Sex, lust, adultery, all anathema to him.' I picked up the *Foxe's Book of Martyrs*. 'Read this book long enough and you'll start to dream about torture and persecution and that whole medieval worldview. I'm afraid our Reverend is completely stuck in a pattern of righteous retribution. Do you know he kept our secret confessions?'

'What?' said Emily.

'He burnt them,' said Suzanne, paling. 'I saw—'

I marched across to the dining table, picked up the Reverend's Bible and brought it over to the fireside. I pulled out the pile of folded notes from the back pouch. 'A conjuring trick. He used them to shape our punishments.'

Emily and Suzanne stared at the notes on the table. No one wanted to pick them up. Suzanne looked at me sharply. 'Have you read them?'

'No.' But I hesitated a little too long.

'You read them!' said Suzanne. 'You read mine, didn't you?'

'We have to read them,' said Emily. 'It'll give us a clue about his thinking.'

'I just wrote bullshit,' said Suzanne. 'What did he really think? That I'd confess all my sins?'

Emily agreed. 'I had so many sins, I couldn't fit them on the piece of paper.'

'So what are we going to do?' said Suzanne. 'Shouldn't we have something to defend ourselves with if he attacks again?'

I looked at the open doorway. 'We stick together, and we arm ourselves. We don't go anywhere alone. And we find where they're holing up. At least we know who our enemy is now.'

'What happens if we need to go pee?' said Emily.

'Do you?'

'I'm bursting. All that coffee.'

'Me too,' said Suzanne.

I considered. 'Let's all go together,' I said. 'I'll stand guard outside the loo, you two go in first, then me.'

'We need weapons.' Emily walked over to the dining room cabinet and pulled out a carving knife and fork. 'Here.'

Suzanne took the fork. Prodded it into the air. 'Can't see myself using this on anyone.'

'You will, if some hand grabs you around the throat like he did me,' said Emily. 'I wished for a weapon in my hand.'

'I have mace in my room,' said Suzanne.

'Good. Let's get it after we go to the loo.'

We stayed close. Instead of a fearful silence, I decided to fill the silence with our presence. We chatted overly loudly, as if to spook any silent attackers in the shadows.

'Have to look on the bright side,' said Emily. 'He bungled my execution.'

'I'm next, if his sermons are anything to go by. Eight maids a-milking,' I said.

Suzanne gasped. 'He gave us our death cards at that first supper. Little did we know.'

'What card are you, Suzanne?' said Emily.

'Eleven pipers piping.'

'Oh, you're safe then, for at least a few days.'

Suzanne sighed. 'You guys are so glib, so facetious.'

'Only way to deal with it,' said Emily.

I interrupted their chatter. 'Wait, shh. What was that noise?'

We froze.

A creak on the floorboards, a slamming window. 'The wind?'

'After you go to the loo, I think we'd better secure all the windows. Lock the doors to each room.'

At the women's toilet, we stopped and listened. The door was closed, but the wind blew under the gap underneath it. 'I'll check for lurkers before you go in.'

'We all check for lurkers.'

I pushed open the door, peered in every corner, every

cupboard. A window banged open and shut. I closed it, secured it with its latch. Suzanne and Emily checked the stalls.

'All clear.'

They closed the door and left me outside. 'Lock it,' I ordered.

I stood outside and waited. I listened carefully for creaking footsteps, wind. I could hear both women peeing, it was so quiet.

The next moment I felt a bee sting in my neck, a stinky cloth clamped onto my mouth. I dropped to the floor, feeling myself go soft, as if I had no muscle strength. In my falling into unconsciousness, I thought I heard screams – far away – and pummelling on the door behind me, but they faded into blackness. My limbs felt heavy, my body like jelly, and a bright light receded at speed in my brain, a blackness like squid's ink enveloping me.

A throbbing head, my body clammy and hot. Claustrophobic. Pressure on my face, and my nose burning. Rose and musk perfume itched my eyes, seared my nostrils, as if someone had wiped it on my face. 'Suzanne,' I muttered, as I opened my eyes, 'is that you?'

The sting on my neck burned. But that was the least of my worries. I smelt burning cotton. A metallic flavour in my mouth. I reached up and sensed I was in an enclosed space that radiated heat. I touched a scalding hot metal roof and quickly pulled my hand away. My eyes were burning now too. I looked up and saw two glowing diffuse lights. As I grew used to the darkness, I worked out the shape and texture of my prison.

Suddenly, I knew where I was: encased in the brazen bull. Above my head was the hollowed out inside of the mouth and head and the two lights were its nostrils. I had been placed on top of the inside of the udders with its four teats, lying face up.

And worse, whoever had captured me had lit the fire underneath. The brazen bull was heating up, cracking and expanding.

Death by milkmaidens. Not the iron maiden, but the cow that produced human fluids through its udders. I was going to be roasted alive.

You're going to be the milk, Rafe, I thought. I felt for the trap-door hatch that I remembered seeing on the first day here. That's how I had been placed inside. I could make out with my fingers a rectangular section, but it was getting too hot to touch and there was no way to open it from the inside. The torturers who built it had thought of that. Thank God I was wearing heavy clothes. But I could smell that they were beginning to singe. And the oxygen was fast disappearing. It was already hotter than I could stand. Soon I would be bellowing in pain, out of the bull's nostrils, amplified by the hollow interior.

I was going to die.

NINE LADIES DANCING

I couldn't breathe. My skin blistered. And the pain throbbed in my left thigh. I wriggled around and felt a hard object in my pocket. Of course, the dagger I had taken from the torture museum as a weapon. It was so hot it was burning my leg. I wrapped my hand in my sleeve and pulled it out.

I groped around me, but wherever I touched was burning hot. The bull had been moulded as one continuous piece of bronze, smoothed and shaped so that the victim would have nothing to grip on to.

Except for the udders – these were a later addition to the bull, and I could feel the uneven plate where the bowl had been grafted on to the underbelly. I felt for screws or bolts but found none. Maybe I could pry the two searing sheets of metal apart. But the heat was strongest at this very point.

Think, Rafe, don't panic. Try to be logical about this.

But I could not think. My brain sizzled. I knew there was a critical temperature at which the human body could no longer function and after that point I would deteriorate rapidly. The brain would be the first to go. I had to focus my energy in spite of the throbbing pain.

I clanged the side of the bull with the dagger. 'Help! I'm in here! Get me out!'

The echo of my voice mocked me. No one could hear, I was sure. And who would be listening but the murderer himself? 'Reverend James!' I called. I banged again on the side with the dagger.

Calm yourself. Think rationally. Pain, I knew (along with other similar bodily sensations), was a response of the brain to nerve endings. If you could detach yourself from the circuit and understand it, you could stop feeling it. The sensation of pain is separate from pain itself. Pain is subjective. Experiences are in the head, if they are anywhere.

Detach yourself, Rafe, from the pain. Detach. Push down that rising scream in your throat.

I fought back claustrophobia. I hated confined spaces, metaphorical or physical. Trapped in a metal container that was heating up, with no air, was my worst nightmare. But I had to conserve both air and energy. I wriggled to escape the heat on my legs, moved my weight across, and the bull shuddered a little. This gave me the idea. I hurled myself with full force against the side, felt the bull lift into the air, hover for a second on two feet, then fall back on all four. *Four legs good, two legs better.* I shoved myself again at the concave inner stomach of the bull, and it lurched again, hanging in the air, and as I pushed all my weight against it, felt, yes, that it had reached tipping point, and was falling. It crashed and my body was jarred onto the side of the bull, which was now I imagined – I hoped – sideways on the cold floor of the torture museum. I arched my body away from the red-hot underbelly and inside of the udders but there was nowhere that did not scald me.

Was it just my wish for it to be so, or was the bronze slowly cooling? Yes. I had moved it far enough away from the fire to have an effect. After a few minutes, I could sit more comfortably and my brain began to clear. I took breaths of air inside the skull where the two nostrils had been fashioned so the cruel torturers could hear the bellowing of the dying victim. The metal cracked and ticked as it cooled, and I began working on the plate with my dagger. I steadied my hand, wrapped my fingers in my sleeve as I found purchase and tried to prise open the metal plate. But it would not move.

I cranked it on all sides, banged it with my fist, and finally I felt a slight give. Encouraged, I worked around and around the plate until at last the casing separated and I could lever the metal away from the shell. It pulled away reluctantly, and in a matter of minutes, I had removed the metal plate and the whole udder came with it, inside the bull. I shoved it towards the tail end and breathed the cool air sweeping into the gaping hole it left.

The euphoria was short-lived. The square hole I had created was large enough for a fist, maybe even my head, but never my whole body.

Now claustrophobia kicked in again. There was no way I could escape this way. Above me, the door, bolted, was the only way out.

Unless...

I reached my arm out of the udder hole as far as I could stretch it and felt for the bolt that held the door shut. I could not quite reach, but if I strained and caused a tearing pain, I could touch the bolt. I needed to move this bolt and wiggle it out of the slot. I couldn't. I needed an extra few inches. I held the dagger out through the opening, stretched and tapped, just touching the bolt. I could lift it up but not push it across to open it.

I rested my cramping arm. My skin scorched on the still-burning hot metal, and I felt short of breath. But I had to do it or die. The body and mind can perform miracles when needed. I had to believe it. Summoning all my mental and physical reserves for the final move, I pushed the dagger and felt the bolt move in its groove. One more push and it was open all the way.

The door groaned, lifted, clanged open as it hit the metal side of the bull.

Air. Cold. I fell out, slid down the side of the bull and collapsed onto the stone floor. The scene in front of me looked precisely how I'd imagined it: fire burned in trays once positioned under the bull, which now lay on its side.

I could not catch my breath at first, but was grateful for the cold air in my lungs. My chest hurt, my body felt on fire, my skin burned. My eyes would not open properly. And I could not lie still. I had to be alert. Whoever had drugged me and placed me in the bull could still be here, watching. Reverend James. Reverend James and Linda.

I squinted up at the eight dangling dummies, at the beheaded corpse, at the iron maiden. I inhaled the crisp air more freely now, grateful to be alive, grateful to breathe, grateful to be free of that hell. Slowly, my brain cleared as oxygen made its way through my system. I could stand again, so I smothered the fire by spreading out the coals, crushing them, stamping them out. My hands stung even more with cold. I could see welts and blisters already forming on my skin, and my face throbbed.

I had dropped the dagger on the floor. It was cool now, so I pocketed it, but I hunted along the display for a more formidable weapon. I deliberated over the cat-o'-nine-tails, executioner's axe and a long spear. I chose a beautifully polished, doubled-bladed axe. I wondered how many heads this axe had severed. Maybe it was just a modern replica. I tested the blade with my finger. This would do. Although heavy to carry, it felt good in my hands, an extension of my rage, my pain.

I pushed open the door, wary, looking into the dark corridor out of the corner of my eyes where the light was best. If they thought I was dead, I had the element of surprise. But I had made such a racket, I doubted that. I kept to the shadows and made my way back to the women's bathroom where I had been attacked. I wondered what had happened to Emily and Suzanne.

How long had it been? I had no idea. Hours? No light came from the end of the passage by the living room. I stood by the door, wary of what I would find. 'Emily. Suzanne.'

The thumping on the other side of the door told me they were alive. Thank God.

Emily's voice: 'Rafe, what the hell?'

'You're still here!'

Suzanne's voice: 'We can't get out. Our key won't turn the lock.'

'What happened to you, Rafe?' called Emily. 'We heard you cry out, then nothing for hours and then a terrible ruckus. What happened?'

'Rafe, get us out of here!'

I took the dagger out of my pocket and played with the lock, fiddled with two tiny screws and managed to loosen one and pull off the cover. I saw three wires leading into the lock. Maybe if I ripped out these wires, this would release the lock. But maybe it would seal the women in the room instead.

'Here goes nothing.' I cut all three wires out with the dagger and the lock clicked.

I pushed on the door. It did not open.

Okay, so I was not a locksmith.

'Plan B, Emily and Suzanne. Stand back from the door, please.'

I heaved the heavy axe above my head and struck the lock, splintering it from the wooden door. I felt a searing pain in my chest, and my arms hurt like hell. Maybe I had done more than burned myself in that bull. Maybe snapped a tendon. But I raised the axe and struck again. My skin burned as if it was on fire. My chest felt crisped and my lungs full of black ash. But I pushed through the pain. Again. Again. I chopped to the side of the door handle until the whole lock mechanism fell onto the floor. Then I pushed the door – or what remained of the door – open.

Emily and Suzanne had pressed themselves against the back wall of the toilet. 'Come,' I said.

'Rafe!' I must have looked a sight, because they both recoiled. 'What happened?'

'I took a sauna. A little hot, but it clears the sinuses.'

Emily touched my face and I flinched. 'The brazen bull. Someone stuck me in the brazen bull and tried to roast me alive.'

Suzanne winced. 'Your face looks terrible.'

'Someone drugged me and I woke up inside the bull. Obviously, I was meant to be burned alive. But I escaped.'

Emily touched my arm. 'Ow. We need to put something on your arm. And face.'

'Let's get to the living room, where it's warm – not that I want any more heat, but you look blue with cold.' I grabbed the axe and led the way down the corridor. Now the real pain kicked in. No one needed to tell me that burned flesh is one of the most painful of wounds; all the nerve endings lie close to the surface of the skin. I pulled a chair from near the fire to the centre of the room where the heat could not reach me and the cold could not freeze me.

'I'm going to the kitchen to get some cling film,' Emily said.

'Be careful.'

When she returned, she gave me three paracetamol tablets and wrapped the burned skin with cling film.

Suzanne watched, a distant air returning to her demeanour, her eyes alternately on my free hand, which rested on the axe, and on Emily's face as she went about her work. 'It's going to sound like a horror story,' she said, 'but how did you get out of there alive?'

'Through the udders.'

Emily stopped dabbing and considered the scenario. 'Seriously?'

'Remember, we saw the tits on the brass beast on our guided tour of the museum. They were a later addition, so I could pry them off.'

'Like *Survivor*,' said Suzanne. 'Only here the camera crew is not about to appear and say, "well done, you won".'

I grimaced at the ceiling, disassociating from the pain as Emily wiped the wounds, but also annoyed at Suzanne's analogy. *Survivor!* As if everything was a movie or TV show to her. 'The terrifying thought is that if the murderer had succeeded, Emily and I would be dead and you, Suzanne, would be the only one left. You'd be the survivor.'

She turned and gave me a look – of fear, of guilt, I was not sure. 'Rafe, you said something earlier that doesn't make sense. How exactly was the murderer planning to keep me going on my own until the eleventh day? It's only the eighth day now.'

I shook my head. 'I have no idea. Maybe things are not going according to their grand plan.'

'I think we've already messed up the plan,' said Emily. 'Only trouble is, they'll want to finish the job. Do you think they know they botched the job, that you escaped?'

'I'm sure,' I said. 'Notice how you're saying "they" now.' I pushed her hand away. 'And thanks, you can stop wrapping me up now like a mummy.'

'Reverend James and Linda,' said Emily.

'It's hard to imagine Linda being part of all this,' said Suzanne. 'I can't picture it.'

Emily's expression was grim. 'I can.'

'I still can't believe they want us all dead.'

I stood up, carefully, and reached for the Bible on the dining room table. I leafed through it to the notes. 'The sermon for day nine. Nine ladies dancing. The nine fruits of the Holy Spirit.'

'How does that help us?' said Emily.

'On the eighth day, it was meant to be me. Eight maids a-milking. He used the brazen bull, the idea of milking. So all we have to figure out is what torture device is associated with dancing.'

'Who is number nine?'

I consulted the Reverend's notes again. 'Linda. And James is ten. Maybe they plan a double suicide.'

'It doesn't make any sense,' said Suzanne. 'Especially if I'm number eleven.'

I shut the Bible and sighed. 'I could use a meal.' I put the Bible back down and hobbled to the kitchen, brought back left-over curry and rice and canned rice pudding. We ate it cold. I kept a wary eye on the door and the axe close at hand. Now I knew how wild animals feel when they feed.

After supper, I yawned. 'I'm exhausted.'

Suzanne gave me and Emily a suspicious look. 'But how do we sleep?'

'We sleep in one bedroom,' I said. 'I disable the locks on the door. We barricade ourselves in.'

Emily and Suzanne exchanged glances. 'So we all sleep in the same room?'

'Yours, Em,' I said. 'I get the floor. And we take turns at guard duty.'

We collected our clothes, and I gathered my mattress and bedding and dragged them into the corner of Emily's room. I searched everywhere for anything suspicious – hidden cameras, secret entrances, spy holes.

Now the door. I unscrewed the lock as I had done before, pulled the wires out and the door clicked and remain locked.

'Safe enough for us to get some sleep,' I said without conviction.

Night fell. Emily's room creaked and groaned in the wind. Ghosts of the castle walked upstairs, rattled at the window to get in. Reverend James and Linda also lurked somewhere between these castle walls. So many questions: What were they doing? Where were they? Did they know I had escaped?

As the two women slept, I took the first shift. I managed my pain, as I had read in books on Zen philosophy, by watching it from the outside, feeling it, observing it as a foreign thing, and that way I was in control. *You are not your pain, you simply have a pain. Your body is not who you are.*

I watched them sleep. Emily, her duvet tucked tightly around her, Suzanne lying on her back, hair over her face. I observed something else at work here in me. The ache that I had carried all my life about Suzanne had dissipated. Perhaps the suspicions of her involvement in these deaths had dried up any feelings I had. Or maybe just seeing a real, un-idealised woman had done it. In my heart, in that place I had nourished and kept alive for all these years, was a hard, dry stone.

What of Emily? It was true that Emily and I were friends – close friends – but I was old enough to know that in life, boundaries, like arguments, were messy and frayed around the edges. She had loved me and I had kept her love at bay, seeing her as a friend only.

I could not sleep, even though I was exhausted. Pain kept me alert and conscious. I puzzled over the moral fibre of a pastor and his wife capable of carrying out this outrageous killing spree. I listened to every creak, every howl of the wind, every thump on the floorboards, waiting for them.

I had failed miserably. I had not prevented Alison's death. I had been too slow. Perhaps it was failure of my imagination. I had not been able to conceive of such sadistic evil – and the lengths it would go to. Since I had no personal experience of wanting to kill anyone, I could not relate.

I thought of the story of *The Wizard of Oz*. The story was profound, philosophically speaking – it was about the unmasking of God. What Dorothy and Scarecrow and Lion and the Tin Man feared was the omnipotence, omniscience and omnipresence of this great Oz whom everyone worshipped and feared. But Dorothy unmasked him and revealed that he was just a puny man whose powers were all illusion.

Reverend James was Oz, a weak little man playing God. We had to unmask him, find the screen behind which he now hid.

Where could he be?

I began to make plans. If we were still alive in the morning, I would carry them out. At midnight, I woke Emily and she took over guard duty, and I slept like a dead man.

I woke on the mattress on the freezing cold stone floor, wrapped in a blanket. My burns stung. It was still dark, and Suzanne was prodding me on the shoulder. 'You okay, Rafe? You were having a nightmare.'

I sat up, felt the pain return, and winced. 'Thrashing around. You were drumming on the floor with your feet and groaning.'

I pressed my fingers to my eyes, which felt roasted.

Emily opened her eyes. 'Good morning!'

'How did you sleep, Em?'

She rubbed her face with her hand. 'Nightmares too. I still feel that thing on my face, his creepy hand on my neck.'

'I have a plan.'

'What?'

'First we have to get out of this room.' Though I had disabled the lock, I pried the door open with the axe, and we ventured out into the corridor. Emily took the carving knife, and Suzanne took out the can of mace she had collected earlier from her bedroom.

We tiptoed down the corridors like thieves. My heart beat rapidly, and I was prepared for ambush. I held the axe out in front; Suzanne brandished her mace spray and Emily brought up the rear, her knife at the ready. We made it to the living room and I peered in. Sunlight was pouring in through the windows. The wind had died down. It was eerily quiet. The snow was bright outside, like the first morning of creation. I was fully expecting an attack, but a cursory glance showed it appeared to be safe. I closed the door behind me and we searched every possible hiding place. We secured the kitchen and made breakfast and coffee, then sat and nursed our fear all morning.

I had told the women a white lie: I didn't actually have a detailed plan. Yes, we had to leave this house of horrors, but while we worked out how to do that, we had to create a safe space here.

My mind turned on itself. How would a murderer think? An accomplice? I had to imagine what they were planning next. If their plans had backfired and Emily and I were meant to be dead, then Suzanne was the next target. But we were all targets.

If we stay together, I thought, *we will be safe, for now.* Until I recovered sufficiently to do battle. Until we could come up with a strategy.

Although I knew that Emily and I weren't ones for sitting around waiting for something to happen to us, I was weak and in pain. I took painkillers, bathed my wounds, and drank glasses and glasses of water to avoid dehydration, under Emily's instruction. But I was restless, so I racked my brain to think of a plan. They had to be hiding somewhere in the castle, but where?

After lunch, I took the key and tried to unlock the passage door. It would not open. I pushed it. Tried the key again. In panic, I tried the kitchen door. It was also locked and I could not open it with the key.

'Damn,' I said.

'Shh,' said Emily. 'I hear something.'

The crackle of the loudspeakers, the hiss of a recording beginning, and the same computerised voice we had heard days before began. But this time, the voice began singing: 'On the ninth day of Christmas, my true love gave to me…' And then stopped.

Then it repeated the line with an inflection at the end: 'On the ninth day of Christmas, my true love gave to me?'

'He's live,' whispered Emily. 'He can hear us.'

'I doubt it,' I said.

'On the ninth day of Christmas, my true love gave to me?'

'Nine ladies dancing,' said Suzanne to the speaker.

'Correct. Nine ladies dancing,' repeated the voice.

I froze. Emily was right. He was live.

'Shit,' said Suzanne. 'He *can* hear us.'

'Who are you?' I demanded.

'Eight maids a-milking, seven swans a-swimming, six geese a-laying, five golden rings… You want to know who I am? I am your guide, fellow travellers on a journey to hell.'

I listened intently. The voice was disguised electronically, but I was checking for intonations, pauses, characteristics of Reverend James' speech patterns.

'I trust the three witches are brewing fear nicely in their stomachs. And Macbeth, are these three ladies you see before you? Triple them!'

'James Miller, stop playing games,' I called. 'We know it's you and you will not escape. Your attempts on our lives failed.'

'Beware!' said the voice. 'Women have always been the downfall of man. Eve tempted Adam. Suzanne, Emily, Linda, witches three, multiply by three and you have nine ladies dancing around you.'

'What are you talking about?' said Emily. 'Linda is with you. Don't pretend she isn't part of this.'

The voice continued as if she hadn't spoken. 'The nine ladies dancing are the nine fruits of the spirit. You know what they are, I hope. This is another test for you. A riddle. Tell me what they are. Nine fruits of the spirit? Anyone?'

I picked up the Reverend's Bible and opened it to his sermon for the ninth day of Christmas. I read aloud. 'Love, Joy, Peace, Patience, Kindness, Goodness, Faithfulness, Gentleness, Self-control.'

The voice waited until I had finished and then continued. 'Exactly, exactly. Now ask yourself, all of you, honestly, how many of these virtues do you possess? These virtues would have saved you, but alas, you have none of them. I know your hearts, your blackened hearts. You are the unbelievers. I have isolated you. Spared your lives to give you a chance to repent. All you need to do is repent. Give up your life to God. Stop worshipping idols. Mammon. Self. Reason.'

A pause. Emily twirled her finger around her ear. 'Seriously?'

I spoke to the speaker, as I assumed the microphone was placed there. 'You killed the others who were all believers. If you want an argument, a logical, rational argument, I can talk to you. But you're not even listening.'

'And you, Rafe, the female sex will be your downfall. I

know all about you and your affairs. Even under this very roof, you have polluted the retreat. I know. I know everything. Debauchery. Sin. Immorality.'

Emily nudged me. 'He doesn't know about platonic relationships, obviously.'

'I know about Linda's affair with Glen. She will be punished. Suzanne, I have watched you debauch the female species, you whore of Babylon. Emily, you temptress who seduced and ruined and polluted the Church. Rafe, your loose morals and affairs. And so you are condemned to death if you refuse to repent. All of you. Suzanne, Emily, Rafe. And Linda *in absentia*. All of you.'

'He's speaking as if Linda is not with him,' whispered Suzanne.

'Where are you?'

'I am everywhere. The cellar, the kitchen, the living room, in every room. I am omnipresent, omniscient. Dance, ladies, dance.' The microphone clicked off, the hissing in the speakers stopped, the door locks slid open, and the performance was over.

Suzanne stared at me. 'Shit! What the hell do we do now?'

I folded my arms. 'Game on.'

'Where are we going, Rafe?'

'There is one place we didn't look. The cellar.'

'What cellar?' said Suzanne.

'He just told us. The cellar, he said.'

'I didn't even know there was a cellar,' said Suzanne.

'I think there's a set of steps going down from the corridor as well as up,' said Emily.

'And Glen mentioned it on the first night. Said it was a no-go area. This could just be where it all happens. They have to be hiding somewhere, and this is the only part of the castle we haven't explored.'

We armed ourselves and set off in a convoy. The hallway was already dark and the afternoon light slanted across the passage. Emily was right. We found a set of cold stone steps going down, and at the bottom, a door, wide open. Light flickered inside.

Emily clutched her coat. 'He's expecting us. He's been watching us.'

'It's a trap,' said Suzanne.

I held up the axe like a wand to dispel all evil. 'Come.'

Now Emily was shaking. 'We can't go in there!'

'Shield your eyes.' I raised the axe and smashed the lock on the open door. The wood splintered onto the floor. I hit it again and the door collapsed.

'Rafe, the door's open.'

'We don't want to be trapped inside after we go in.'

'We're not going in,' said Suzanne.

I stepped over the debris I had made and they followed me. 'Trust me.'

The cellar was lit by crude neon lights overhead, one flickering and sparking. The room was a low-ceilinged, damp dungeon of a place, but sparse so that I could see there was nowhere for anyone to hide and waylay us. I kept to the side of one wall, and stared at the rows and rows of wine bottles. They were dusty. Stickers with dates told me the wine was homebrewed.

The room was not heated, and should have been cool, but heat emanated from a separate room at the end of the shelves. And a noise. Shuffling, rustling and creaking. Someone was here. I peered around the shelves and looked into the room.

A quivering voice greeted us. 'Wh-who is it?'

I expected Oz. I expected the killer's lair. I expected an attack, a booby trap, but not this.

This was a voice in distress, a pleading, terrified voice. A muffled, gagged voice. And one I knew very well.

'Reverend James,' I called out.

The Reverend was in the centre of a bare storeroom, tied to a rack, the rack we had all seen upstairs in the torture museum. His arms were stretched above his head, his legs splayed out. His clothes had been removed, but he was covered in a hairy coat.

'Thank God you've come,' he said, his eyes wide, his head covered in sweat.

I reeled. Was this a trick?

'Please, I'm in agony.'

The rack had been designed to stretch and break the victim's bones. Emily pointed to the top of the device where a handle ratcheted up the pressure. She turned the handle. It was tight. 'Other way, other way,' I said.

'Slowly, please.'

'Hold this.' I gave Suzanne the axe. 'Guard him, be alert. Watch the doors. This could be a trap.'

Reverend James shook his head. 'It is a trap. He's waiting for you. For us all.'

'Who?'

'Satan.'

He couldn't have tied himself up. Did Linda do this? He looked to be in real distress, and the rack had been tightened just enough to keep him in pain but not enough to break anything. I loosened the pressure.

'Untie him,' I said.

'You sure?' said Emily. I nodded.

She used the dagger to slit the cloths that bound him. When I helped him off the rack, he could hardly move and collapsed onto the floor. Emily went to work, examining him for injury, but keeping her guard up in case he attacked. I spotted the characteristic red dot in his neck.

Suzanne gripped the axe tight, guarding the doorway.

'Where's Linda?'

His eyes were wide with terror. 'She isn't with you?'

This was not the Reverend James we had conjured up in the last day; not the murderer, the voice playing games with us.

'How long have you been here?' I asked.

'You locked me in my room, then I felt Satan's presence, the fiery darts of Satan, and found myself here. I thought hell. Forever. I don't know. I've been praying, for a miracle. An angel.'

'We thought,' said Emily. 'We thought—'

Reverend James looked down at himself. 'I'm sorry you have to see me like this. But I need to get this thing off me.'

I recognised the hair shirt we had seen on display upstairs. It had been worn by monks so they would not become too comfortable in the flesh, designed to irritate the skin, made of coarse horsehair, and this had reddened his skin. 'Here, I'll help,' I said.

'I'm not decent.'

I found his clothes in a pile on the floor. Suzanne and Emily looked the other way while I assisted him to get out of the hair shirt and into his own pants and shirt.

'I know where there are some painkillers,' Emily said, 'if you need some.'

We helped Reverend James to his feet. He could not stand by himself, so I supported him.

'That only leaves Linda,' said Emily.

Reverend James gave her a dazed look.

'She disappeared shortly after we locked you in your room. We thought she helped you escape.'

'Who did this to you?' said Suzanne.

'Demons,' he said. 'Lots of them. Satan himself presiding.'

'He's not right in the head,' whispered Suzanne.

'The drug,' Emily said to her. 'It can make you feel woozy and hallucinatory.'

I nodded. 'Tell me about it.'

'Linda?' Emily said to me.

I shook my head. 'Not by herself.'

'I still think this is a trap,' Suzanne said. 'The cellar door was open. We were led here. As if we were meant to find the Reverend. We were lured into the cellar. He gave us the clue in that speech.'

The hair at the back of my neck stood on end. I saw shadows leaping out of the dark corners of the room. But we managed to help Reverend James out of the cellar and up the steps into the living room without incident. The light outside was already fading.

In the living room, he sank into the couch. I wedged the doors open. Stood guard.

Suzanne made him a coffee, which he held with trembling hands. Emily found the first-aid kit and dispensed the painkillers.

He fell into a feverish sleep, and Emily examined his wounds. We sat beside him, in shock at discovering that our prime murder suspect was a victim. He woke an hour later in the gloom of twilight, bewildered and still trembling. Emily felt his forehead. 'Maybe a hearty meal will help, Reverend?'

Suzanne leaped up. 'I'm onto it.'

'Not alone.'

'You rest, Rafe. You're also recovering.'

We ate supper in silence. Colour came back into the Reverend's cheeks. I felt a whole lot better too.

'We thought it was you,' said Suzanne. 'Rafe read all your sermons, and how each one pointed to someone's death by torture.' She picked up his Bible and leafed through to the notes on each day of Christmas. 'And when you disappeared when some of the murders were committed, we thought it must be you.'

Reverend James snatched his Bible from Suzanne. 'I know what you were thinking. But I swear, whoever is doing this is mocking me, is mocking the Lord, using my sermons to do evil. No wonder, for even Satan disguises himself as an angel of light. I simply meant to give a homily on "The Twelve Days of Christmas" and what they mean. Not... this.' He looked sincere, bewildered.

'I thought it was you, Rafe,' he said. 'The unbeliever come to get revenge on us believers. Your book...'

I frowned. 'I'm a philosopher, not a murderer. I was nearly killed too.'

He looked afraid. 'I didn't know that.'

'The brazen bull,' I said. 'Eight maids nearly turned me into milk.'

His face was sour. 'He took my sermons and used them against me.'

'Who?' said Suzanne.

'Satan.'

I tried to steer him away from his supernatural hallucination. 'Listen to me, Reverend, concentrate. You set up the order of those cards. You planned this whole thing. Each death matches each of our transgressions, matches the *Foxe's Book of Martyrs* and matches the days of Christmas. So neat. So obvious. It had to be you.'

I thought he was going to have a fit. He leaped up and dribbled from the mouth as he stammered, 'Satan himself! Look!'

He pointed a shaking finger at the dining room table. I did for a second expect to see hellfire and brimstone, but he was pointing to Linda's placemat. I rushed towards the table, and Emily and Suzanne followed. Reverend James tried to lift himself up from his chair, but fell back again. 'Linda...'

On the table, on Linda's placemat, stood a knife stand that had not been there an hour before. From each of nine hooks on this stand hung a naked Barbie doll attached to fishing line.

I spied the nine ladies dancing card, which had been slipped under the knife stand. On it, a Bible verse had been written, as always, in Suzanne's handwriting and smothered with her sickly perfume. I read it aloud: 'Then when lust hath conceived, it bringeth forth sin: and sin, when it is finished, bringeth forth death.'

'Jesus,' I said, and looked at Emily, at Suzanne, at the Reverend whose pupils looked dilated.

He pointed a finger at the air, stared into nothing. 'Begone, Satan, in the name of Jesus Christ. Jesus Christ is Lord. Flee, Satan, flee.'

'Who did this?' said Suzanne. She walked over and then looked pale as I showed her the card with her handwriting. She sniffed it and shook her head.

'Linda's card was the ninth day of Christmas,' said Emily. 'Remember? And today is...'

'The ninth day of Christmas. January 2nd.'

'Where is she?' said Reverend James, clutching his heart. 'Where is my wife?'

'We thought,' Emily answered him, 'that you two were working together, so we don't know where she is.'

'So she's the one,' said Suzanne. 'She's the murderer.'

'We have to find her,' said Reverend James. 'I know what is going to happen to her.'

'You know because you're in on it,' I said.

He tried to stand up again. 'She got the dancing ladies card. She showed me after supper that first night. She shouldn't have, but we talked about it. It was ghastly–'

'What?'

'About Herod, about Salome dancing seductively for John

the Baptist's head. I was going to use it in my ninth-day sermon. But then after John was beheaded—'

'Stephen, you mean.'

'Stephen. Then we knew, we ɔoth knew that Satan was here, he had taken our words, and she felt she had caused his death by sinning, by... dancing. A metaphor for lust, seduction.'

'Satan's fault, no doubt,' I said, unable to keep the caustic tone from my voice.

'No, look,' said Reverend James, standing up and tottering towards me, wincing with the pain as he leaned on his left leg. 'Dancing. I know where she is.'

'Where?'

And then I knew too.

We found the torture museum just as I had left it when I had escaped – ice cold, a bellowing bull broken and on its side, the iron maiden casket holding a frozen, sagging corpse, the head of Stephen on the floor in blankets, his body wrapped in blankets on the guillotine, Alison lying by the window in a thin sheet, and an abandoned Catherine wheel broken and dismembered too. A gap where the rack had stood, the cabinet raided and toothless. A mummy in a shroud.

But this was not where Reverend James and I were looking. We were gazing up at the rafters where there were eight unclothed store dummies strung up with nooses. Only now there were nine torsos dancing there, the latest addition an emaciated woman hanging by her neck.

TEN LORDS A-LEAPING

Reverend James stared, his face ashen. 'Linda?' he whispered.

My throat constricted.

She hung limp like a dead bird, her hair over her face, a leather noose around her neck, wearing the clothes we had last seen her in when she disappeared. How long had she been here?

Suzanne's teeth chattered. 'I'm going to throw up.'

The Reverend grasped my arm, and then collapsed on the floor in a faint, dragging me down with him. My arms stung with the pain from the burns, but I stayed there and held him gently. Emily rushed over and supported his head. 'Easy, Reverend. Just take slow breaths.'

I struggled back onto my feet, looked up again. The other dummies swayed gently, but Linda hung heavy like a rock, her head drooping, her shoulders slumped in what looked like disappointment. The beam looked old. Would it support her weight or come crashing down? I reached up and touched her foot. She was ice cold. 'She's been here for hours.'

Emily left the Reverend and stood by me. We both knew

that hanging by suspension, strangulation, is a slow death. It can take up to twenty minutes, and the victim can struggle as they try to breathe and hoist themselves up to escape the noose. A painful death. But Linda looked peaceful and calm. I searched for the telltale red dart mark on her neck. When I found it, I pointed it out to Emily.

'I think she was dead already before being strung up,' Emily said, more to comfort the Reverend than anything else, I realised.

Reverend James sat up. 'He was a murderer from the beginning. He will destroy, but be broken without human agency.' Then he collapsed back down, closing his eyes.

'Easy there, Reverend,' called Emily. And to me: 'He's lost it.' I had to discount Reverend James now, this blubbering wreck of a man on the floor. And Suzanne looked incapable of such machinations.

As I looked up, I noticed that above the rafter where Linda hung was a square hatch above the door. It looked like a possible entry into the ceiling. 'She's been lowered from above, not lifted up. There's a trapdoor in the ceiling.'

'You're right,' said Emily. 'The police will have to look into that.'

'We'll all be dead before the police get here,' said Suzanne.

'Don't say that,' said Emily.

'Let's get out of this vile chamber,' I said. 'And contemplate how to make it through another night in purgatory.'

It was a grim night. All of us in one room, but this time Reverend James as an uncomfortable addition. I secured the room with as much furniture barricaded against the door as I could, locked the door (a futile gesture) and laid the mattresses out in a row of four, Reverend James tight in the middle.

Emily stayed awake. I too, was unable to sleep.

'It's unreasonable, but I still have the feeling that these two have something to do with it all,' Emily whispered.

'Hard to think of him as innocent, that's for certain. His reactions seem inconsistent,' I said.

'And she's just a class act,' whispered Emily.

I gave her a puzzled look. 'What do you mean?'

'Her behaviour. She's harbouring guilt. Not shock. I'm not saying she's the killer, but she knows something, feels guilty about it.'

'We'll see.'

Eventually Emily fell asleep. I woke Suzanne around three. She opened her eyes in terror at my touch. 'I need to get some sleep. Can you just keep an eye on things?'

'Shit. I've had such nightmares,' she said. 'Yes, of course. Go on, go to sleep.'

But I still found it difficult to sleep next to people who could be, I still believed, complicit in some way in this terrible business.

In the morning, I woke from a dead sleep. The others were just waking, looking haggard and confused. 'The Lord has given me strength,' Reverend James said. 'Praise be the Lord.'

'Well, we're alive,' I said.

'Not Linda,' said Suzanne.

'Not Linda.' Reverend James stared at her as if he only now remembered his wife's death. Then he clutched the air and fell back on the bed, pale. He closed his eyes and his mouth twitched.

'Come, Reverend, we'll get you some coffee,' said Emily. 'I wish I had some Valium.'

I removed the furniture enough for us to get out of the

door, and I stood guard while each used the toilet, this time gripping the axe tightly. I pressed my back against the toilet door so no one could jump me. We moved quickly in single-file down to the kitchen. No one was going to be out of my sight for a second, I vowed.

I was at a loss, back at square one. No, not even square one; minus one.

I worked alongside Emily and Suzanne in the kitchen as we made eggs, bacon, toast and coffee. Reverend James sat at the dining table staring into the mirror as if he did not recognise himself.

He has nothing to do with it, I thought. My prime suspects are either dead or their minds are wrecked.

Minutes later, we sat down. I sipped my syrupy coffee.

'What?' Suzanne said. 'Rafe, you're staring at me.'

'I don't mean to,' I said, and shook my head. I had not looked closely at the ceilings before, but now I saw it: a trap-door right above me, carefully designed to blend in with the ceiling boards. It had a small keyhole.

Suzanne passed me the toast. 'Rafe, I need to ask you something. You were number eight. Linda was nine. What was supposed to happen on day ten?'

Reverend James stared blankly ahead. 'I never meant this to happen. I never meant–'

'Well?' I said. 'What *did* you mean to happen?'

'The Lord told me to bring you all together and He would show you the error of your ways. To use "The Twelve Days of Christmas" to flush out sin and drive you back into His arms. I was just doing His work – repent and return to the Lord.' He looked up at the ceiling. 'Forgive me, Linda, I was going to make you confront your adultery.'

Did he really believe she was there, after death, listening to him, hovering near the ceiling of the room?

'And yours?'

He reached into his pocket with a shaking hand and brought out a piece of card folded over and over and creased, a picture of ten men in top hats, leaping over a hedge like so many racehorses.

I nodded. 'Ten lords a-leaping.'

Reverend James stared at the card he held in his hand. 'I wanted Suzanne to be ten and me eleven. That was my plan, but somehow the cards got mixed up.'

I gave him a sharp look. 'Who mixed the cards up?'

'I don't know.'

'And who's number twelve?'

'No number twelve,' said Reverend James. 'It was meant to be a wrap-up of what we learned during the retreat. There are – were only ten of us at the retreat. The partridge in the pear tree was meant to be the beginning – putting Christ at the centre of our retreat. Then ten verses. Twelve drummers drumming were to be the triumphant end of the cleansing, forgiveness of the Lord, all our sins purged. Meant to be. Not this, not this.' He swallowed and his eyes teared up. 'I didn't mean this to happen, I swear. Any of it.'

'Again, just tell me what you meant to happen.'

'I sat down with Stephen and we ordered all these days, put The Twelve in order of each day. I thought it would be a neat way of learning about "The Twelve Days of Christmas". A perfect twelve-day sermon. We even talked about using the torture instruments as teaching visuals. One for each day.'

I stood up in shock. 'What? You knew?'

His eyes looked terrified as I leaned over him. His lips quivered as he spoke. 'Yes. Each person had a day, a torture instrument assigned. On the second day I was going to talk about adultery and stoning, the third day I was going to show us all the guillotine to talk about beheading, the fourth day–' He held his heart. 'If I had only known that–'

I jabbed him in the chest. 'So you planned these macabre deaths.'

Emily held my shoulders and I pulled back, winced at the pain. Took a deep breath. 'Go on.'

'No. Linda made all the cards, I planned the sermons: they fitted so neatly, and I felt God guiding my thoughts. I never thought... it would really happen. I can't believe it. And Linda... Linda. We planned the correspondence between the deaths of martyrs and the torture instruments. Sorry, Rafe, the bull... But we never dreamt of actually carrying any of it out. It was meant to be a morality play.'

I faced the large living room mirror and stared at his reflection. 'So you knew, as each death happened. As if you had foretold each one. It was no surprise to you. You knew what was going to happen next. And you never said anything. That's despicable.'

He stared into nothing.

'Who else knew? Who did you tell? Who did you plan this with? The concierge? Did you sit down with the owner and discuss which torture instruments would correlate with each day?'

'No, no. Only Glen, Stephen and Linda. And now it's all coming true. Like a prophecy. A ghastly Satanic prophecy. And now we are all going to die, just the way I planned it.'

'The Pear of Anguish didn't work, thank God,' said Emily, putting her hand on his shoulder. 'And Rafe escaped death too. It's not inevitable. Not predestined, as you used to say in Church.'

He squeezed the blanket over his chest and spoke in a strangled whisper. 'Linda didn't escape.'

'I'm so sorry.' Suzanne took the Reverend's hand. He looked a million years old.

Strange this, I thought. This odious man had ruined our lives, and here we were, comforting him.

I, however, was not so merciful. 'Reverend, tell me what the *Foxe's Book of Martyrs* says about the tenth day,' I said. 'Who was martyred on the tenth day of Christmas, and how?'

He shook his head. 'No one. I didn't plan to expose my own... sins.'

I ran my hands though my hair. 'Of course bloody not! So what is going to happen today, do you think? What is the torture weapon you planned for today to teach us sinners some God-awful lesson?'

'Don't blaspheme, Rafe.'

'Goddamn. I'm serious. There's a system here, and whoever is doing all this is going by your book, Reverend James. Your sermon. Has worked it out to the letter. Nine ladies dancing, seven spokes of the Catherine wheel–'

'I don't understand the eight milkmaids,' said Emily. 'I didn't see how the bull had eight anything.'

'I counted,' I said, 'while I was inside. Eight apertures: four teats, two nostrils, two eyes. Believe me, I was grateful for those apertures. They kept me alive long enough to escape. I could breathe through them.'

'So what torture instrument upstairs has ten features?' said Emily. 'The rack? It has a number of rungs. Was it ten?'

'I can't remember,' said the Reverend. 'I wasn't counting, I can tell you that.'

'Or that device I saw in the cabinet where each finger is crushed in a device,' I said. 'Ten fingers?'

'Who is this sick person?' said Suzanne. 'Who?'

'The recording said he was one of us,' I said, looking at each in turn. 'Which one of us?'

'Don't be stupid, Rafe,' said Suzanne. 'It can't be one of us.' He just wanted to pit us against each other.'

'I agree,' I said. 'Maybe that was indeed a red herring. Reverend, did you meet the owner, the mad collector of these exhibits?'

Reverend James shook his head. 'It was arranged on a website, advertised as a B&B. Stephen and Glen made all the arrangements.'

But Stephen and Glen were dead.

'What about the concierge?' said Emily. 'We all met him. He organised the whole trip for us, chauffeuring us all in, bringing food. Did he...'

I pictured the small man, with his delicate fingers and birthmark on his hand. 'But what motive would he have? Unless one of us put him up to this? You, for instance, Reverend James. And now you create your own alibi by having him tie you up on the rack so you look like the victim.'

'Come to think of it, the concierge was rather creepy,' said Emily. 'As if he had some interest in keeping us here.'

I looked at her sharply. She shrugged. 'Just a feeling. No concrete evidence. Just creepy. Hanging around.'

'What motive would anyone have to kill all of us?' said Suzanne.

'I'm sure you made enemies at some time,' I said to the Reverend. 'Be honest. Someone might have had a vendetta against you.'

'Some disgruntled parishioner who didn't get his way?' said Emily.

He pursed his lips. 'Our only enemy is Satan himself.'

We sat in silence. But I now had a plan. 'I believe Linda's body was lowered through the trapdoor in the ceiling. I am going up there to investigate. And you are all going to stay put and let me get on with it, because whether the murderer is among us or someone from the outside, we are all going to be dead soon if I don't.'

Suzanne and Emily sat at the table, sipping coffee. Reverend

James sat between them. I took a flashlight and a butcher's knife from a kitchen drawer and slipped into the shadow of the corridor. I waited, listened, then climbed up the steps, negotiated the darkness of the corridor to the torture museum and pushed open the door. The place was ink-dark. I switched on the flashlight. Held my breath. Listened for any movement or presence, but heard only the silence of death.

The open window looked out on to whiteness. Stillness. And the room was a fridge. As Emily had said, it made a good morgue, and the dead bodies were being kept cool. I stuck the knife into a loop on the back of my pants and put the flashlight in my shirt pocket so my hands would be free.

Linda's body dangled slowly in the air, with her eight partners. I positioned one of the display cabinets under the square hatch in the ceiling and climbed up. If I stretched, and held on to the top of the door, I could reach the lip of the trapdoor and push it open. A black hole opened up behind it. I pulled myself up and into the ceiling near the doorway.

Catching my breath, I listened.

A gust of cold air blew into my face, and as I shone my flashlight around, the shape of the attic became visible. I could see a criss-cross of wooden beams; this part of the castle had been renovated and bolstered with modern wooden supports. With disbelief, I noted something incredible: along the beams ran a planked pathway that seemed to travel the full length of the space. And running alongside and flush with the path was a metal railing. I realised what this was – some sort of monorail. I had heard of mansions and castles with systems of pulleys and rails so servants and tradesmen could transport goods to the various locations inside. And I knew that some houses had a network of servants' passages above the vast dining rooms and kitchens to facilitate the movement of goods and food.

And here, to facilitate the movement of dead bodies.

I flashed my light down the line to the left which came to

an abrupt stop at the other end of the torture museum where I
noticed the top of a ladder. I walked along the rail, balancing
myself by pressing my hands against the roof above me, and
peered over the edge. The ladder was very long, and I
surmised that it must lead down to the trapdoor I'd seen in the
living room ceiling.

I shone my light to the right and the line gleamed silver.
It looked used, not rusted or dull. I decided to follow it. I
edged my way along, balancing on the rail and steadying
myself by pushing my hands along the roof beams, and
came to a fork where the rail bifurcated. I remembered the
layout of the rooms. The left branch led to the women's
wing, the right to the men's. I was about to take the left fork,
when I saw that the left rail was blocked by a dark
rectangular shape.

I stopped. Caught my breath. Listened. Touched the
object. It was metal. A trolley, I saw now, an open carriage. I
gave it a shove and it slid along the rail easily. Well oiled. Well
used. Silent. And, I thought, it was strong enough to carry a
dead or unconscious body. Now I knew how he – they – had
done it all.

Seeing as this passage was blocked by the trolley, I inched
my way along the right fork, above the men's rooms, I guessed.
Was it my imagination, or was I seeing little flashing red lights
at odd intervals? And then I saw the next thing that stunned
me: not just one, but a whole series of trapdoors on either side,
which I presumed led down to the various rooms below – the
Reverend's, Danny's, Stephen's, Mike's, mine.

In each trapdoor I spotted a tiny spyhole in the middle, a
lens grouted into it, wires leading to a flashing red light to the
side. I crawled along, checking each trapdoor, trying to guess
which room it led down to.

I was amazed. It seemed that each room in the castle had
access from above, even the ground-floor living area.

I saw it all now. The castle had been chosen because it allowed precisely this secret mobility for the killer.

I followed the rail line to the end of the passage where I guessed the men's bathroom was, and stopped suddenly. A flat rectangle of light seeped from underneath a door at the end. I held my breath. Listened. Tried to make out what this was.

I heard the hum of some equipment inside.

I pulled the knife out, held it in my right hand and flattened my body against the door. It was, of course, possible that the killer was not one of us. That he was in this room, at this very minute.

I was shaking badly, my heart racing, my breathing shallow.

I counted to three and pushed on the door, gently. But it would not open. I shoved it harder and though it clicked and rattled, it would not budge.

Damn. I backed away, watching for any movement.

I could try smashing it. But I knew I would not get far enough if someone was inside. If someone already knew I was here. I turned and tracked back, and as I got to each trapdoor, I yanked out the wires and the cameras, and the flashing red lights died. One room, two rooms, three rooms, four rooms, five rooms – all the men's bedrooms. Then I crawled along the other fork, pushed the carriage silently ahead of me and took out the cameras spying on the women's rooms: one room, two rooms, three rooms, four rooms. The bathroom at the end.

Then I turned back, found the trapdoor where I had climbed up, and pulled out those wires. Opposite the rail was another trapdoor – leading down to the library, I presumed, as that was adjacent to the torture museum, and I pulled out that camera and wires too.

Whew. I was trembling, but glad I had done this. I peered down the right fork again to see if I had been observed, but the rail was silent, and the door at the end still shut.

I peered down and readied myself to climb back into the

torture museum, to lower myself and jump onto the desk I had placed below, when my sixth sense – my intuition, that finely tuned scientific and rational machination of the brain – told me that something was amiss.

The air was different under me; a foreign smell, the sound was different, as if something had been displaced. All this told me to stop. As I shone my flashlight down and made sense of what I saw, I flicked off the light and pulled myself up quickly, my heart thudding in my ears.

The desk had been removed below. In its place, the killer had positioned that deadly torture device, the Judas Cradle, directly underneath the opening in the ceiling. If I had dropped down, I would have been impaled on it.

The Judas Cradle was a tall, four-legged wooden stool with a sharply pointed metal pyramid on top. Used primarily in the Spanish Inquisition, victims would be lowered onto the 'chair', making the pyramid enter the vagina or anus.

The only way down without being impaled on that device was to climb down the rope where Linda was hanging. My fall would not be that long if I used her as leverage. I pocketed the knife, and then made sure the beam would support my weight by hanging on to the rope that was tying her to the beam. So far, so good. I slithered down, felt her icy face and shoulders as I threw myself wide of the cradle and landed hard on the floor.

I immediately sprung up into attack position, pulled out the knife. The killer could be in the room waiting for me.

I listened. Could hear nothing.

What I was feeling – apart from shock and pain from landing on a cold stone floor from the height of the ceiling – was outrage. Not fear. Not terror. Anger. How dare this person try to do this to me? And was this killer in the close inner circle of survivors, or an outside madman hiding in these castle walls? What sadistic bastard would think of this? The owner of the castle, a mad collector of torture instruments, itching to use them on an unsuspecting group of guests? His concierge a gleeful accomplice? Whoever it was, this was personal now. This killer had stalked me, knew my every movement, had declared war on me. In that instant, I made a vow to get this person, no matter what it took.

Harnessing that anger was easy. My will swelled to righteous size. I was capable of anything now. I could kill with my bare hands if necessary.

He could still be in the room, or could have returned to the living room. Call me paranoid, but for a moment I thought all three remaining could be in on this.

I shone the flashlight in every corner of the room then edged towards the door, aware that there might be other booby traps set here for me. I checked for wires across at throat level, metal traps at my feet. But I reached the door without incident. Maybe the killer was an outsider in the control room, watching his cameras go out one by one. Or lurking somewhere in the passage planning his next murder.

The exit door from the torture museum was closed.

A cold chill of claustrophobia shivered through me. I pushed against it.

The door was locked.

Of course.

I slid along the wall, felt my way to the library door. But that was also locked.

The killer knew my every movement. He had locked me in. Maybe it was my turn to die now.

But not yet. I looked for a better weapon. I browsed the various implements. Tongue-remover. Fingernail-gouger. Spiker. Then I found my weapon of choice. A wooden hammer with a spear-like spike on the fore-end of the haft. 'War hammer, or maul', read the label. 'Fourteenth century'.

I gripped the maul tight in both hands and raised it above

my head. *Let's see what you're made of, hammer of Thor.*

The door was hard and would not splinter or break. I made no dent on the lock at all.

I looked at the wide-open window. An obvious exit. But it was on the first floor and there was a sheer drop to the courtyard. And the cold was inhibitive.

But the snow was deep.

Here goes. Ten lords a-leaping.

I flew out of the window, the maul in my right hand. Felt for a second that deceptive buoyancy before gravity kicks in, then I was plummeting straight towards the courtyard. I hoped the snowdrifts would be deep enough.

I crashed through an icy layer and sank up to my armpits in snow. Quickly, I struggled up so I would not be buried. Beneath the surface, the snow was powdery. I crawled, pushed, waded towards the front of the castle.

The cold was starting to bite and I was wet. And freezing.

I hunted for the maul. I had let it go as I landed and it was buried somewhere in two metres of snow. No hope of finding it now. I dug my way across the courtyard, around the side of the castle, towards the front door.

I was so intent on getting there that I almost missed it – a single garage, tucked away at the back of an old horse stall. The garage doors were ill-fitting, rusted away, and chained together with a new padlock – but they had been pushed half-open by a snowdrift. At eye level I could see a glimmer of red inside.

I saw the gleam of a bumper, a licence plate, a tyre.

First thought: we drive out of here! Emily and Suzanne and me. Or just me. Get the police. But as I wrestled through the snow, I could not imagine anything but a snowmobile getting us very far at all. And this did not look like one. But still. I waded through the snow and peered into the garage, where drifts had piled up inside the doors.

And then I felt giddy. I stared again, not quite believing what I was seeing.

The car was a Fiat Uno. If I was not mistaken, the very same car I had arrived in ten days ago.

But the concierge had driven away. Or so Reverend James had told me.

The whole ten days rewrote itself. That niggling suspicion about him, Emily's intuition – all gelled now. Reality – what we call reality but is only a kaleidoscope of impressions and assumptions and narrative constructions – shifted and adjusted itself. Pieces of the puzzle clicked into place. Not all of them, but enough.

The front door was unlocked. I shook myself off in the hallway and walked over to the living room. I found my three remaining fellow guests exactly as I had left them, huddling by the fire.

I decided to keep the discovery of the concierge's car to myself, for now – until I figured out exactly what it meant. But an idea was forming in my mind.

'Thank God you're safe,' said Suzanne. 'We were so worried about you.'

'Rafe, you're soaked,' said Emily, leaping up. 'What happened?'

'I just need to thaw out,' I said, moving over to the fire.

'I'll bring you something hot to drink,' said Suzanne.

'You okay?' said Reverend James.

'Did you hear anything upstairs?' I asked. I scrutinised each face in turn. But no one revealed anything amiss.

Emily shook her head. 'I did hear some banging, foot-steps, but I thought it was you. What were you doing outside?'

'I want to know if you were here all the time I was gone. Give me your word that no one left the room.'

They looked puzzled. No one had left the room, they assured me.

I was dry pretty quickly in front of that blazing fire, but the trembling would not stop.

'Thank God you're okay, Rafe,' said Suzanne. 'We were worried.'

'You all right, Rafe?' said Emily. 'You look, I don't know, wild.'

'Tell us what you found,' said Suzanne.

'I need to show you all something. I want you all to come with me. No one stays behind. I want everyone to see exactly what I saw – and then we will find the killer. But first of all we need to find a ladder.'

'I saw one in the back of the pantry,' said Emily. 'Why? Where are we going?'

'Back into the torture museum, and up into the ceiling.'

'What? You went up?'

I nodded. Watched each face carefully.

Suzanne shuddered. 'I'm not going up there.'

'We all are.' I herded them into a group. 'I'm not going to wait for the next clever little trick, the next torture device. We go after the killer. We find an appropriate torture device to string him or her up.'

For a response, Reverend James fell to the ground, clutching his stomach.

'Get him some water.' Emily knelt by his side and felt his brow.

'What's wrong with him?'

'I'm okay,' said Reverend James, struggling to speak. But he clearly was not. He leaned over to one side and retched, vomiting up the contents of his last meal. His brow felt clammy and he looked feverish, and kept shivering even after we moved him near the fire and wrapped him in a blanket.

He sat, mute, on the couch. It was clear he was going nowhere today.

Instead of leading the charge to the hidden room, I had to wait in awful tension, anticipating attack. Reverend James was delirious, spouting Bible verses, pointing at me and Suzanne, and pushing Emily away when she tried to give him water to sip.

'It's all been too much for him,' said Suzanne, 'and me.'

My stomach suddenly clenched with fright. 'Was it something he ate?'

Emily said, 'Could be. Either some bug he picked up or food poisoning. If it's food poisoning, it should pass through his system soon.'

'Food poisoning,' said Suzanne. 'But we ate what he ate, and we're fine.'

'You prepared the meal,' I said to Suzanne.

She glared at me. 'Meaning?'

I shook my head. 'I'm just saying.'

'Do you think I–' Suzanne gave me a look of pure venom. 'After all we talked about. I trusted you! I–' She stormed off into the kitchen.

'Suzanne. Please. Stay here. We can't trust anyone anymore. It's nothing personal.'

I found the aluminium ladder propped up against the back wall of the pantry. I pulled it out and hauled it to the living room. This would allow us to go up into the living room ceiling and into that recess I had seen from above at the end of the rail.

But by afternoon, Reverend James had fallen into a feverish sleep on the couch. Emily mopped his brow with a damp cloth. 'He's burning up and dehydrated.' She kept giving him sips of cold water, but most of the time this dribbled down his chin and he pushed her away.

Suzanne hovered around the couch where he lay. 'Will he be okay?'

Emily nodded. 'If it's a normal case of food poisoning, yes, in twenty-four hours.'

'We don't have twenty-four hours,' I said.

'But,' she added, 'if it's something more serious…'

I did not want to go off again and leave him here alone. So we waited.

I feared sabotage. I feared that this was his death sentence. Poisoning. That because he didn't die on the rack, the murderer had devised another form of torture for him. Maybe one of the early Church martyrs in the *Foxe's Book of Martyrs* had been poisoned on the tenth day of Christmas.

Some hours later in the afternoon, he was sleeping more peacefully, but still not fit enough to move let alone climb into the attic. As it was getting dark, I resigned myself to holding out for another long night. What use was it that the pieces of the puzzle were coming together when we were still trapped here at the mercy of the killer?

We stood in the kitchen that evening making supper. We were wary of the food now, but I took charge, searching for alternatives to the food that had been prepared for us. We were starving and had to get our strength up for the final assault, which would be, I decided, early the next day.

'I'm not accusing you of anything,' I said to Suzanne, who was still not speaking to me. 'Just looking at every possibility.'

To replace the pot roast designated for tonight's meal, labelled and frozen in a Tupperware container, I found some cans of chicken soup, which I figured would be safe because they were sealed, had not expired, and on inspection, had not been opened and resealed. Emily gave the Reverend some dry crackers, but he could not hold anything down and could only manage a few sips of water.

We served the soup in the dining area and ate cautiously. And we agreed that from now on, we would avoid the food left for us by the concierge. Just in case.

I had to figure out the safest place to sleep. Every room had a trapdoor in the ceiling, and even though I had ripped out as many cameras as I could, there still might be more, and the murderer, or murderers, had access to any room they chose. I decided that my room was safest. So we spent the evening hauling mattresses into my room, then pushing the desk to the centre of the room and wedging a bed against the ceiling so the trapdoor could not be opened.

Reverend James could hardly walk, but with two of us supporting him, he made it up the stairs and collapsed on a bed. Emily tucked him in. 'Food poisoning is intense but short. Let's hope that's all it is and he'll be all right in the morning.'

Now that we were all inside the room, we shoved the heavy wardrobe in front of the door. While Suzanne was making her bed in the other corner of the room, Emily whispered to me: 'Tell me about this plan of yours.'

'It would spoil the surprise.'

She pouted. 'You still don't trust me?'

I pointed up. 'I pulled out the camera wires I could see, but the room could still be bugged. Just trust me. Do you trust me?'

'Of course.' But the look she gave me told me otherwise.

ELEVEN PIPERS PIPING

'Rafe, Rafe, wake up.'

A grey light poured in from the window. Morning. Suzanne was shaking my shoulder. She looked like a ghost. Emily was crouched over Reverend James.

I sat up. 'How is he?'

Emily's face was expressionless as she turned to me. 'He's dead.'

I sat up. 'My God! What happened?' I immediately looked up at the trapdoor then at the door. Both remained secure, as we had left them.

She shook her head, then opened his mouth and examined his tongue. 'I was so stupid, I really thought it was just food poisoning. But his heart stopped. He has been deliberately poisoned, Rafe. With something powerful.'

I reached over and took his pulse. He was stone cold. 'Right in front of us.'

'We couldn't have done anything,' said Emily. 'Truly. He needed hospitalisation.'

I swore. 'The tenth day. Bang on schedule. Right under our

noses. So there was poison in his food. But we were all in the kitchen. When could this have happened?'

The way we looked at one another, I knew now that we all harboured suspicions of one another. Emily shot Suzanne a quick glance, Suzanne returned a hostile one, then they both stared at me. Any of us could have easily slipped cyanide into Reverend James' food. I wished I could tell them what I knew, but that would have to wait. I was not sure of what I knew yet.

Suzanne bit her lip. 'Hey, we all helped make breakfast. And I swear, I'm not eating another thing here. Not now.'

'Suicide is also a possibility,' said Emily. 'I mean he just saw his wife hanged, his flock tortured and murdered. And maybe he knew more than he was letting on. Maybe he took cyanide or something. Maybe…'

I nodded. 'He knew something, all right. But now he'll take it to the grave with him.'

'What do we do?' said Suzanne.

I considered. 'We leave him here. Open the window to keep his body cold. And we go downstairs.'

I dragged the dresser away from the door and, armed, we moved in a tight trio down the stairs and into the kitchen. Again, we went through the motions of a normal morning. I made coffee, being careful to use sealed coffee packets, bottled water and ultra-pasteurised milk in packets. We sat at the dining room table, opposite the mirror. 'Not for me,' said Suzanne as I poured her a cup. 'I told you, nothing is touching my lips from now on.' She glared at me.

The Christmas tree still blinked its garish lights, and the tinsel sparkled in the firelight. 'Can't we take that stupid tree down?' said Emily.

'According to tradition, not until the twelfth night of Christmas,' said Suzanne.

I marched over and unplugged the lights. An eerie glow still emanated from the mirror, like an afterimage of the tree lights.

'Look!' Emily pointed at Reverend James' place at the table. The mat was newly decorated with ten Sir Topham Hatt figurines from a *Thomas the Tank Engine* playset around a document. I turned on my flashlight to see a list of the Ten Commandments torn from a Bible, and a chilling Bible verse scrawled underneath in Suzanne's handwriting:

Their throat is an open sepulchre; with their tongues they have used deceit; the poison of asps is under their lips – Romans 3:13

'Poison of asps,' said Emily. 'The killer is telling us how he did it.'

'Snake venom under his tongue,' said Suzanne.

'Maybe not literally,' I replied. 'But the killer wants us know that Reverend James was poisoned.'

'And so,' said Emily to herself but so we could hear her, 'the killer moves on, relentlessly, day after day, and we still have no clue who it is. What day is it today? The eleventh day?'

Suzanne shivered and hugged her stomach. 'The fourth of January. My day.'

'He didn't get Rafe or me,' said Emily. 'Suzanne, he won't get you today. We can beat him.'

Suzanne gave Emily a pointed look. 'Or her. Or them.'

'No one dies from now on,' I said.

'That's what you said two days ago.' Suzanne's eyes were daggers. 'You said you'd keep us safe. I don't trust you at all. You said–'

'Calm down,' said Emily. 'We need to all calm down.'

Suzanne now lashed out at Emily. 'Sure. Reverend James dies in the same room we're sleeping in and you say calm down. I'm supposed to die today and we haven't been able to escape this hellhole or stop the killer, and you say calm down. You and your smug little conspiracy, you and Rafe. I swear, I think sometimes–'

I placed myself between them, but I could see in her eyes

what she thought. 'We're all in shock, Suzanne,' I said. 'But we can't lose it. Not now. I have a plan. I know what to do.'

She laid her head on the dining room table and pulled her hands over her head. 'I can't take this anymore.'

Was it just me, or did Emily also sense that Suzanne's behaviour looked like a melodramatic performance? Maybe I was being ridiculously insensitive here. I had not taken her off the suspects list, not since the first murder.

Suzanne took three long breaths, then sat up. 'Sorry, guys. It's really getting to me. Tell me what we can do.'

'We need to see the modus operandi of this killer,' I said. 'The eleventh day. Let me read his sermon.' I reached over to open Reverend James' Bible and leafed through his sermon notes.

'But if the Reverend is dead now, then he didn't orchestrate all this…' said Suzanne.

'It doesn't make sense, I know,' I said. 'I was sure Reverend James was behind all this, had planned this whole thing. He even confessed he had organised the twelve days to unfold like this. But now I'm not sure.'

'What does his sermon for today say?' said Emily.

'The eleventh day of Christmas,' said Suzanne. 'Eleven pipers piping. Whatever that means.'

'Eleven faithful disciples,' I read. 'And one traitor. One betrayer of The Twelve.'

Emily leaned over. 'Read us his sermon, Rafe.'

'It's not a good one.' I skimmed through his notes. 'Babylon. Eve. Seduction. Lilith. How women are temptresses and seductresses of men. A Biblical verse about some great whore committing fornication…' I turned the page. 'Temptresses, blasphemers, adulterers, Hollywood is the new Babylon, sex the new Babylonian religion. This is such shit.'

Suzanne grabbed the Bible notes from me and peered at

them, her hand shaking. 'He always said Hollywood was like Sodom and Gomorrah. Like Babylon.'

I took the Bible from her and slammed it shut. 'We're going on a treasure hunt,' I said. 'Get warm things on. We're going outside.'

Emily wrapped her cardigan tightly around her. 'I thought we were going up into the ceiling.' She pointed at the ladder propped up in the living room.

Suzanne eyed me with distrust. 'I don't know. Why should we come with you?'

'Because I don't want anyone else to die, that's why.'

Through the window, the sun was a white Communion wafer climbing into the weak blue sky. The snow glowed on the ground. The valley was smothered in a deep blanket of snow.

It would be all over soon. I could sense it. This was the endgame.

'Where are we going?' said Suzanne.

At the entrance hall closet we pulled on warm clothes and jackets, plus hats, scarves and gloves, and headed for the front door. I gripped the axe. I would go nowhere now without this weapon. I expected the door to be locked, but it wasn't. I opened it.

The snow looked incongruously beautiful, glittery and white, and as the sun strengthened, I could feel warmth on my face. I took it as a promise. And even though it was well below zero, I felt it refresh my spirit. It cleared the mind.

We stepped into the deep snow and shuffled around the walls of the castle.

'Stay close,' I said.

I would not, could not, risk leaving any of them alone again.

I located the fuse box at head level under the eaves of an overhanging gargoyle, a demon eagle perching on the edge. The door to the fuse box was open, and inside I spied fuses in neat rows and a wheel going around measuring electric current. Main switch. Up: on. Down: off.

I opened the fuse box and switched the main power off. And for good measure, I raised the heavy axe into the air, brought it down and smashed the fuse box.

'Here goes nothing,' I said.

'What are you doing?' said Emily, clutching my arm.

'Are you crazy?' said Suzanne. 'We need power.'

She looked at me, and in her eyes I could see her thoughts. I was the killer. I had led them all outside to kill them. She cowered up against Emily.

But Emily, I was sure, was thinking the same about her. Who had served Reverend James food yesterday? Suzanne. It would have been easy for her to slip some poison into his food or water. Yet she acted so sincere, so afraid today. But the key word was 'acted'. She acted so well in her movies, this role would be a cinch.

Emily shrugged. 'Great plan, Rafe. Would you mind telling us why you've just cut the power?'

I huddled them close to me. 'Simply, we have to render any cameras or electronic door mechanisms inoperable. The murderers need power to control things. And now, our next step.' I led them back to the front door.

Inside, the living and dining room and the kitchen were dark and foreboding. Embers glowed in the fireplace.

I did not want to let go of the axe, so I directed Emily to place the stepladder underneath the square trapdoor in the middle of the ceiling. I watched both of them carefully for their reactions. 'It's going to be dark up there.' I steadied the ladder. 'We're going on a ceiling tour. You first, Em,' I said, indicating the steps.

Emily held back. 'Why don't you go first?'

'I'm going last. And I went up yesterday. It's okay.'

She shrugged. I held the ladder while she climbed.

'Now just give the trapdoor a shove,' I said. 'And then go in. Turn on your flashlight, and move forward so we can follow.'

She climbed up, pushed the trapdoor upwards and loosened it. It gave easily, revealing the dark, musty space above the room. She shone her flashlight into the void then climbed up.

'There should be a tall ladder ahead of you, am I correct?' Emily called down. 'Yes... right here.'

'Now you, Suzanne,' I prompted.

'Me? I'm not going up there.'

'You'll be fine,' I said. 'Em's up there already.'

She shook her head. 'You go. I'll wait here.'

'We're all going.'

'Come, Suzanne,' called Emily.

Suzanne shuddered, but then something seemed to shift in her, as if she had realised we had no choice but to trust each other. She shook out her bandanna hairband and retied as a headscarf. 'It might be dusty up there,' she explained.

I came up behind them, into the cavity between roof and ceiling, one hand still clutching the axe, the flashlight in my top pocket. I placed the axe on the ledge inside the space.

Flashlights flickered, dispelling the darkness and revealing a wall and ladder leading to the secret passageway. This is what I had seen from above.

'Now climb the ladder.'

'I can't make out what this metal thing is,' said Emily when she'd reached the top.

When we had all reached the top, I urged her forward on

the rail. 'A secret railroad of sorts,' I said. 'Leading to trap-doors that lead to all of the rooms.'

'I never would have thought…' said Emily.

I urged them forward, keeping Suzanne in the middle.

Across the passageway we went, over the torture museum to the right, the library to the left, and then taking the right fork, over the men's bedrooms.

Until we came to the door.

'Stop!' I hissed. 'Let me go ahead now.' I squeezed past Suzanne, balancing on the metal line to get to the door. I gripped the axe with one hand, pushed the door with the other.

It opened a crack.

Light flickered on the inside.

But I had turned off the electricity. Maybe this room had its own source of power. If it was what I suspected it was, that would be likely.

I burst into the room, axe at the ready.

Emily and Suzanne stood behind, holding on to me.

No one was there.

The room, the size of a small bathroom, glowed and flick-ered with candlelight. Candles stood everywhere – on a wide desk, on top of a computer and to the sides of two computer screens. An empty console chair stood in the middle. A control room. With no controller to be seen.

The scent hit me hard – Suzanne's perfume.

No shadows for a killer to hide. No cupboard he could spring out of. No trapdoor. This room was hermetically sealed and this was the only entrance.

But such light! The candles illuminated the walls. And the many pictures on display, looking like a gallery of revered work, some holy of holies.

'You've been here before,' said Emily.

'It was locked last time,' I said. 'Come in, Emily, Suzanne.'

They stared.

'I'll guard the door,' said Emily. 'It must be a trap.'

Suzanne pointed. 'Look.'

The pictures were not works of art. They had been cut from the pages of high-flying glossy magazines. There were newspaper cut-outs, enlarged copies of those cut-outs. And other, older photos.

All featuring one person.

The fear of being attacked or discovered was forgotten.

'My God,' said Suzanne.

'It's you,' said Emily.

I could not believe what I was seeing either. The heady perfume intoxicated me. This was sensory overload, a garish nightmare.

'I'm looking, I'm looking.'

Suzanne at the Oscars. Suzanne on holiday. Suzanne in her major role in that Tahitian movie.

All Suzanne.

Polaroids of Suzanne at school, as a sixteen-year-old, marching with the drum majorettes. Suzanne on the stage for her crowning of the Miss Riverside High School pageant.

'I don't know what this means,' said Emily.

Suzanne trembled as she moved from image to image, recognising her past, sometimes puzzled. 'Who took this picture? This is me in my old room at home from my school days.'

I pointed to the computer desk, at a display, surrounded by candles. 'Look.'

I gripped the axe tighter. In the centre of the console was the message.

A miniature ballerina dancing on a carousel, and around her – and I had no need to count – eleven little figures, plastic fawns playing flutes and panpipes.

'Eleven pipers piping,' whispered Emily.

'I'm scared,' said Suzanne.

The inscription underneath was not flattering. Emily read the verses aloud, her voice trembling. 'Come hither; I will shew unto thee the judgement of the great whore that sitteth upon many waters: With whom the kings of the earth have committed fornication, and the inhabitants of the earth have been made drunk with the wine of her fornication.' She paused, and then continued, 'And the ten horns which thou sawest upon the beast, these shall hate the whore, and shall make her desolate and naked, and shall eat her flesh, and burn her with fire.'

I nodded. 'Straight from the Reverend's sermon I read today.'

Suzanne whispered, 'What does it mean?'

'It means that someone is taking Reverend James' sermons very literally,' I said. 'All planned to the letter. Even after his death.'

'And it means someone knows our every move,' said Emily. She pointed to a red light flashing on the console above a tiny fish-eye camera lens. 'We're being watched. Someone can see everything.'

'Not anymore,' I said. I walked over, pulled a bit of adhesive putty off the side of the table and stuck it over the camera lens. 'Any more cameras?'

I spotted a spherical camera on top of a filing cabinet in the corner and used more adhesive putty to obscure the lens. I looked at the faces of my two companions. They were blank with fear.

'Interesting how this must have a separate source of power,' I said, examining the console. 'We may have turned off the main power to the castle, but this room is still wired.' I flipped a switch on the console and the room flooded with light. The computer fired up and the monitors sparked into life. A row of switches on the console glowed green beneath the printed words: *Door One. Door Two. Door Three.* All the way up to *Door Twenty-four.*

'This is what I want.' I studied the console switches.

'Look!' said Emily. 'The monitors.'

Dimly lit hallways.

I flipped a down switch and a lock clicked behind me.

'He's locked us in,' said Suzanne.

'No,' I said. 'I've locked us in.'

I flipped all the switches. 'This is how it works. Now all doors are locked – those still operational. And closed. Don't look so worried. You're safe here with me.'

I played with the monitors. 'Here are the views – what's left of them – of the castle. The living room. Oh, and the kitchen. Library. But none of these others work – they must be the bedroom cameras I disabled.'

'My God.' Suzanne picked up a shiny object from the desk.

'That looks like your ring,' I said. 'The one Glen was wearing on his little finger. I saw it on his body in the snow.'

'You didn't tell me that.'

'Whoever is doing this is doing it because of you.'

Suzanne looked pallid. 'You mean he took it off Glen's corpse?'

'As a trophy, perhaps,' said Emily.

'I think I'm getting it now. Glen was punished for his obsession with you.'

'That's what this is all about,' said Emily. 'It's all about you, Suzanne.'

I nodded. 'All those notes you supposedly wrote. They were to lure the victims, but also to judge them, to expose their true intentions.'

'The perfume—'

'I swear, I never did this.' Suzanne backed herself up against the back wall. 'I'm scared. Really scared.'

Emily embraced her.

'I thought at first Reverend James, or whoever the killer is, was trying to frame you,' I said. 'That you were there at each death. But then I thought, *No, this is someone's obsession.* And it is.'

'I also thought it was Reverend James,' said Emily. 'Punishing us all for what we did.'

'We're all part of the game,' I said, 'like interlocking pieces of a puzzle. Suzanne, Reverend James, Emily and me. We're all needed to play this game. But who is controlling it?'

'You know it's not me,' said Emily.

'Nor me,' said Suzanne.

'So there is an outside killer after all,' said Emily. 'There's no way any of us are involved here. It's the concierge. The owner of the castle.'

Suzanne nodded. 'I knew he was creepy.'

'Was he a fan of yours, perhaps? The concierge.'

Suzanne shook her head. 'When he was serving food, he ignored me completely. I don't think he even knew who I was.'

'Maybe the owner is an obsessive fan,' said Emily. 'But we don't know what he wants.'

'Obviously you, Suzanne,' I said. 'And obviously to punish us all for our various crimes – including being involved with you in some way. The Twelve. I don't know. He never meant to kill you. The eleventh day is for you.'

She shook her head. 'No.' She pointed out the last part of the verse we had read on the console. '"…shall make her desolate and naked, and shall eat her flesh, and burn her with fire." Does that sound like he never meant to… doesn't mean to kill me?'

I now hugged her too. 'We'll never let it happen.'

Emily sat at the console, brushed the display of the eleven pipers piping to one side, and tapped the keyboard. A computer screen blinked to life.

I peered at the screen. 'Emily, what are you doing?'

'If we have computers up here, we may have internet

access. Maybe we can call the police, dial 999, or whatever it is in Italy.' She hunched over the keyboard and began typing. 'My God, we have internet access, I think.'

'Get the police,' said Suzanne. 'Get the cops. Quick.'

'And the ambulance, fire engine, helicopter, the lot,' I said. '*Squadre volanti*.'

Suzanne grabbed my shoulder. I turned and she pointed to one of the monitors. 'Watch out!'

On the monitor of the corridor outside, some dark shape was hurtling full speed towards the door.

'The cart!'

The door shook and a loud crash jolted the room like a thunderbolt.

'Jesus, it's being used as a battering ram.'

The cart reversed, and again backed up along the corridor and hurtled towards the door. This time the door shuddered, but it did not break.

'Shit,' I said.

'We're under attack,' said Emily.

I stared at the monitor. Tried to see where the trolley was.

'I'll hold the door. Emily, you try to get the police. Suzanne, watch the monitor and tell me what's going on.'

I heaved at the cabinet in the corner and rocked it across the room, pushed it against the door. The trailer struck again with such force the whole room shook. One picture of Suzanne fell off the wall. But the door held, the lock intact.

Another hit would do it.

'Emily, any luck?'

'I've found the website for emergency calls. Just says dial 112. The whole of the EU. Or 113 *Polizia*.'

'And if you don't have a phone?'

'I'll find a way,' Emily said.

Suzanne gave a cry. 'It's reversing and coming back again.'

I held the cabinet against the door, waiting for the next blow.

'Got it,' Emily said a few seconds later. 'Calling now... where is the mic on this thing?'

The computer speakers clicked and we heard a voice on the phone. '*Pronto? Qual è la vostra situazione di emergenza?*'

'We need help!'

'*Pronto?* What is your emergency?'

'Damn. They can't hear us, the mic's not connected.' She fumbled with the microphone lead and plugged it into the computer.

'Watch out!' yelled Suzanne.

The impact of the next blow to the door bowled the cabinet over and I had to hold it up to stop it falling onto the console. I pushed it level again. But the door had been breached. I knew because a cold draught of icy corridor air entered the heated room. The lock beeped once and clicked as it was torn from the wood.

'Shit.'

I pushed the cabinet back in place, and Suzanne kept an eye on the monitor for movement. 'Nothing out there.'

I gripped the axe tight. 'It may be all remotely controlled.'

'Not from this control room. He must be in another part of the castle.'

Emily yelled into the mic. 'Come quickly, 112, emergency. Please come quickly.'

And miracle of miracles, a woman's voice responded in English, with an Italian accent. 'Please stay calm. Tell me where you are and what is the emergency.'

'There's been a murder. Several murders. We are trapped in the Castello di Rocca. Emilia. The killer is trying to get us...'

We waited while the emergency respondent absorbed the information.

'Stay calm, and stay on the line. Please give us your exact location.'

Emily looked at me. 'I have no idea where we are.'

'*Castello di* Bloody *Rocca*,' I shouted into the mic. 'They should know where that is. Near Reggio Emilia. Ciano d'Enza. The river Enza. Get them to trace the call.'

'Ciano d'Enza,' shouted Emily. 'Come quickly, he's going to kill us.'

The computer went dead. The monitors died. The lights went out.

'Power is gone,' said Emily. In the flickering candlelight, her face looked red and ghostly.

'I will kill him,' I said. 'Whoever he is, he won't enter this room. I promise you that.'

I held my rage like a cup of hot liquid that was about to spill over. I itched to wield that axe now. I was ready.

Suzanne leaned over Emily. 'Are the police going to come?'

'They will,' I said. 'Well done, you two. We just have to hold out. Keep vigilant. We'll keep him at bay.'

I said this for their benefit. The sinking feeling in my gut told me that the message had not got through, that the emergency services had no idea where we were and might even treat it as a crank call.

The smell alerted me before the sound of hissing that we were being outmanoeuvred, that whoever this killer was, he had many tricks up his sleeve. He wasn't going to enter the room, not with me wielding an axe. But he didn't need to. The truth, the horrible truth was, I realised, he was going to gas us.

'Quick, try to block the gas coming in.'

'What is it? Poison?'

'Cover your nose and mouth,' I said. But I saw that Suzanne already had a bandanna around her face.

'There must be an air vent. Those candles need air.'

I pushed the cabinet away from the doorway to breathe

fresh air from the corridor. But then I smelt a pungent perfume coming from the caboose. The killer must have set up a pipe leading into the hole in the door made by the caboose and now was pumping gas into the room. I had to stop it. I had to–

My last thoughts were, *he's gassing us with Suzanne's perfume. Or he has mixed the chloroform with her perfume.*

I woke up, the room spinning, metal handcuffs cutting into my wrists, to find myself shackled back-to-back with Emily on the console chair. The cabinet had been cleared away from the door, which was now open wide.

'Emily, you okay?'

Emily moved her head back and bumped my head. 'Ow.'

'Suzanne!' I craned my neck around the room. 'What was that stuff?'

'I think it's some gaseous form of etorphine,' said Emily. 'I told you. The stuff they use to tranquilise wild animals.'

'At least we're still alive.'

'Suzanne!' I called again. I wriggled.

'She's not here, Rafe.'

'Christ.'

'She–' said Emily.

We were thinking the same thing, I knew.

'She must be part of it,' said Emily.

'She had that bandanna on her face before we even knew we were being gassed.'

'But… this shrine? What's that all about? None of it makes sense. She's been targeted. She's a victim.'

'And I want to know why we are still alive,' I said. 'He– She– They could have killed us… again. We're being played with here.'

'Don't speak too soon, Rafe. We're handcuffed to this chair.'

'Handcuffed. Hmm.' I strained my head to see the hand-cuffs that shackled us. 'These are the same ones I used on Reverend James.'

'He wants us alive,' said Emily, 'to torture us at the end. On the twelfth day. I feel sick.'

'If these are the same handcuffs I used on Reverend James, then we have a key,' I said. 'In my pocket.'

'Praise the Lord.' Even in the circumstances, her ironic response made me laugh.

'Can you reach into my left trouser pocket?' I called. 'I can feel the key there. I'll try wriggling it towards you.'

She contorted her hand and stretched her fingers. I felt her hand groping for the key. 'Got it!'

'Now the difficult part,' I said. 'Can you get it into the lock and turn it?'

'Easy peasy,' she said.

It was not easy. Emily strained and swore, chafed the hand-cuffs, had to take a rest, and then clicked the key in the lock. She turned it slowly and it snapped open.

I pulled the handcuff off my wrist. 'Wonder Woman,' I said.

'Now you uncuff me.'

I did it.

'My hands are completely numb,' said Emily. 'But we're free. Now what?'

'We get the hell out of here.'

'What about Suzanne?' she said. 'We have to find her.'

'If she's been kidnapped, yes. If she's in league with this madman, no.'

'Either way, we have to find her.' Emily pointed to the display of eleven little fawns playing flutes and panpipes she had pushed aside to get to the computer. 'Whoa!' The plastic ballerina in the centre was smashed into pieces.

'It could have been the caboose hitting the door – it shook the whole room,' I said.

'Or it could mean she's dead already.'

'Come. I know where to look.'

Our weapons were gone, but we still had our flashlights. Even so, we were blinded in the dark passage after the brightness of the candlelit room. I stumbled against the train carriage and banged my shin. An ambush was likely. We squeezed past and I led Emily by her hand to the trapdoor that I remembered led to the torture museum. I pulled off the trapdoor covering and peered in.

I did not know what to expect. Maybe our eleventh day of Christmas victim.

I played the flashlight on Linda's corpse below. The cold air blew strong across the room. The room lay in darkness; the windows were wide open. 'It's the middle of the night,' I said. 'We must have been out for hours.'

'Don't make me go down there,' said Emily as she saw me lower myself down the trapdoor.

'Better than up there.' I aimed for a clear patch of floor and jumped. Rolled over. 'Jump. I'll catch you.'

Emily manoeuvred herself over the opening and leaped towards me.

'Gotcha.'

We shone our lights across the room: the guillotine, the open window where the curtains danced like graceful ghosts, the iron maiden, the draped head, corpses.

I was expecting more. Anticipating some other diabolical torture instrument used on her. A corpse impaled on the Judas Cradle. But the room was empty of new victims.

My stomach was in a knot. I raided the cabinet for weapons. 'Here, Emily.' I passed her a tongue-extractor and took a knuckle-duster for myself, and the breast-ripper for good measure. 'Careful, someone might be waiting for us.'

I froze at the sounds of laboured breathing, the groaning of wood. A flickering light casting shadows of demons on the back walls came from under the closed door to the library.

'In there,' whispered Emily.

I nodded.

'It's a trap,' she whispered. 'Don't—'

But I did not hesitate. I pushed the door open, weapon out in front of me.

Burning candles dotted the floor.

The Catherine wheel had been placed in the centre of the library. I should have noticed it missing from the torture museum. Suzanne was bent backwards over the wheel, strapped by her ankles and wrists. She opened her eyes, first in terror then in relief. 'Thank God. Rafe! Emily!'

Around her a hundred candles glimmered, dripping wax onto the floor. 'Where is he?' she moaned.

'Who?' said Emily.

'I don't know. I never saw him. I woke up tied to this monstrosity. I've been here for hours. But I knew he would be coming for me at dawn.' She cocked her head to the wall behind us where a message had been pinned up:

'Dawn. Twelfth day of Christmas my true love sent to me, twelve drummers drumming.'

She shuddered. 'I guess I am to be the final sacrifice, the climax of his killings. After seeing that room with all the pictures of me, I know—'

'Not anymore.' I untied her hands, Emily her feet, and together we helped her off the wheel.

I held out her left hand. 'Look.'

Suzanne jerked her hand back in surprise at seeing the ring on her finger – the ring Glen had worn, the ring the killer had removed from his body and placed in the computer room.

I stared at her. Such conflicting feelings. And suspicions. But she had to be innocent now, I was sure of it.

Yet she had been left here to live, not die. As a trap. I scanned the room, checked the entrances. And then I heard a booming noise above us. A thudding. It echoed the beating of my heart.

Thud. Thud. Thud.

'What the hell?' I said.

'Twelve drummers drumming?' said Suzanne. 'Oh God, no, he's coming for me.'

I listened to the thudding. Then I knew what it was. 'Time to get outside. The courtyard. Quickly!'

TWELVE

TWELVE DRUMMERS DRUMMING

Darkness still shrouded the castle, but as we burst out of the library and ran down to the living room to stare out of the window, we saw streaks of grey on the horizon – the dawn of the twelfth day of Christmas.

A searchlight from the sky scoured the courtyard, and we looked up to see a helicopter thudding over the castle walls. We shone our flashlights up in the sky through the window, and moments later the chopper began to descend over the courtyard.

My heart lifted. 'Well done, Emily, they took your SOS call seriously.'

As the whirlybird lowered, the snow blasted the windows and obscured our view. The blades whipped up a new ministorm and the throbbing of its engine and blades rattled the panes. But we welcomed the battering of the air, the pelting snow, the thudding of the blades as the chopper manoeuvred its skis onto the frozen drifts and the blasts of air under the chopper splattered snow against the walls of the castle.

The air cleared. I saw the chopper now in all its detail: a twin-engine Kawasaki BK117. I could see it was fitted with searchlights, cameras and winches for search and rescue operations. As soon as it touched down, three uniformed paratroopers, with assault weapons, leaped out and ran towards the front door. I ran to the entrance, opened the door and raised my hands. 'Thank you for coming!'

The lead man lowered his weapon. '*Qualcuno ferito?*'

'There are seven dead bodies,' I shouted. 'We believe the killer is in the castle.'

It was impossible to be heard while the rotors were spinning. I stepped aside to allow the paratroopers to run through the front entrance. 'How many?' one of them called out.

'Three survivors,' I shouted, holding up three fingers. Emily and Suzanne huddled around me.

Two medics with packs jumped out into the snow and followed the paratroopers inside, followed by a man dressed in an electric blue ski jacket, as if he had a day on the slopes in mind. '*Energia?*'

I shook my head.

In the living room, the medics quickly checked over Emily and Suzanne. One placed a large electric lamp on the mantelpiece.

The civilian man introduced himself as Ispettore Tivoli. '*Cos'è successo?*'

'Where do I begin?' I said. 'Maybe the torture museum. There are four dead bodies in there; but there is also a body in a bedroom, one in the pond and one in the snowdrift under the tower. I can show you the exact location.'

'*Madre mia.*'

'But first, the killer is still in the castle. You will need to secure that. There are secret corridors above the rooms and a secret control room. I'll show you.'

The inspector translated this all to the waiting paratroopers, who held their weapons at port when they heard the last piece of information.

'Rafe!' called Emily. She pointed to the dining room table. 'He's not finished. He's—'

The head of the table was decked out with twelve little drummer boy figurines and a scroll on which was printed the Apostles' Creed. I finished her sentence. '—still playing games.'

I walked over to the table, picked up the scroll and read the familiar twelve articles of faith that were the foundation of the Christian Church.

And underneath, scrawled in what looked very much like Suzanne's handwriting:

And thus the whirligig of time brings in his revenges.

I'll be revenged on the whole pack of you!

'Another Bible verse,' said Emily.

'No,' Suzanne gasped, 'that's not from the Bible, it's Shakespeare. From *Twelfth Night*. The last line of Feste's speech and then Malvolio's line.'

I stared at the mirror, trying to work it out. Stared at the reflection of myself in the mirror. Reflected on mirrors. You could look at the mirror or you could look through the mirror at what was being reflected. Or you could look behind the mirror, as Dorothy looked behind a curtain in *The Wizard of Oz*.

Twelfth Night? Some memory echoed uncomfortably in my mind, out of my conscious grasp. Until Suzanne said, 'Remember the school play we acted in? *Twelfth Night*. Maybe that has something to do with this.'

Twelfth Night was about reflections, doubles, characters disguising themselves as other characters. About appearances and deceit and... revenge.

'Yes, everything,' I said, suddenly realising the truth. 'Everything. It was all about mirrors. Reflections.'

I was busy all morning walking through the castle with the

paratroopers and the inspector. He demarcated the crime scenes, and I explained the sequence of events, how the murders were discovered.

Then we braved the morning air and I pointed out the whereabouts of Mike's frozen corpse in a now completely snow-buried pond. Same with Glen. I indicated the place he had fallen, and the markers I used to identify the exact spot. 'He is the important one,' I said. 'The key to this whole mystery. Please tell me when you have located and recovered his body.'

I told them about the concierge and his car in the garage, and the inspector nodded. He knew Signor Antonio Alfieri from the village.

By midday, the castle and its surrounds, according to the inspector, were 'secure', he said in his very formal English. No trace of the killer had been found, though they had combed the secret corridors and searched the control room and the cellar. Forensics would arrive later, once the survivors had been airlifted, and he promised they would take this place apart. The bodies of the deceased would be treated with respect, removed to the nearest morgue, and next of kin informed. But this was for now a crime scene, and we had been right not to attempt to move or tamper with evidence.

'But they haven't found the killer,' said Emily. 'They've searched every room, the corridors, the secret passages.'

I shook my head. 'They're looking in the wrong places. I know exactly where he is.'

'You do?' said Emily. 'Then pray share.'

'I have just worked it out. Or rather, Suzanne worked it out for me.'

'I did?' said Suzanne.

Emily and Suzanne were standing around the fire, still wrapped in blankets. I paced up and down. The pieces were finally in place. I just had to prove it.

At that moment, the inspector and his crew joined us in the living room. The irony, and I did not believe in synchronicity, was that I counted twelve people present at this gathering, this epiphany when all would be revealed: three of us, four paratroopers, the two medics, the inspector, the chopper pilot… and the murderer, still somewhere in the castle, I guessed.

No. I knew. I knew exactly where he was.

Lunchtime: our rescuers had brought food. We were not going to touch the concierge's delights for fear of poison, so we contented ourselves with a few *paninis* and some *brodo*.

After lunch, we sat in a circle in the living room, sipping coffee. I stood in front of the mirror and called everyone's attention. 'As we all know, the twelfth day of Christmas is the day of the Epiphany, when Christ revealed the truth about himself to the world.'

The inspector nodded, looking puzzled. He hadn't come here to listen to a sermon.

'Don't worry, *ispettore*, I am not claiming to be Christ. Or Christ-like. As a philosopher, I do not believe in the paranormal, or God's predestined plan for mankind, or the cosmic significance of numerological signs. Or coincidence. First introduced by psychologist Carl Jung, the notion of synchronicity maintains that simultaneous occurrence of events with no causal relationship can be "meaningful coincidences" and thus the events are related.'

Emily furrowed her brows. 'Get to the point.'

'These twelve days are my point. Maybe even Reverend James believed that God arranges events this way, or Satan maybe. But what happened here was a mockery, an imitation of a plan. The killer exploited Reverend James' naïve and medieval superstitions in a meaningful pattern whereby the universe is numerically consistent. And this is what I am going to reveal. Why this killer did it this way, how he did it, and most importantly who he is.'

I was still not sure I was up to the task. I had been piecing it together all along the way, and the clues now made sense. But maybe this was self-deception, making a meaningful pattern out of random insignificances. Maybe I was also guilty of 'a causal parallelism'?

I addressed the inspector. 'We are the remnants of the disciples of a cult called The Twelve led by Reverend James, who organised this retreat to isolate us and make us repent of our sins. But one person wanted revenge, judgement, wanted us all dead. And if you give me a few minutes, I will try to explain.'

The inspector crossed his legs, sat back. 'Go ahead.'

'Exhibit number one is the recording played on the fourth night of Christmas. This was planned. And this one who wanted us dead claimed that he was one of us. A Judas, a betrayer of The Twelve. That threw us all into turmoil, because we began to accuse one another. But he made one mistake. This is not an Agatha Christie closed-room mystery. One of us could not have carried out all these murders. The murders we have witnessed required great engineering skill, planning, collaboration. As you all now know, there is an elaborate network of passageways and surveillance equipment in this castle, of unwieldy torture instruments, which would make it impossible for one sole murderer to carry out all these crimes.'

'So if it was not one of us,' interrupted Emily, 'then who? The owner of the castle? Only he would know about those passageways. Or the concierge.'

I nodded. 'One person wanted us all dead. One of us. But I suspected collusion. He or she had to have had an accomplice. A hitman. The concierge, perhaps?'

'Are you saying that we are still suspects?' said Emily.

I nodded. 'A murderer who wants the satisfaction of seeing his victims die horrible deaths would want to be there to the very end to see the results of his handiwork... or her handiwork.'

She looked at Suzanne and I returned their gaze. Then they both looked at me. Maybe they expected me to confess that I was the murderer.

'The twelve days of Christmas did not yield twelve deaths,' I said. 'Only seven. Maybe we three were supposed to survive? Maybe he was just playing with us. He could have killed us but didn't. He wanted us alive at the end. For what?'

'I'm confused,' said the inspector.

'Let's go back to the first murder. Or accident. Or hoax gone horribly wrong. Or deceit.'

The officer listened. Occasionally, the others whispered to one another, translating into Italian.

'We all came here with secrets, and many of us had the intention of exposing those secrets, or making others accountable for past actions. We know, for example, that Glen, the first man murdered, was having an affair with the Reverend's wife, Linda. We also know that Suzanne had broken his heart, that he was still not over it and was planning to confront her at this retreat. He wore her ring to his death.'

Suzanne nodded.

'Because Glen called me aside, showed me your ring. He wanted in these twelve days to sort things out with you. He told me. You showed me a letter that said as much. And he was not the only one. Most of the men here had crushes on you and were hoping to talk about it with you. You received notes and whispered conversation from Danny. And even I, I need to confess, had something to resolve.'

Suzanne opened her mouth to object. 'Those were fake notes. I didn't write them.'

'Further, Glen knew something. He told Emily and me to lock our doors. He knew something would happen. He knew there was a plan to murder us all. Maybe he knew the murderer. But he died before he could tell me.'

'He was murdered to stop him spilling the beans,' said Emily.

'Spilling the beans?' said the inspector.

'*La fuoriuscita di fagioli,*' whispered the man by his side.

I continued. 'It was no accident. The balcony had been tampered with.'

'So who killed Glen?' said Emily. 'Do you know?'

'Obviously, Reverend James would be a suspect. He wanted revenge for being cuckolded by his wife and Glen. But he was horrified when you found out that Glen was really murdered. Or maybe Linda did it. I saw someone with Glen just before he was murdered.'

'*La trama densa,*' said the inspector.

'I suspected Linda. Ali. Even you, Emily. But on his body there was a trace of perfume. Your perfume, Suzanne.'

Suzanne shook her head. 'I was being framed.'

'Maybe. Maybe not. Maybe you and the killer had made a plan, and created this red herring, a clue so obvious it could not be believed.'

'*Che?*' said the inspector.

'Murder number two. Stephen came to me, terrified. He knew something too, but was murdered before he could talk. A pattern here. He knew of Reverend James' plans, and so when he saw Glen murdered, he thought the Reverend was out to kill us all.'

Emily nodded. 'That was my guess.'

'Yes, we realised then that this was a pattern, and it followed Reverend James' sermons. Glen was stoned to death for adultery, Stephen was beheaded, just as it happened on the first and second day of Christmas to early Christian martyrs. We began to suspect some scheme at work.'

Suzanne shifted uneasily in her seat.

'But Stephen was behind all the arrangements, Reverend James told us. He allocated which day we were, he worked with James on the sermons, he came here in advance to set things up. So maybe he was the organiser of all this, but then got a guilty conscience and so had to be eliminated.'

Emily shook her head. 'I thought so too. But—'

'Then the series of murders, as planned. One per day. And they each had one thing in common.'

'The twelve days,' said Suzanne.

'Your perfume, Suzanne. Every one of those crime scenes smelt of your perfume.'

'I told you, he was trying to implicate me.'

'I thought so at first, but then I realised — each murder was *because* of you. He wanted to implicate not you but the victims. Each one had dealings with you. Each murder was a message to you. And this is how I solved the mystery.'

'You solved it?' said Suzanne.

'Yes. The affair with Glen. He never let you go. He was obsessed. Stephen loved you. Never got over you. Danny, Mike, obsessed. I too.' I paced the room to avoid her stare. I felt my own face redden. 'I fell in love with an image, kept that ghost alive for twenty years. Not anymore.'

She looked red in the face. 'No!'

'Danny asked to meet with you.'

'But I never wrote that letter.'

'Mike was a puppy dog whenever you were around.'

'What are you saying? He killed them because of me?'

I nodded. 'You saw the shrine. This was all because of you.'

'Then why kill the women?' said Emily.

'They were all sworn enemies. Suzanne, they were jealous of you. Linda hated you. Ali hated you. Cloaked their hate in pious Christian judgement. You were the whore of Babylon.'

Suzanne shuddered. 'But the concierge didn't even know me.'

'Think carefully. It was one of us.'

'You still think that?' said Emily. 'But we didn't have the means. And we can rule out the dead as suspects.'

'Maybe not,' I said. 'Glen died conveniently. So did Stephen. And Reverend James admitted he and Stephen did plan this to flush out our secrets, our sins.'

'But he didn't plan the murders,' said Emily.

'Died conveniently,' repeated Inspector Tivoli. 'Why conveniently?'

'Did anyone see Glen's dead body?'

'We all did.'

'Are you sure?'

'Inspector, please tell us what you found, and what I have suspected for some time but was not sure. And then when Suzanne reminded me of the school play *Twelfth Night*, it all came together.'

The inspector stepped forward. 'My men have retrieved the body that had fallen off the balcony. The body has been identified, as you suggested, as the man missing from the village for the past twelve days, Signor Rafe, that of the concierge, Antonio Alfieri.'

Both Suzanne and Emily leaped to their feet. 'What?'

I nodded. 'I assumed it was Glen's body. We all did. But later, after I began to suspect that all was not as it should be, I returned to the scene of the crime and had another look. And I discovered that the hand with a ring on it also showed a birthmark, shaped like a lady. I saw this very birthmark when the concierge dropped me off on that first day.'

'So Glen–'

'Was not killed. The person I saw with him before he "died" I mistook for a woman. I was so primed to think it was some nocturnal affair, but it was the small frame of the concierge I saw going into his room. There followed an argument. Then Glen must have killed the concierge and planted his body for us to find, therefore eliminating himself as a suspect. Glen's warning to me was to throw me off the scent and point blame at the Reverend.'

'I see. No one would accuse a dead man of murder,' said Emily.

'I later found the concierge's car hidden behind the castle in a carport. He never left the premises.'

'You never told me this,' said Emily.

'I'm sorry, Em. We were being monitored. I couldn't afford to let him hear I had found him out.'

Suzanne sat down again, hugged her stomach. 'I feel sick. It's all because of me.'

'So what happened to Glen?' said Emily.

'He took Reverend James' plan and ran with it. All those sermon notes were real, but the murders were not part of the Reverend's plan. Or Stephen's. No wonder Reverend James thought Satan had come to haunt him.'

'So if Glen did all this, he's still—'

I nodded. 'And his clever engineering feats were designed to frame all of you, to make you panic, to make you suffer fear.'

Suzanne wrung her hands. 'Why? Why?'

'He hated Reverend James, he hated Ali, religious bigots who condemned him, drove him out of the Church. And Linda turned her back on him. He was jealous of me, hated the men who were in love with you, Suzanne. Wanted you for himself. Revenge, murder, hate, bitterness. Reverend James created a path for him to follow.'

Emily pressed herself against her seat. 'And where is he now? Glen?'

'He's watching us. As we speak. Listening to me.'

'In the control room?'

I shook my head. 'But something still puzzles me. Why he let me and Emily go? And Emily twice. We were his friends, his allies. Maybe he showed mercy. Maybe he relented. Maybe he was having second thoughts. Shall I ask him? Glen?'

Next to me, a paratrooper held an enforcer in his hands, a bright red manual battering ram used for gaining forcible entry. '*Permesso?*' I took it from him and in one swift movement I smashed the huge mirror that took up the whole wall behind me.

The police aimed their weapons, first at me then at the hidden room behind the mirror. As the glass shattered and fell to the floor, a gaunt figure stood before us, dishevelled, unshaven, but not shocked at being discovered.

Glen looked as if he had been expecting it. He raised his hands and stepped forward calmly at the prompting of the paratroopers' weapons.

Behind him we could see a room, bedsit, fridge, computer, settee. His secret camp, where he had been living all this time. The mirror was one-way glass, so he could see everything that happened in the living room. From the very beginning, he had been watching our every move through the mirror. I had inklings all along, intuitions based on strange feelings. One-way glass is not always one way. In the night. In the silence, I had heard strange sounds. When I turned off the Christmas tree lights, a reflection of light still glowed in the mirror. But it wasn't a reflection. 'Was I right, Glen? Did I get it all right?'

'How did you know?' Glen stepped forward into the room.

'Your Malvolio clue. In the school play, you played Malvolio. I knew that it was you – I guessed that when I saw the lady birthmark on what was supposed to be your hand. And the mirror? We've been staring at you all this time. Only at the end did I realise that mirrors can also stare back. Or, as in *The Wizard of Oz*, there can be people hiding behind screens. Or one-way glass.'

Glen nodded. His smile was crooked. 'You're so smart.'

The cancerous tissue on his arm seemed worse. His face was a blotchy map of grafted skin and coloured patches. He looked haunted, his eyes sunken and with black rings under them. Or as Reverend James would say, he looked demonic, possessed.

Suzanne pressed back against the mantelpiece. 'Rafe, you were right. Glen, we thought you were dead. We were heartbroken. We—'

'It was you,' said Emily. 'All those murders.'

Glen folded his arms. Did not flinch.

'We didn't deserve this,' said Suzanne. 'What did we do to make you hate us so?'

Glen shook his head. 'To even have to ask that question means you deserve everything I threw at you. You have no idea what anguish I have been in all these years. The definition of true evil is that you do not even know the pain you are causing.'

'What pain did I cause?' said Suzanne. 'I never did anything to you.'

Glen flashed a macabre smile. 'You destroyed my life. You played with me, teased me, led me on; and when I was hopelessly in love with you, you dropped me. I was a game to flatter your ego. You played men, you destroyed lives. Don't tell me you don't even know what you did.'

Suzanne paled. 'You stalked me for years. I tried to make friends with you, but it made it worse.'

'You made me suffer. I could not get over you. Ever.'

'Don't listen to him, Suzanne,' said Emily. 'You can't be held responsible for a man's obsession with you. He's the predator. You didn't do anything.'

Suzanne bit her lip.

'And those others,' said Glen. 'They destroyed me too. Your so-called Reverend James may as well have taken a mallet and smashed my legs. His poisonous sermons, he destroyed my self-confidence, condemned my youth, made me sit Sunday after Sunday purging my desires, my own impulses. Destroyed my mind, made me feel like scum for any impure thoughts. All while he was being so holier-than-thou, having it off with Emily! And who knows who else. So I decided to teach him a lesson. Linda was my first vengeance. It felt good. But he smeared my name, him and Stephen. And Alison and Linda turned on me.'

'You had an affair with his wife!' said Suzanne.

'You lot made sure my reputation in that little town was ruined. I couldn't get a job. No one would hire me, so I left the area and signed up with the army. The only way I could purge myself of the Church of the Joyful Resurrection's vile shit and Suzanne's treachery.'

'I did not—'

'It was good, so good. I became fit, transformed myself, and on my first tour, I learned to kill. How to torture enemies of the state. I liked the feeling it gave me. And so I began to fantasise about revenge. About how to get you back, all of you smug little Christians. I learned about booby traps. I learned a lot about myself and who I am.'

The inspector moved forward to silence him, but I held out my hand. 'Let him speak. We need to know all this. It's a confession. Go ahead, Glen.'

He nodded. 'So when the Reverend began talking of a reunion, I made my plans.'

'But why me?' said Emily. 'I was a victim of this Church too. Much more so.'

Glen's eyes were cold and steady on her. 'I was going to kill you, Emily, but I couldn't do it. I did feel you were also a victim. You two were my allies. The dissenters. But the rest of them, I wanted them all to suffer. Even you, Rafe. You were all so smug about death, about everlasting life. The Twelve was all so pious and uppity. "Death hath no sting," Reverend James used to preach. Well, it does now. My lesson – what death is really like.'

'So you had to kill all of The Twelve,' I said. 'What about Sean and Jack?'

He turned to me. 'No, I didn't kill them. When I heard of their deaths, that's what set me thinking. What if there was a curse on The Twelve, and they all got bumped off one by one? Then the Reverend came up with this retreat idea and I ran with it, found this castle, planned my revenge.'

'And me?' said Suzanne. She could not look at him, but stood her ground, arms folded, tossing her hair back.

'I was in total control. I would never harm you, Suzanne. Never. This was all for you. This whole thing. I wanted you to feel fear, yes, but I would never hurt you. You know that.' His look was tender, disarming.

'Did you think this would impress me?'

Glen walked forward to her, arms out. 'Suzanne, I came to rescue you!'

She shrank back.

'Get against the wall,' called out the inspector. Glen complied. He was smiling, calm, not at all perturbed.

'So you orchestrated the whole thing?' I said. 'You used Reverend James' sermons, you set up the castle, rigged up the cameras, all those torture instruments.'

'The castle was already set up with cameras and secret rooms,' said Glen. 'That's what gave me the idea. I visited a number of venues months before, scouted this one out and found it ideal. The owner was quite mad. Used to spy on his guests and watch orgies from behind the mirror. Bondage S&M parties. And his fascination with torture instruments was most educational. He showed me how each was used. And so the idea blossomed. This is how I would take my revenge. How I would wake you up to the terror of what you had done to me. I planned everything, and listened to your every counter-plan, used them against you.'

'You're sick,' said Suzanne.

The police held his arms as he strained towards her. 'Love is a disease that eats and eats you if it's not reciprocated. Like cancer, it burrows into your soul, into your heart. Until you have to do something. Cut yourself. Cut others. Burn it away. But you have no idea, do you, what you have done to people? No idea.'

Suzanne cowered away from him. 'You monster.'

'Enough,' said the inspector.

I stayed him with my hand. I wanted to hear everything. The police moved back and Glen walked to the middle of the room again, centre stage. Suzanne stood two metres away, arms folded. Defiant. I admired her now. She was standing strong, confronting him. We stood in a circle around them, as if we were watching a play, some tragedy.

'You made me out to be the monster! You, Emily. You, Suzanne. And you, Rafe, you always had all the girls eating out of your hand. Rafe this, Rafe that. Suzanne dancing around you. And those vile men, Danny, Mike, and their disgusting thoughts about you, Suzanne. And Alison, the pious puritan. The Twelve spat me out, and so I spit you out, all of you.'

'You're crazy,' said Suzanne. 'If you thought that this would fix things up—'

Glen smiled. 'But it will. I will have my revenge on the whole pack of you. You've read your Shakespeare. You mocked me like Malvolio. You teased me, played silly games with my heart.'

'No, Glen, I never—'

'You did. You all did. But on the twelfth night of Christmas, the fool becomes the king and the king becomes a fool.' In one deft move, he launched at Suzanne, grabbed her around the neck, pulled out a slim pistol from his sock and aimed it at her head. 'No one moves or she dies.' Using her as a shield, he broke through the circle and dragged her towards the front door. The police raised their weapons again, but he was too quick. He lunged into the door frame, pulling Suzanne behind him to block any clean shot from a weapon.

'Oh, and Nurse Emily,' he called, 'it was fentanyl I used, injectable solution. But it does come in other forms too, such as a gas. Lethal if used in a confined space. Good luck!'

He slammed the door and locked it from the outside.

'Stop him!' called the inspector.

I heard a hissing sound from the room behind the now-broken mirror and then the clicking of the internal doors as they locked. He had the system operational again. He had planned even this!

The endgame.

'Shoot!' shouted the inspector. The police ran to the window, weapons raised.

'No!' I shouted back. 'He has a hostage.'

'He can't go anywhere,' said Emily. 'He's stuck here. There's no way out.'

The hissing gas, invisible, odourless, was filling the room. 'We have to get out of this room,' I said. The doors were locked – to the kitchen, to the living and dining room, to the passageway.

'Cover your mouth and eyes,' ordered the inspector.

Coughing and spluttering, we all bottle-necked at the door. I felt itching, burning, all over my face.

Then Emily called out, her mouth covered with a scarf, 'Listen.'

A drumming outside the window. A slow thudding. Slow at first then faster and faster. I knew immediately what it was. So did the pilot. '*Madre mia.*'

'He's taking the chopper!'

'Stand back.' One officer fired at the lock, and the bullet

ricocheted dangerously in the hallway. Wood splintered into the air. He fired again and the lock shattered. The door sprang open.

We swarmed outside, taking huge gulps of cold, fresh air and grateful to get away from the gas.

The scene was dismaying, surreal. Glen in the pilot's seat of the helicopter, its blades rotating, faster, faster, and Suzanne in the front seat. He had tied her up and now was navigating the controls of the aircraft.

'*Quale idiota ha lasciato l'elicottero incustodito?*' shouted the inspector. '*Pazzo.*'

'He must have learnt to fly a chopper in the army,' said Emily.

'Damn,' I said. 'He planned this to the last detail. Even his escape should we find him out.'

The police raised their weapons.

The chopper rose slowly then nosed up into the air.

'*Sparare! Sparare!*'

'No, don't shoot!' I called out.

The police fired but missed wide, then fired again. A blade twanged and a bullet ricocheted into the courtyard. The helicopter lurched but continued to rise six metres or so off the ground. I could see his plan now – to escape into the valley below.

'No!' Emily screamed.

'Stop firing!' I yelled. 'The hostage!'

'We can't let him escape,' replied the inspector.

Either the chopper was damaged or Glen wasn't an expert pilot. He lurched towards one of the walls of the castle, regained control and surged away into the centre of the courtyard again. He then yawed horribly before climbing a few more metres.

I watched Suzanne wriggle out of the passenger seat and push herself out of the open cockpit door. Glen was busy trying to regain control of the aircraft, but he grabbed her with one hand as she leaned out of the chopper. She screamed. I saw her open mouth but heard nothing above the throb of the engine.

'Jump, Suzanne,' I called, seeing her plan. Of course she could not hear me, but she knew what to do. Although the chopper was now ten metres in the air, below was the same deep snowdrift I had landed in. It would cushion her fall. I pointed to it, signalled wildly to her. I didn't know if she saw me, but it looked as if she was going to make the attempt. She struggled out of his grasp, but he held on to her hair as she pushed herself out the door.

I saw my moment. 'Give me that '

I grabbed the weapon from the nearby policeman and aimed at the right-hand side of the chopper, high at the blade, and fired.

It was a distraction more than a direct hit, and the chopper lurched to the right. Glen let Suzanne go in his effort to right the chopper, and she used that second of freedom to jump far and clear of the door. She floated like an angel for a few seconds, her hair spreading like fairy floss, then she disappeared into the expanse of white snow below.

The chopper rose and spun as the blade could no longer keep the aircraft going straight ahead. Over the tower and into the valley it went. I knew Glen's intention now, to fly high above the Enza Valley. But the chopper was damaged. It spun and then dropped fast down the slope.

He tried to right it, but it veered, could not correct itself and smashed against the side of the mountain, bouncing up again before it succumbed to gravity and hurtled at speed into the valley below.

We watched the impact, heard the crash, and then saw the fireball rise and paint the sky red and orange.

EPILOGUE

On the sixth of January Emily, Suzanne and I stared out at the snowy mountains of Reggio Emilia from the warmth of the hotel foyer. Behind us, suitcases were stacked, ready for when the taxi arrived. Suzanne was staying another day, to meet some fan club delegation. The press too had caught up with her and was camped out at the hotel.

'Well, some reunion,' I said.

'Yes,' said Emily. 'Never again.'

'They detained the owner of the castle too, for questioning,' I said. 'I'm glad we declined their offer to stay and debrief. I told them we needed to get home to our families.'

'You don't have a family, Rafe,' Suzanne said.

'What are you doing after this, Suzanne?' Emily said.

Suzanne sipped a hot chocolate. 'New movie. A thriller called *In the Deep Mid-Winter*, I believe.'

'Really?' Emily said.

'I wish I could skip this one, though,' said Suzanne. 'I need a break from snowy settings.'

'One thing I don't get,' said Emily. 'I don't think Glen meant to kill himself. What was his plan, do you think?'

'To kill us all, and have Suzanne to himself for ever and ever in the castle, with rotting dead bodies around,' I said.

'No,' said Emily, 'I think he had planned even the helicopter escape. Glen and Suzanne ride off into the sunset together and live happily ever after.'

Suzanne shuddered. 'He never could let that schoolboy crush go. Or his grudge against The Twelve.'

'Some people never change,' said Emily.

'Thank God it's over,' said Suzanne. 'I can't wait to go home. But I'll have to face these guys first.' She pointed to the vans parked across the road outside the hotel – Rai, Canale 2, Sky News. 'They found me at last.'

'Here's the taxi!'

Emily, freezing, ran from the hotel to the waiting car and climbed into the back seat. The driver shut her door then piled our suitcases into the trunk. Cameras flashed from across the road. I couldn't understand how Suzanne could live with people preying on her very existence.

Suzanne rested a hand on my arm. 'Rafe, before you go, one last thing…'

'Sure.'

'Did you ever wonder why I accepted the invitation to the reunion?'

I pointed at the media crews on the other side of the road. 'You were waiting for that big scandal to blow over.'

She smiled. 'Forgotten. Anyway, they always have a new story – now it's about an obsessive lover who lured me to a castle in Italy and killed himself over me.'

'I honestly didn't think you'd come. Was surprised when I heard you were here. Then I guessed it was to avoid the media attention. Was it?'

'Not the only reason. I had some ghosts to put to rest.'

I looked into her eyes. 'What do you mean?'

'You.'

She touched my lip with her finger. 'Didn't you know?'

'Know what?'

She sighed. 'I loved you, Rafe, you idiot. For years. At school. In The Twelve. Even after. You never noticed. You were that self-involved.'

'Not possible!' I studied her face for any sign of insincerity. She was smiling ironically, yes, but her eyes were true. Was this possible, that I had been so wrapped up in my own obsession I hadn't taken note of this minor fact?

'All the other guys knew. They were insanely jealous. But you were so enigmatic, so aloof. And I was too proud to ever let you know how I felt.'

'I had no idea, Suzanne.'

'No, of course not. For a while afterwards I imagined fame would impress you, that you might finally come running to me. But you were immune, beyond my reach. Anyway, I came here to lay my own ghosts to rest, and I'm glad to say, they rest.'

'Suzanne.'

She shook her head. 'It's fine. I'm fine. It would never have worked anyway. You and I, we're too much the same. You'd better go.' She leaned over and kissed my cheek. 'Look after yourself, Rafe. Someone's waiting for you.' She inclined her head toward the taxi. 'Take good care of her, she's worth it.'

She walked inside the hotel entrance, turned once, waved, and the door swung closed behind her.

ACKNOWLEDGEMENTS

Thanks to Shelley for being co-conspirator; and to the wonderful Bloodhound team, especially Betsy, Tara, Clare, Heather and Sumaira for their excellent work on this book.

Lightning Source UK Ltd.
Milton Keynes UK
UKHW010115220820
368600UK00001B/199